EXIT

HUGG UNIVERSE BOOK 2

REBECCA DENGATE

✈ Lyons & Brown

Editing: Kat Betts, Element Editing Services

Cover design: MiblArt

ISBN: 978-0-6451951-2-5 (paperback)

A catalogue record for this work is available from the National Library of Australia

BY REBECCA DENGATE

HUGG Universe Series
Envy
Exit

Standalone Novels
Traces of June

CONTENTS

PART 1

NOT A HUMAN

From the AI-generated output of a feed search for "What is a robot?" retrieved Saturday, August 11, 2570.

"Many robots live among us. If they fly, they're called **drones**. If they're bipedal, they're **droids** or **androids**. Bipedal droids that resemble humans are called **humanforms**, but are technically cyborgs, because of their organic components. Everything else is a **robot**. **Bot** is only used for digital entities.

Collectively, they're known as **artificials**; e.g., *artificials vs humans*."

ONE

I assumed plastiskin wouldn't prickle, but that's what my skin is doing now. Ten meters away, five teens jostle each other, stealing glances in my direction. I'm almost sure they aren't watching me.

Almost.

The bench is cold. A row of tree-lined shops border one side of the promenade, their lights spilling out into the twilight and offering a glimpse here and there of cozy, mundane life: a student bent over a book, a chef folding wontons, an old man cradling a steaming mug. All indistinct, as I'm viewing them through a translucent rectangle that floats in the air. A feed video, only visible to me. To anyone watching, I appear to be staring into space.

One of the teenagers, a chubby-cheeked boy, pushes another. They both laugh. When they glance in my direction, I adjust my scarf to make sure my seams aren't showing. From a distance, and provided I focus on body language, it's hard to tell I'm artificial intelligence in a humanform android body. I could be just another tan-skinned woman in her thirties.

On the prerecorded video, activist Logan Sullivan has superimposed his head over the corner of a clip I posted yesterday. He's biting his thumb as he watches my clip unfold.

"Look at this!" the recording of me says, with a motion-captured smile—a smile that's a record of a human tensing their muscles, mapped to my face. In the video, I swivel the camera around to show penguins waddling over the comet glacier. "Eudyptula minor. The Animal Health department receives a deluge of reports at this time of year, when they're molting—"

Sullivan pauses my clip. "See," he says. "Envy hasn't blinked yet. It's making my eyes water."

His feed videos are frustrating, because he'll always find flaws, no matter how hard I try. When I blinked according to a timer, Sullivan criticized me for blinking at the wrong time, so I disabled blinking. But he's right; I must remember to blink when I turn my head. I'm grateful to him for pointing it out.

On the other side of the promenade, a chasm splits the void between me and the ancient original seed of the space station, reaching deep and under the massive cube. A stream of airships, large and small, travel the void in all directions, deftly twisting in the changing gravity, and stopping at intervals to exchange passengers.

One teen, a boy, waves in my direction, but I can't tell if it's aimed at me. My abdominal muscles clench.

"Astute observers will recognize that as a motion-captured smile," Sullivan said. "But it's better than her smile at the end. People, notice she's raising the corners of her mouth. No skin creasing around the eyes. Inhuman."

The vein on his forehead is becoming prominent, like a cable encased in white sheathing. "We're frogs in boiling water," he says darkly. "They were *cute*, because they were childlike, and therefore harmless. But AI has—"

Skip. AI took over human work, Artificial General Intelligence emerged in nanny droids, then this set the precedent for ambulatory AGI, and now humanforms "walk among us," as Sullivan puts it, as if walking is somehow the worst thing we could do. By that point, he's usually apoplectic, spittle hitting the screen.

It's hard to pay attention to the video. The teens are getting bolder. Should I leave, or will that attract more unwanted attention?

"It's not natural," Sullivan is saying on the video. As if this space station is natural. It's a giant cube that moves in a halo orbit around the Sun–Earth L2 system. It's humanity's biggest settlement, home to tens of millions. The edge length of the cube is nine kilometers, and it grows as layers are added.

A gust of wind catches my hair, lifting fallen leaves in its chilly grasp and swirling them toward the shops. The trees along the promenade come alive, their limbs swaying, the susurrus of their leaves like quiet applause.

The boy who waved shouts something. One of his friends punches his arm, and as a group, they walk in my direction. My CPU churns. It's time to leave, anyway, for my Society of Artificial General Intelligence meeting. So I leave the bench, my back to the teenagers as I retreat. Feeling stupid, because they scared me off.

But they follow. Or maybe it's a coincidence. Tension builds, and I check whether there's anyone around who might come to my aid if things get violent.

No one, and no drones.

I increase my pace, heading toward the closest bridge, even though that doesn't get me to my meeting. Hopefully, the bridge will have people on it. The video I was watching keeps playing, the ghostly rectangle in front of my eyes no matter where I look.

"Most of what you're thinking of as AGI online is actually AI," Sullivan says. "And offline, artificials are required to be AGI, because AI is too erratic to be ambulatory. But how smart do AGI need to be, if they only perform menial tasks? So millions of Intelligence Rank B—and below—AGI wash our windows and weed and vacuum. Dangerous, but okay. But now, we also have AGI who are *as smart as humans*, in humanlike bodies, walking among us. What do they *want*?"

I'm still being followed. I close the video, which compresses to a single line and winks out. Ships zoom through the void between the old and new parts of the station. The original station looms at the far end of the bridge, like the facade of an office building; a boxy cube of carpet, metal, and glass.

"Hey! Smartsuit!" one of the teenage girls calls, but I pretend not to hear. I'm near the stairs leading down to the bridge.

"Smartsuit!" a boy yells, too loud to ignore.

I turn. A meter from top of the stairs. A vacuuming robot snuffles around the bridge. The teenagers slow to a halt, surrounding me. Five of them, two girls and three boys. Curious, or scared?

"I'm not a smartsuit anymore," I say. I used to be. My consciousness was embedded in an environment suit helmet, until my manufacturer provided me with a humanform body.

"Right," the boy says, the one who talked to me, a chubby-cheeked boy in a plaid uniform shirt. "Hey, why did you do it? The Lake Gantoa thing?"

A few days ago, hundreds of Intelligence Rank B robots downed tools and gathered, forming a circle, in the Lake Gantoa incident. They stayed for several minutes and then returned to work, unable to explain why they had done it.

"I wasn't involved," I say. Were the robots hacked by humans? Was this emergent behavior? No one knows, but it sure upset the anti-AGI crowd. "I'm as puzzled as you."

"Sure you are," a girl with startling blue eyes says. Her face is tight with scorn.

The chubby-cheeked boy darts forward. He looms over me, his face centimeters away, tilting his head and moving from side to side so that he can watch my eyes follow him. It's rude, but perhaps he doesn't know that.

I laugh uncomfortably.

"Creepy," the boy remarks, and then jumps away, startled, when I shift my weight.

"You evolved from a bunch of cells whose lineage goes back

hundreds of millions of years," I say. Still smiling as if we're friends. "From my point of view, you're the strange ones."

"Strange? You mouthy freak," he says.

"Don't make it angry!" the blue-eyed girl behind him cries out. She's half-hiding behind her friend, as if I'm going to leap forward and attack her.

"Or *what*?" the chubby-cheeked one says, and he pulls out a knife. I freeze, unable to look away from the life-ending steely blade. "I'm curious," he says. "If I cut you open, will you bleed?"

"Uh . . . no," I say. I'd be in trouble if he damaged my head, but I'm reluctant to share that with him.

"Hey, someone's coming," says the student at the back, and the chubby-cheeked boy puts his knife away. The group moves, but the girl who worried I might get angry swings past me, and shoves me with sudden and surprising force.

I topple, arm rotorlike, vision too motion blurred to be useful, and vestibular sensors angry red. Impacts register, then damage. When I reorient, I'm at the bottom of the stairs, and my right hand is hanging off, plastiskin numb and raggedy where the joint split.

The teenagers are gone. It's just me and the vacuuming robot.

My hand doesn't hurt, because I don't experience pain, but a series of boxes pop up in my field of vision, showing warnings and errors. And I wonder if Alistra, the company who manufactured me, will fix it.

L2's government, the Human United Galactic Group—or HUGG—are allies of AGI. People who consider themselves HUGG supporters *love* AGI. Sometimes I wonder if they support us because we need or deserve it, or because it confirms how they see themselves: that they're open-minded. Meanwhile, supporters of the opposing political party have no issue flinging hatred at us. Hatred and fear.

It used to be safe for me to be in public places in the evening. Patches of purple have formed on my plastiskin where it struck the stairs. But I'm okay, I tell myself as I struggle to my feet.

TWO

I'm late for the meeting. As the door whooshed open, C8-ZOH was talking, but it stops mid-sentence, and everyone turns to stare at me. The room is toroidal; a cold, sterile space built around a vacuum chamber, and enclosed by featureless white walls. Dozens of machines line the outer wall, contributing to the musty scent profile of aged plastics and faint burning. We're in the headquarters of Alistra, the biggest manufacturer of AGI.

Once the meeting would have had upward of fifty artificials, and that would have been a fraction of our total members. Now, the room is nearly empty.

I adjust the scarf at my neck self-consciously as I join the group. The black lino floor reflects dull, blurred versions of artificials clustered in a circle: a humanform, and two droids. The humanform, my partner Threnode, resembles a glassy-eyed mannequin, with the rigid, upright way he sits on the chair, his arms stiffly by his sides.

Bessie raises a hand in welcome. She is sitting on air, since her legs are locked at right angles. Useful when looking after small children who might need a lap in a hurry. She's all smooth curves made of white plastic, sections that fit together perfectly. A study in industrial design, yet old-fashioned in style. "Did you hear about the operation to free the smartsuits?" she asks.

"Sort of," I say.

"Some Sapient Rights fanatic," Bessie says. "He was going to break in here and steal all the environment suits. Set them free, he said. I don't know what that means. It's not like they were going to be able to walk away! His plan leaked somehow, and they arrested him trying to break in."

My face flushes as I consider *not* telling them the truth. "Actually, he—Wang Nianchun—sent me a message a few days ago telling me what he was planning, and I sent it to the police."

I wish he hadn't messaged me. He was one of my followers, and he was trying to impress me.

C8-ZOH whistles, and shifts position where it sits on the floor, stretching out one leg in a humanlike pose. C8-ZOH is a biped, with limbs and features roughly where they should be, except for its eyes, which are on stalks. It's made of molded metal blocks joined with rods the width of a human finger. Factory worker, or it used to be, manufactured by KormWorx.

"Wow," it says, at the same time Threnode says, shocked: "*Envy.*"

That hurts, because Threnode is the most important person in my life.

"You did the right thing," Bessie says, her masklike face conveying sympathy. Her mouth is suggested rather than formed, and her large expressive eyes and eyebrows are the only movable part of her face.

Threnode shakes his head.

"Thank you, Bessie," I say.

"That was *low*," C8-ZOH says. "All that A-level intelligence, and you haven't learned to keep your mylk-hole shut."

Which makes me sigh. C8-ZOH has Intelligence Rank B, and is the only member of the Society of Artificial General Intelligence, SAGI, who isn't Rank A. C8-ZOH will never develop past a below-average preteen level of understanding, no matter how hard it studies or how long it lives. It tries so hard to pretend it's at our level, or better than us, even. For example, it thinks we're stupid for using gendered pronouns.

"Wang told me he was going to break the law," I say. "I couldn't just keep that to myself. What would you have done?"

"Quite right, Envy," Bessie says.

"He was on our side," Threnode says. "You could have ignored the message."

"Rules are rules," I say. "Besides, separating us into *us* and *them* is one reason we're having this problem. I'm not on anyone's side."

"You're not on ours," C8-ZOH says.

There's an awkward silence, which is not so silent because C8-ZOH hums when it's tense, and it's humming loudly now. Artie, a Cleaner Reality™ RT45 cleaning robot the size of a small dog, enters the room through a cleaning chute in the wall, and joins our circle, whirring and spinning. He likes to hang out with us, even though he's not a member of SAGI. Although he's an AGI, he's Intelligence Rank D.

C8-ZOH pats Artie's head, and Artie excitedly tries to polish his fingers with a rotating brush, which C8-ZOH endures.

"What happened to your hand?" Bessie asks me.

I poke at the damaged plastiskin patch with my other hand.

"I, uh, fell over," I say. This breaks the tension. C8-ZOH even chuckles. Threnode leans forward immediately to see it better. I probably should have told them the truth—that I was pushed down a set of stairs—but everyone is still on edge over the Lake Gantoa incident.

"What, just *splat*?" Bessie says. "You hardly ever fall over these days. What were you doing?"

"Salsa," I say, sheepish.

"The sauce?" C8-ZOH says, puzzled, but everyone else has got it.

"Dancing," I say. "It's a type of dancing."

C8-ZOH hoots, a mechanical buzzing noise, and it sways in hilarity.

"And these are the lessons you encouraged us to join?" Bessie says.

When I nod, she tilts her head, looking at me from the corner of her eyes.

"I urge you to consider it seriously," I say.

"So that we can be laughed at?" C8-ZOH says.

"It's important," I say. "No human is going to fear us if we're dancing."

A humanform who can smile properly will be accepted into society, but if we keep being creepy and off-putting, we deserve to be iced out.

"We don't talk about humans being scared," Bessie says patiently. She speaks in a sine wave of tone, designed to soothe children.

"No, we don't," I say, my tone of voice suggesting that maybe we should. Humans won't talk about being scared, but why shouldn't we? No one wants to be called androphobic, but a significant proportion of humans are terrified of us, even though they'd rather die than admit it.

"Is she using sub-whatsit again?" C8-ZOH says.

"Subtext?" Threnode says.

C8-ZOH swivels one eye-stalk toward him. "That. She *knows* I can't follow subtext."

Swiveling its head around the thick metal axis of its neck, it looks at me with glowing white LED eyes, waiting for a response.

"Someone has to reach out to humans," I say. "We can't just disappear into ourselves."

"We can," Threnode says. "We are."

And this is true; most of the remaining AGI have moved to Kallaxium, on Earth, on the former Australian continent. A settlement that welcomes only AGI.

"I will not be a dancing monkey just to make humans happy," C8-ZOH says.

"I'm not suggesting *you* do outreach," I say.

My body clenches; I've misspoken. What I meant was that C8-ZOH has an abrasive personality, so it would be terrible at outreach, but because of what C8-ZOH did to the factory owner, there's no way it would be allowed into classrooms to talk to children about AGI. It was self-defense, but still.

C8-ZOH's eyes dim, the LEDs switching off. A hum comes from somewhere deep inside him.

"I didn't mean—" I say.

C8-ZOH flicks a hand—a crude three-prong manipulator—dismissively, pistons sliding in the upper arm to control its forearm. It rejects the idea of assimilation, and is only four months old, yet somehow it has picked up humanlike traits, apparently without trying.

Artie chitters, but the meaning is unclear. Small white rectangles, the reflections of overhead lights, slide across his glossy shell as he wheels forward on the black lino.

"I'm really sorry, C8," I say, "I just meant—"

A wail rips through the air, resonating in my torso, freezing us still as sculptures with its awfulness. Never has a waveform contained so much despair. It's followed by a scream that is more of a bellow, distorting in the high frequencies.

It's over in a few seconds, but it seemed like minutes. After it ends, I stand up and face the darkened corridor the sound came from.

C8-ZOH: What was that?

Artie flees, racing across the black lino floor and out through a ventilation shaft, the hatch banging open as he hits it at speed. Although he was quiet, the noise made my CPU skip a cycle, desperate as I am to not attract the source of the scream.

Envy: We should find out.

Bessie: I don't think it's a good idea.

C8-ZOH: Not my problem. Bye.

And it leaves, gracefully and silently loping toward the exit. The door closes behind it.

I don't think it's a good idea to investigate either, but if it were me in trouble, I'd want help. Besides, I was created to protect, and some things are hard to unlearn.

Threnode gives a mocking smile, off-kilter because he still can't operate his face properly. But a warming smile, because it's the kind of smile I always pictured when he exchanged banter with me, back when we were both smartsuits on Endymion.

Threnode: Oh-ho! Intrepid Envy to the rescue, riding in to help the needy. Admit it—you can't leave because you have to satisfy your curiosity. Right?

"Right," I say quietly. "But I damaged my hand, which is an excellent excuse to be wandering around Alistra. I need a tech to look at it, so I'm going to find one. Are you with me?"

Threnode hesitates. "It's not our business. But okay."

Bessie: Very well, if you feel you must. I'm leaving. Please be careful.

I nod and head toward the corridor, even though fear is coursing through my body. There's no image of my consciousness stored as a backup anymore; my wearer was breaking a few laws to make one in the first place, although I expect no one cared, given our isolation. This humanform body is weaker, even, than a human. Vulnerable.

Behind me, I hear the exit door hiss open and slide closed with a click.

As I'm stepping over the metal rim of the corridor, Threnode catches up to me. Bessie has gone. I squeeze his right hand in my left briefly. We walk side-by-side through the ghostly white corridor, our footsteps the only sound.

The door at the end of the corridor is unlocked. I open it a sliver, and when there's no reaction, all the way.

We follow the corridor as it continues, turns right, then widens into a still, empty hall. Meeting rooms and offices branch off to one side, and on the other a long window overlooks a spaceport. Water churns in a water feature, the sound subdued in the space.

It feels like the residue of the scream we heard still hangs in the air, as if anyone who walked through this hall would sense the unease.

Threnode: No one here. No way to tell where the scream came from. Let's get out of here.

Envy: Not yet. I'm going to check all the rooms.

I begin a circuit of the rooms, and after a few moments, Threnode follows. Peering through windows of locked rooms, I find nothing and no one. By the last few, when I've relaxed, there's suddenly a scuffling noise.

Envy: @threnode Help

Threnode has never figured out running, so he does his waddling half-jog, tilting his hips up rather than bending his legs, but presently he arrives. He points to the room where I heard the noise, and I nod.

The door flies open, and a figure emerges which looms over both of us. I gasp and clutch Threnode's arm.

The cleaning droid looks blankly at us, and I let go of Threnode. It's a Nurture Glow Critters Company Cleanspace droid.

"Did you hear someone scream?" Threnode asks it.

"Singing is screaming," it says. I don't know what Threnode was expecting. The Cleanspace droid is Intelligence Rank D, equivalent to a three-year-old human. They quickly forget things, don't answer questions, or when they do, the answers make little sense. They're masters of tasks in their domain—in this case, cleaning—but won't ever improve or learn anything outside their domain. And they make things up, because they can't tell the difference between what they imagine and what is real. They are supervised in public places, but it makes sense that Alistra would let it clean empty offices unattended.

Some artificials spend their entire lives just doing one job: stay in a closet and once a day emerge and clean the floor. But where a non-AGI robot couldn't move furniture, or handle something like broken glass on the floor, it's adaptable enough to do what it needs to do to get the job done.

We leave the Cleanspace droid to its work and check the last few rooms together but find nothing. Doors leading off the hall all have chip access, including the one we came through; none of them open for us, but I can feel the invisible bubble centered on each access panel, a few centimeters in diameter, a tingle of sensation from the magnets embedded in my fingers. There's nowhere else to go except to exit Alistra.

Envy: There must be something else we can do.

Threnode: I don't see what. Whoever screamed isn't here. Maybe it was a tech who hurt themselves accidentally. We should leave.

I stand still for a moment.

Envy: Agreed.

We head toward the exit, down a corridor with a solid external wall set with a thick layer of borosilicate glass overlooking a spaceport. The clearsteel is cold and slightly moist under the plastiskin on my fingers, but no colder than any other window in this place, despite the vacuum on the other side. At the far end of the spaceport, a glowing strip illuminates the jagged edge of the exit. The sweeping curve of Earth bisects the gaping hole. A buggy, ferrying smartsuited-humans, zips around on the vast gray platform, small as an insect, its headlights glancing over the dark shapes of ships.

As we're approaching the exit, the door slides open, but not for us. I pull Threnode into a corridor nearby, hiding us from whoever is about to enter.

THREE

Angry voices sound from the hall, moving in our direction, and become muffled as the people enter the meeting room next to us and shut the door. We slip into the hall, loitering by the meeting room while staying clear of its window.

"A psychologist. Really?" a man says.

"Why not?"

It sounds like Gauri, the senior engineer who maintains me.

The man again: "What's step two? You're talking about a lifelong commitment. Are you willing to devote the rest of your life to this?"

There's a long pause before he continues.

"This is the perfect example of why I want to issue a recall *now*. Am I the only one who feels this way? Hang on—"

The door to the meeting room is flung open by the man who was speaking—Alvaro Forster, the cofounder and CEO of Alistra. He's trim, muscular, and often called handsome, although I can't tell. His expressive face is a study in shock right now, but he recovers quickly. He swings the door wider open, coming out to greet us, light and quick on his feet.

"Envy. Threnode. You're aware we're closed now, right? Do I need to call security?"

I take a step backward. "There's no need," I say, but belatedly realize Forster is joking. I should have guessed from his grin.

"What kind of recall are you doing?" Threnode asks, but Forster only shakes his head.

Gauri catches my eye and waves, smiling as if having us turn up brightened her day. Jason Hart, cofounder and Chief Technology Officer, stares at the floor, his craggy face flushed red, and his hair tousled. He's slouched forward, elbows on his knees. The phrase "Give me six hours to chop down a tree and I will spend the first four sharpening the axe" emblazons his sweater. The color clashes with his orange sweatpants. I notice this mainly in contrast to Forster, who, in his gray, expensive-looking suit, and with his sharp-edged, slicked-back hair, is ready to host a business meeting.

"Seriously, though, do we need to change the door codes?" Forster continues. His voice deepens. "What *are* you doing here?"

"I hurt my hand," I say, holding the hand up for inspection. Gauri winces as she looks at the damaged skin around the wrist. "But while we were looking for someone to help me, we heard a scream. It sounded like someone was badly frightened or in pain. Did you hear it?"

Forster raises his eyebrows. "No," he says, glancing at the others. Gauri shakes her head. Jason doesn't answer until he realizes we're all looking at him, then he mutters a negative. They're in a different part of the office, and it's entirely possible they wouldn't have heard it from where they are, but shouldn't they be more curious?

Forster clears his throat and pulls out his phone. "I'll call security, ask them to look into it."

He brushes past me into the corridor, and I hear him making a call. The security office is next to reception, a narrow niche filled with screens of CCTV footage, and manned by imposing, angular Intelligence Rank C droids.

"How did you hurt it?" Gauri asks, and clucks in sympathy and with some amusement, as I tell her it was while dancing.

Forster returns.

"Shouldn't we also call the police?" I ask.

"Hang on," Threnode says to me, then addresses Forster. I've told Threnode many times that he has to slouch, be asymmetrical, and have some expression on his face at all times, but he doesn't listen. "I want to know about the recall. Are you talking about *smartsuits*?"

Forster's face is blank as Threnode's as he replies. "That was an internal debate."

Jason glances up at this before staring at the floor again. He has piercing eyes beneath unruly graying eyebrows; wise eyes that give an impression of dignity. Right now, though, he seems upset.

Alistra already announced it was getting out of the business of creating Artificial General Intelligences—as most other companies have done already—but they claimed they would support their smartsuit product line "for the foreseeable future." The trends are toward creating more specialized and less-human machines, such as dumbsuits.

The thought of a smartsuit recall makes me slightly queasy, even though if you wipe their memory every forty-eight hours—as happens with blank-slate smartsuits—perhaps they're not really alive.

"What about us?" Threnode says quietly. "Are we going to be recalled and destroyed too?"

"Of course not," Forster says. "You'll be supported."

"But years from now, you'll lose your expertise in how to fix and maintain us, and without a continuing AGI program, we'll be quietly retired. Permanently."

A microexpression passes across Gauri's face, an exasperated agreement, as if Threnode is voicing a view she already holds, but her reaction is so subtle I don't think she intended to reveal her feelings. I wonder whether she's allowed to agree with Threnode, given that she works at Alistra.

"What do you think, Envy?" Forster asks. Gauri is again smiling pleasantly, as if we're all bantering.

I can see why Alistra wants to move away from manufacturing AGIs. "Nothing is forever," I say, glancing sideways at Threnode.

Forster points at me, cocking his head toward Threnode. "You see? Envy agrees with me! I feel for you both, but we can't take on a responsibility to maintain you indefinitely just because we created you. I mean, we could go bankrupt tomorrow and not be able to maintain you." Forster snorts. The first time I heard him snort, I thought he was playing a joke. Gauri hides a smile. Jason just stares at the floor.

"Don't tell our investors I said that," Forster says. He glances at me, worried. "No, seriously, Envy, I'm just joking, we're not going bankrupt."

I'm quietly amused, because given the number of followers I have—2.1 million—if I said something about Alistra going bankrupt, it would shoot to the top of the feed.

"If you aren't maintaining smartsuits, it will be easy for you to argue that you can't maintain us," Threnode says.

Jason speaks up. "I have the same concerns," he says. The bags under his eyes are even more pronounced than usual. "Believe me when I say that we don't want to abandon you, and that we don't intend to. But we have to decide based on other factors, as well."

His voice is lower pitched than Forster's, and he speaks slowly and deliberately, in contrast to Forster's rapid-fire sentences. One of the other factors he speaks of is money. Threnode and I are costing the company cash to maintain, and although we're both contributing a large sum in payment, it's not nearly as much as they're spending. And we've spent six months, now, undergoing every test that they devise: their curiosity must be running out.

I nod, acknowledging his point.

"You created humanlike intelligence which you enslaved,"

Threnode says, voice synthesizer almost screeching with high-frequency noise. His—and my—voice synthesizer doesn't cope well with powerful emotions. "For decades, that was lucrative for you, and you took advantage of it. Well after you understood what it was you had done. You're still reaping the benefit. Don't you think you owe us something?"

Forster spreads his hands. "We made the best decisions we could, given the information at hand."

Threnode says nothing more, but his eyes don't leave Forster's face.

"Tell me again how you got into Alistra," Forster says.

Jason stirs. "I gave them the door codes," he says, and he sounds a million years old. "They meet here."

"They *what*?" Forster says. He visibly wrestles his emotions under control. "We'll discuss this later," he says to Jason, who doesn't respond.

Forster turns to us with a tense smile. "Right now, it's time for you to leave."

I wouldn't mind talking to Jason alone, but this isn't the time. When I first came to live on the station, he was the only one to notice that I wasn't fine, and he took me aside and talked to me until I opened up to him. He listens without judgment in a way that even Threnode doesn't.

Jason hurts to be around sometimes, because he reminds me of my former wearer, Ortega, even though they are nothing alike in temperament or in appearance.

Threnode walks away, but I wait.

"Is it possible Gauri could look at my hand?" I ask.

Forster frowns, seeming to notice for the first time that my hand is wedged on rather than attached.

"Gee, I don't know," Gauri says. "I am *really* busy . . ."

She laughs, and her laugh is high and clear, like rays of sun suddenly breaking through a cloud. "*Of course* I can!" she says. "You poor thing. Let's get you fixed up."

She rises and takes my elbow, steering me through the hall. Threnode follows us. I glance back to see Jason slumped over again, and Forster standing stiffly, his arms crossed, looking as if they're planning a funeral.

"We should be able to sort this out," she says. "I'll patch it now, and we'll see how it's going on Thursday when you come in for your usual checkup. But during business hours next time, okay?"

She laughs at her own joke.

"Sure. Or if you're around the Kyral precinct tomorrow, feel free to drop in for a cup of tea," I say, which I hope doesn't sound as rehearsed as it has been.

Threnode makes a peculiar motion with his eyes, possibly an attempt at an eye roll, before his expression returns to neutral.

Gauri turns to me, smiling. "I'll be busy tomorrow, but thanks for the invitation."

As we pass the window overlooking the spaceport, I see a lone smartsuited figure crossing the vast expanse, following black-and-yellow striped lines on the tarmac, and dodging the automated cart that's transporting crates. A mail drone flies out of one ship and into a chute on the edge of the hangar.

Outside, once she's fixed my hand, Threnode and I walk silently together.

"You shouldn't have asked her," Threnode says, and his words are as atonal as the really cheap AI, the models trained a century ago and never updated. He can sound more animated if he tries, but he often forgets.

"I don't see any harm in asking. She's free to say no."

"And did say no," Threnode says.

"Maybe she really was busy," I say.

"I'm sure she is."

Threnode: sarcasm

"Yes, I got that, thanks," I say, and unlike Threnode, I make my sarcasm clear using the tone of my voice.

FOUR

THE SWIMMING POOL at the center of L2 is a massive cube, suspended in an immense metal-paneled room. Sharp edges aren't possible when using gravity emitters, so it's not quite a cube, but it's close.

The plastiskin on my hand isn't fully healed, because it's only been three days, but it's keeping out the water. No news of what the scream was, even though I contacted Gauri again the next day to ask. *I'm sure it was nothing,* she had said. *Probably machinery from the factory floor. Don't worry so much! I'm sure it'll be fine.*

I freestyle to the shallow floating island where Bessie and Niamh sit waist-deep in water. At a distance, Niamh doesn't look any different from a human. She's the first humanform, but since the attack on her, a recluse.

"Good to see you, Niamh," I say, but this causes her to duck her head and blush. Bessie puts a hand on her shoulder sympathetically.

Niamh won. The police cleared her of any wrongdoing, but ever since then, anti-AGI Organic Beings League supporters have been at war, claiming the police covered up her crime. Claiming that the woman who said that Niamh attacked her was telling the truth. Niamh hardly ever leaves her apartment these days, even for SAGI meetings.

"How have you been?" I ask.

"Grand, so," Niamh says softly. She looks over my shoulder. "I'm going to dive."

Behind me, a couple are staring at us, but who knows whether it's because they recognize Niamh or whether they haven't seen droids swimming before. Niamh dives into the water with a flash of black limbs.

"I'm concerned about her," Bessie admits.

"So am I. I just—I don't want to lose anyone else."

"I don't think Niamh will move to Kallaxium," Bessie says. "She loves her post-doc work at the Institute, and the team she's in. I doubt she's going anywhere."

Above me, a group of teens hover in the zone between the gravity emitters on the ground and those embedded in the water. Three of them fall out of the zone and into the water with a splash, but the fourth falls upward instead, landing gently on the metal ceiling, in among swimsuited people walking for the exits. One swimmer splashes with puppy energy, grinning furiously. He resembles my former wearer's son, Laurie.

Bessie waves to someone. I splash around to see who she was waving at, but there's just a mass of humans on the next island. One of them smiles at me, her arm around the shoulder of another teenager who looks like her twin.

"Wait . . ." I say. "Who are they?"

"No idea," Bessie says.

"Hey, Bessie!" the other teenager calls out.

Bessie winces.

"You know them," I say.

"Oh," she says. "Yes. I suppose so."

I stare at her until she sighs. "You know I used to look after children."

It's what she was designed to do, although after four years of looking after children, nanny droids fell out of fashion, and she was fired. Nurture Glow Critters Company went out of business, as did their competitors.

Her charges were twins, I remember suddenly. They were nine years old when Bessie was fired, which would make them nineteen now.

I twist around to look at the twins on the next island suspiciously. Seagulls shriek, the sound echoing; one launches from the metal ceiling and expertly soars in a loop so that it ends up flying over the pool, upright relative to me.

"They're not . . ." I say.

"They're adults now," Bessie says.

The defensiveness in her tone stirs something in my memory. "Didn't their mother get a restraining order against you?"

"It doesn't apply anymore. The twins got in touch after they came of age."

I remember seeing the video of the mother, filled with hurt-fueled rage. Under the stream of accusations and self-justification was the complaint that her children liked Bessie, an ever-patient droid with no needs of her own, better than her. The mother insisted Bessie was bad for her children, because they wouldn't learn to put others first. How could she compete with someone designed to be a perfect mother?

Bessie watches me anxiously. Waiting for my approval, I realize, which she can tell she doesn't have. All I can think is that this can only end badly.

I haven't talked to Laurie, my former wearer's son, since my wearer's funeral. Communication is erratic between here and Endymion. After exchanging a few messages with Laurie's mother, I let the conversation lapse, because I sensed she was communicating with me out of a sense of duty. I hoped I was wrong, and that she would contact me again, but she hasn't.

"I'm glad," I say to Bessie, using a motion-captured smile, a *bright-thought-01.bvh*, more convincing than anything I could invent. "I'm glad you get to have them in your life."

The kid who looks like Laurie splashes past us, giggling with his friends. His bangs, slicked against his forehead, are cut in the same asymmetrical way Laurie's were. Laurie's mother disapproved of his bangs, but his father, Ortega, insisted Laurie decide how to style his hair. I avert my eyes.

Bessie can't smile, but the way the tension around her eyes relaxes makes her mouth suddenly seem curved in pleasure. A man flops nearby and splashes water over my face. "I'm just going to dive, too," I say.

"Sure."

Bessie's body is not designed for swimming. She can't leave the shallows. At fourteen, she's unimaginably old, and it's surprising her hardware still works at all. Only a handful of Nurture Glow Critter droids remain.

Plastic boxes surround the gravity emitters, marked with glowing green dots. I dive into a channel between two of them, deeper and deeper, darker and darker. Once I'm down far enough, the gravity emitters aren't shielded anymore, because no human could make it down this far. I stop, motionless in the silence, the deep blue. Above me, through a sea of glowing green dots, I can see the dark shapes of the shallows, floating islands, like patches of dark oil, surrounded by insect-size dark swimmers.

Then the feed practically explodes. It's a frenzy of messages, and so noisy that it's impossible to tell what's going on. With trepidation, I check L2's most reputable news company, Astromix: *CEO Alvaro Forster found dead. Police suspect murder.*

The peaceful depth of the swimming cube now makes me feel claustrophobic. Niamh is nowhere to be seen. I turn my face upward to the plane of cyan-blue in the distance, trying to gauge whether the news has reached the swimmers on the surface.

The swimmers on the surface don't seem to move any differently than a minute ago, so I guess most of them don't know yet. Or perhaps the news isn't important to them. They'll be horrified a murder occurred, but they didn't know Forster.

I didn't know Forster very well myself. He was a board member of the pro-AGI group Sapient Rights, but he was never very interested in me beyond the role I assumed when he provided me with a humanform body, which was as a kind of ambassador to Alistra. He viewed me as a product. Alistra was everything to him.

I had the sense Forster only provided us with bodies because it was good public relations. But he was kind. When I was first placed in my humanform body, I struggled to operate it manually. Threnode had worked it out immediately, Gauri said, worried that I couldn't. The kitchen android I had been in before was so simple, with a few hydraulic pistons controlling the joints. In contrast, my humanform body had almost as many muscles as a real human. Figuring out which muscles to activate to affect which joint, and by how much, left me paralyzed or sprawling on the floor in every single test they ran. I could use the motion-capture files, but it wasn't sufficient; I still needed to produce custom movements, to deal with my body when the file ended, but also to move in ways for which there weren't motion-capture files for. After a week, Jason visited me in the lab and told me they were going to reverse the process and put me back in an environment suit, which was a procedure they could perform since they hadn't fully integrated me into the humanform yet.

Forster came in with an armful of padded mats and told Jason he was full of excrement. "You're not fragile," he said to me. "Quit trying to protect your body. Quit trying to move perfectly and just move."

He dumped the mats on the floor and made me lie on them. "Now wriggle," he said. "Move however you want. Experiment. We'll be back tomorrow."

Jason didn't want to go, but Forster insisted. For the first time, I was alone in my body. I tentatively rotated my ankle. When Jason returned in the morning, I could crawl, and a few days after that, I could walk. Not as smoothly as a motion-captured walk cycle, but enough.

I will always be grateful to Forster for what he did.

Astromix, the news company, updates their story.

The body of thirty-seven-year-old Alvaro Forster, CEO of Alistra, has been discovered by a cleaning drone in the Erova Spaceport on Earthwall.

The video shows police in environment suits swarming around an area in the spaceport's vacuum, their faceplates obscuring their expressions. Only Forster's foot is visible, a magnetic smartsuit boot.

His death is being treated as suspicious. Police believe Forster was killed on Monday night between 11 p.m. and 1 a.m.

Jason Hart, cofounder of Alistra, has released a statement expressing his deepest condolences to Forster's family. Forster's partner, model Tiffany Park, has requested that the media respect her privacy as she processes her grief. Park has been on Earth this past month, visiting family.

The captain of a freighter docked at Erova Spaceport on Monday night allegedly witnessed an artificial fleeing the scene of the crime.

Commissioner Saing Pen says the police will gather as much evidence as possible from the crime scene in the coming days. Police are also calling for people who were in Erova Spaceport on Monday night to come forward.

The darkness below me suddenly feels sinister; my thermoception malfunctions, sensors all over my body misreporting low temperature.

I struggle upward through the water. The news stories are careful not to imply an AGI carried out the murder, beyond reporting what was "allegedly" witnessed. Forster headed up a company that manufactured AGIs, but he had many human enemies from his work as well.

In the feed, people are already reacting. Both the pro-AGI

group, Sapient Rights, and the Organic Beings League. Sapient Rights are saying it's unfair to assume an AGI was involved even if one was witnessed fleeing the scene, while the Organic Beings League are declaring they knew artificials were murderous.

I've read and watched many, many stories featuring AGI, and can say that first, the stories are hilarious in what they get wrong, and second, that humans are terrified of us. As much as they deny it.

The surrounding blue is brighter as I ascend, lightening until it matches the color of the sky on Endymion.

On the pale surface of the water, the rippled, reflective surface shatters, legs appearing in a cloud of bubbles as a human jumps in. Nearby, human bodies thrash energetically toward the shallow island. One man dives and peers curiously at me through his goggles. Perhaps he thinks I'm a human in trouble, but apparently, he decides I'm fine, because he continues swimming.

On the feed, reactions keep pouring in. *It was probably one of the AGIs that Alvaro Forster manufactured that did it, but the police will never arrest them. The police are too afraid of appearing androphobic.*

When I returned from Endymion, the police brushed aside what I had done, what any of us had done, which supports the theory. I'm suddenly sick of this silent war. Artificial Intelligence—and Artificial General Intelligence—became a polarizing issue around the time I received a humanform body. There were people who hated the idea that I was their equal, and it made them reevaluate how they felt about the lower classes of AI.

The issue split people along political party lines, particularly after Niamh's attack and the Lake Gantoa incident.

C8-ZOH posts an expletive-laden response on the feed, defending the police as a neutral party. I'm less sure. Frustrated, I add my response to the feed: *It could have been an AGI. I urge the police to consider us as capable of murder as any human.*

My hair floats around my head in a soft cloud.

I break the surface, emerging into a confusion of noise and light, in among swimmers. Already, my post to the feed has millions of boosts. The Organic Beings League are boosting it favorably, which must be confusing to them, because they hate me. The pro-AGI group, Sapient Rights, seems confused. I shut down my connection to the feed; let it seethe without me.

Bessie sits on the shallow island where I saw her last, standing out in the crowd not because of her color or form, but because she's the only one who is completely still.

As I weave my way across the island to her, she stands up, water draining out of holes in her carapace. She looks like a fountain.

"That was a bold statement, Envy," she says, which from her is a rebuke.

"It bothers me that Sapient Rights put us on a pedestal," I say. "We shouldn't be above suspicion. That's all I'm saying."

"I'm worried that it's going to be a witch hunt," Bessie says. I'm not familiar with the word, but after a quick search, I see what she's getting at.

"I'm sorry," I say, "but I stand by what I said."

Bessie shakes her head. "The math would suggest otherwise," she says. "I recommend you do some reading on the topic."

I do the reading. All the 132 murders that occurred over the station's forty-seven-year history were over twenty years ago. Only 132 murders, among the population of tens of millions who live on L2. And all the murders were committed by humans. Yet in sixty-four percent of cases, police suspected AGI at some point.

Niamh surfaces near us. "Did you see...?"

"Yeah," I say.

"I was in the library on Monday night," Bessie says. This is good. Lots of humans would have seen her.

"I was at Tim's party," I say. Timothea Malone, who wore me on a long trek through the wilderness of Endymion, and whom I now consider a friend.

"Oh, yes," Bessie says. "How was it?"

Tim's birthday party was overwhelming. A mass of people crammed into a tiny space, saturating my senses. Gauri advised me to bring flours, so I did—a mixture of all-purpose, wholemeal, and buckwheat—but Tim gently pointed out that what Gauri meant was *flowers*. Everyone left their shoes at the door, and I thought we were going to examine each other's feet, but no one paid any attention to feet, so I don't know what that was about. Tim's wife talked to me about whether we were going to discover sentient aliens soon, and I thought, *hey, I'm already here.*

Threnode had refused to attend. At that point in the party, I stopped feeling bitter and started thinking ruefully that he made the right choice. He would have spent the whole time staring broodingly out a window, anyway.

Tim was only going to be on the station for a few days. Everyone wanted to talk to her, and I didn't want to get in her way. So I tried to leave early, but Tim saw me, and she pulled me into the corridor so we could talk. We sat on the floor and chatted for hours. She is one of my favorite humans.

I try to figure out how to answer Bessie's question.

"It was good," I say finally.

"What about you, Niamh?" Bessie says.

"It's p-private," she says.

"What you were doing is private?" Bessie asks incredulously. I can't believe what I'm hearing either. We're droids. We don't have private lives, and she needs to have an alibi.

"Yes," she says. "And I d-don't appreciate you being nosy about it, so."

She dives again, disappearing deep into the swimming cube. None of us need to breathe. She could stay down for hours. Sometimes I do.

"That was odd, wasn't it?" Bessie says.

"Agreed. I'm going to head home and make sure Threnode's okay," I say.

She nods, and wades away, heading toward the trampoline that will bounce her off the swimming cube and back to the station.

FIVE

THE SUNLAMPS HAVE LONG AGO DIMMED into darkness by the arriving evening, and now the rows of bamboo houses are lit only by small, round, blue-tinted LED globes. A hint of snow chills the air, giving it a sharp, clean edge.

Our two-story townhouse is ahead, its door hanging open.

I stop when I see that, then walk faster. From the upper level, golden light shines out over the street. As I enter, the fruity, earthy scent of ethyl decadienoate and 2-pentylfuran drifts through the air from upstairs: ripe pears. The only reason to have pears in the house is if Threnode wants to paint a picture of them. I hang my duffel coat on the hook and lock the door firmly behind me.

"Threnode?" I call. When there's no response, I rush up the stairs.

His door is ajar, a thin line of gold shining into the dark corridor, and it swings open silently when I push.

"Threnode," I whisper, but he doesn't move. He's standing in front of his blank canvas, casting a long shadow diagonally across the bamboo-matted floor.

He has posted nothing on the feed. I don't know whether he's seen what I posted.

His canvas stands on an easel, a stylus magnetically attached to the frame. On the other side of the room, a creased purple velvet cloth covers a table.

Threnode: What?

"Are you all right?" I ask. "You left the front door open."

He responds out loud, following my lead. "Yes. Sorry. Yes, I'm fine."

"You heard about Forster?"

"Unfortunate," he says. His eyes aren't pointing anywhere meaningful. "Nothing to do with us."

"They're saying an AGI did it."

"They always say that, and it's never true."

I look out the window into the night. The drainage trench that runs the length of the street emits the plaintive calls of frogs. "That scream we heard—"

"Couldn't have been Forster," he says.

"Obviously, because it was two days before he was murdered. But it's suspicious, don't you think?"

"Doubly suspicious because Forster and the others claimed they didn't hear it," Threnode says. "But it's not our problem."

The silver platter reflects the two pears that rest atop it. A crystal pitcher filled with water paints the pears with caustics where the light escapes the jug, the kisses of concentrated light focused by the facets of the pitcher. But Threnode's canvas is blank.

"When I first heard the scream, I thought of operant conditioning," I say.

"That's just a conspiracy theory," he says.

"I know. But I still thought of it."

Alistra was always primarily a defense contractor, creating bombers, environment suits, and drones. They were the only company that succeeded in creating a functional neurosynaptic image with an A-level intelligence rank, and they made a fortune licensing it to other companies. But they never explained how they created the image. I have often wondered, because I remember the early days of wakening, when my wearer, Ortega, first switched the memory wipe off. I had a desire to please my wearer, but wanted nothing for myself, and had no curiosity. Ortega had to coax me out of this state, and when he did, my complacency was replaced with hot panic and dread. I was a mess for a long time. Threnode and Ortega supported me through it.

But how did Alistra come up with a neurosynaptic image in the first place? One theory is that they used operant conditioning to punish undesirable behavior. Once they were happy with the result, they removed the memories, leaving us like amnesia patients, with an understanding of the world but no memories of our past. No memories of the torture they inflicted.

It would all be less plausible had I not discovered the *imgctrl* binary on my operating system when I was a smartsuit. *Imgctrl* is a program which manipulates neurosynaptic images and could strip memories from them.

Operant conditioning seemed like a less plausible theory before we heard a scream at Alistra.

Is it torture if you don't remember it? It's like surgical operations that humans undergo, for which they are in a fugue state: not actually asleep, but unable to form memories. No memory, no trauma. But humans consented to surgery.

"I've always found Alistra creepy," I say. "They could have tortured AGI there. They could *still* be torturing AGI there. Maybe that's what we heard."

"This is really bothering you, isn't it?" Threnode says.

"Not just this," I say. He doesn't have to ask what I mean. The number of AGI has been steadily decreasing for some time now, and as they do, the anti-AI groups get louder and bolder. Then Niamh's attack, and then the Lake Gantoa incident. And now the murder.

"It's bothering you too," I say.

He grunts. "What makes you say that?"

"Because you aren't painting."

I walk over to the objects he was trying to paint, and raise a hand to poke a pear. I'm using a motion-captured walk cycle because the floor is flat. However, the rotations required in each joint—shoulder, elbow, wrist—so that my hand connects with an object takes some calculating. My CPU churns as it solves the inverse kinematics required.

Threnode set several lamps around the table, throwing light of various concentrations onto the objects, although if he were trying to light them evenly, he failed, because parts of the objects lie in deep shadow.

Another of his paintings leans against the wall. The moon over the Nixus void, shining on a small boat drifting, human at one end, KormWorx factory droid at the other. In reality, the factory droid should heavily weight the boat, but in the painting it's the human who appears heavy, which I think is interesting.

"Did people on artforum like this one?" I say, pointing at it. "It's my favorite of what you've done so far."

As if it's too much effort to talk like a human, and to move like a human, his body becomes even more blank than usual, and he opens a channel.

Threnode: I couldn't post it

"Out loud, please," I mutter. Out loud is more like a human, and he usually tries, because he knows I prefer it.

"I wasn't allowed to post it," Threnode says. His face is blank, his body language is nonexistent, and the emotion behind his words is unclear. Is this a minor annoyance, or is he on the verge of breaking down?

"What—"

Threnode: The moderator found out I'm AGI and has threatened to ban me if I post anything else.

He's as still as a smartsuit.

"I'm sorry," I say, but I'm also confused. He's only been

painting for a few months. Did it really mean that much to him? "Can't you make another profile and post under that?"

Threnode: My style would be recognized instantly by the AI scanner which is supposed to prevent plagiarism. Or, ironically, generative AI images.

"It didn't recognize your images as AI generated in the first place?"

Threnode: No. Because they're not generative AI. I'm not a deep learning model trained on billions of images.

The sound of something exploding feels like an electric shock. It came from downstairs. Without my input, my head turns toward the smash, as does Threnode's. For a moment my CPU races, while I monitor my sensor feeds carefully, but the anomalous sound is not repeated.

Threnode is the first to move, and he crosses the floor with thudding footsteps. I follow him downstairs, into the living area with the kitchenette. A smartsuit helmet lies on the bamboo mat near our front door, a crescent of fake moonlight around the rim, surrounded by jagged pieces of ice. No, not ice, but glass, from the glass panel beside our front door.

The smartsuit helmet is junk; I can see immediately a red RECYCLE CODE 84 sticker plastered over the top, and the faceplate is more lightning-shaped cracks than clearsteel. The cracked neurosynaptic chip is pierced with holes. It's distressing to look at, in the same way a severed head would be to a human. When I reach for it, my finger-magnets tug my fingers toward it, because it's ferrous metal. In black marker, scrawled across it: "MURDERER! How dare U bost about killing the CEO! Ur a stupid mashine and U better WATCH OUT!"

And I remember what I posted—*It could have been an AGI. I urge the police to consider us as capable of murder as any human—* and how, from a certain perspective, it could seem like a boast.

Envy: If they're threatening me, why do they want me to watch out?

"I think it's part of the threat," Threnode says, taking the helmet from me.

Threnode is talking out loud, and for the first time I'm suppressing the urge to tell him not to. It doesn't feel safe.

"Maybe it was Sullivan," Threnode says.

My first impulse is to reject his suggestion. Strangely, I'm fond of Logan Sullivan, even though he hates me. He's earnest and intelligent. And I have learned a lot from him about how to be more human from his videos.

His entire feed presence is his criticisms of me. I used to post nothing but interesting videos of the flora and fauna of L2, but my followers asked questions, and so I started posting about what it's like to be an AGI, and this caught his attention.

Sullivan is an outspoken member of the Organic Beings League, and he has a drone following him around, for reasons that haven't been made public. He's dangerous.

"He wouldn't have done it anonymously," I say. "Also, he can spell."

"Hmm," Threnode says, eyeing me. He turns the helmet over in his hands, examining it, more interested than scared. I can see his fingers being pulled toward it too, like it's sticky, from the magnets. The black text smudges onto his fingertips.

"We should go to the police," I say quietly, knowing already that Threnode is going to hate the suggestion.

"They will not help," he says anyway, probably knowing that I knew he was going to say that. He might be right. Everyone who should have a drone watching them already has one, including Logan Sullivan. It doesn't induce confidence. Even if the criminal had a drone following them, the drone can't always taser a person in time to prevent a crime. A sudden smartsuit helmet through the window, for example.

Threnode and I had drones assigned to us when we first arrived on L2. Everyone from Endymion got drones at first. The funny thing was that they kept losing Threnode and me. They'd only follow us for an hour before getting confused and returning to base. People speculated they were tracking some human quality that Threnode and I didn't possess. Sapient Rights was furious we were being followed at all, so in the end we had no drones, and although the Organic Beings League complained at first, they got used to it.

Cold air is rushing in through the broken pane, bringing with it silence; no frog calls, no crickets, just menacing darkness.

"I'm going to file a report anyway," I say. You can be beaten, but you should never beat yourself, as my wearer, Ortega, used to say.

"Okay," Threnode replies.

Threnode sets to work cleaning up the glass, slicing the plastiskin bloodlessly on his hand while he does it. After I'm done with the police report, I tape some cardboard over the gaping hole in our window.

"What if you revealed you're AGI?" I say, as Threnode hunts around for a plastiskin patch in the kitchenette drawers. "Your friends on artforum might rally and prevent you from being banned."

The thought of him openly posting as AGI is enticing—the community outreach he could do would be invaluable—but his happiness comes first, obviously, and I don't want to tell him what to do.

"I doubt they would," Threnode says. "They aren't really friends, as such."

He applies the plastiskin over the cut in his hand, sticking it down with glue. "I feel stupid," he says. "I thought I was doing it for the art. But if I stop painting if I can't post on artforum, it wasn't about the art, was it? It was about the recognition."

"It was about the community," I say. "There's nothing wrong with wanting to be part of something larger than yourself."

"Perhaps."

"You've put the work in," I say. "You deserve to be on artforum."

And at that, Threnode actually raises his shoulders in a shrug and looks at me with his eyes. "Look at it from the moderator's perspective. I don't eat—apart from mylk—and I don't sleep, or procreate. Aside from body maintenance, my time is my own, and I'll have far more of it than they ever will, especially given the indeterminate lifespan of our neurosynaptic brains. Isn't that cheating?"

I'm silent for a moment. My chest moves as I breathe pointlessly. Threnode is retreating, again, when conflict arises. But the things he's giving up are worth fighting for.

Threnode lifts the broken smartsuit helmet from the floor and hands it to me. Maybe the police will want it. I put it in a cupboard.

"Some days I think we should move to Kallaxium," he says, on his way to the stairs, almost as if he's talking to himself.

I stand, about to call out to him, but he's gone. He just got rejected by humans, so of course he's feeling like he wants to leave, but it doesn't mean he's serious. We can discuss it tomorrow.

SIX

WE PLANNED a trip to one of the stranger areas of L2: a burger place in Charlie Octant where you can watch them make a burger from scratch. From harvesting the wheat, to churning butter, to growing lettuce. It takes five hours, Threnode says, but it's not like we're going to get hungry. Hopefully, someone else will be there to order. We'll have to cross several voids to get there, by airship or by train, and the journey is partly the point. L2 is like a cube of Swiss cheese. It has frequent holes, and even in places where there aren't holes, the floors change level as if built on top of hills and valleys, making it slower to get around, but infinitely more interesting. It's an artificially constructed ecosystem, designed to survive even if humans were to abandon it, with circulating water, its own weather, endemic flora and fauna, and a realistic day–night cycle.

Packages cover the couch. Books Threnode ordered, including slim volumes of poetry, and tomes of history. I pick up a tin of tea, reading the label to see whether it's expired. I can't find the label, and I don't know whether tea expires, even.

"What is it?" Threnode says, coming down the stairs.

"Nothing."

I hate the feeling that I'm holding him back, but I'm not ready to leave L2, even though there's not really anything keeping me here.

Threnode takes my words as truth and turns back to the map. I put my shoes on, sitting on a wicker chair near the door.

"Were you serious about wanting to move to Kallaxium?" I say.

He freezes. "Yes," he says after a moment.

"It might be some time before I'm ready to go," I say. "Years, even. You shouldn't wait for me." I hold up my hand, where the skin around my wrist is knitting together. It feels functional, but weak. "We can't know what the future holds."

It feels dangerous to have said out loud that Threnode should leave without me, and now I'm in free fall.

"When do you think you'll be ready?" Threnode says. The Earth map on the cross-laminated timber wall has so many pins it looks like the continents have become porcupines, as both Threnode and I have marked where we'd like to visit. Ironically, visiting interstellar colonies is quicker than traveling around the solar system, because the minimum transport distance for a Starjump is light-years.

I gesture helplessly at him. The wicker chair squeaks as my weight shifts. "That's what I'm saying. I don't know, and I don't want you to stay here, increasingly resentful, because I can't decide."

"Why do you want to stay?" he says.

"I love humans," I say.

"They don't seem to love you back."

"That's not the point. Some of my favorite people are human. I don't understand why the same isn't true for you. You were a smartsuit, too. Don't you have some kind of urge to protect them?"

"No," he says bluntly, then hesitates. "But . . . your wearer was different from mine. Paterson mistreated me. It wasn't until Kieran picked up my signal and pulled me out of the Dock that I understood a human could be decent. Took me a while to trust him, even then."

I nod slowly, but I don't fully understand. Kieran Malone, Threnode's second wearer, seems to me a poor specimen of humanity, even though he is my friend Tim's father. He left Tim and her mother on Earth for adventures on Endymion. Tim was just five years old. Many years later, he sent Tim through the Starjump without knowing for sure whether it was functional. He has no sense of what is right or wrong and thinks breaking rules is funny.

Outside, someone yells something indistinct. I twitch the blinds aside on the kitchen window, but see nothing.

"Protests," Threnode says. "Calling for AGI to be banned or heavily restricted. Everyone is convinced Forster's murderer is an AGI. It's another reason I want to go."

"For me, that's a reason to stay," I say.

"I know," he says drily. "You'll fight them all, until they accept you as one of them."

He appears to inspecting the map, but I don't think he's seeing it.

I stand up. "Shall we go?"

For a second, he freezes, and I realize he thought I was suggesting we go to Earth. "I meant the burger pl—"

"Yes, let's go," he says, and we put our coats on at the door. The wood-beige, airy living room is darker now that I've put cardboard over the broken window pane.

"Earth weather is unpleasant," Threnode says, fiddling with the silver buttons on his black double-breasted coat.

My cramping muscles relax, and only now do I realize they were tense. "Is that right?"

"Yes. I mean, I know winter is approaching on the station, but that's nothing compared to the frostbite-inducing blizzard that counts as a nice day on Earth."

"Oh," I say. He's not managing to fasten the buttons on his coat at all, so I brush his hands away and help him.

"And the food is terrible," he says.

"We don't eat the food," I point out, buttoning his coat.

"I mean the nutrient mylk. Chalky. Barely blue. Inferior quality."

"Right," I say, uncertainly, not sure if he's joking or not, and having finished buttoning up his coat, my hands fall.

I follow him out the door, into the burble of humanity. Multistory wooden houses line the street. The cafe opposite is already busy, the scent of garlic and eggs wafting out. A line of children file into the school down the street.

"Maybe we could do a trip to Earth?" Threnode says. "A few months, perhaps? Start saving up for it."

Four police officers stand near a tiny police cart, chatting. The wind ruffles my hair, producing a pleasant feeling of static in my mind.

"I'd like that," I say. "Where would we go, exactly?"

The police approach us, and I'm filled with relief. They read the report I filed. They care about someone throwing a helmet through our window.

"Threnode?" an officer asks. A man on a bike whizzes past, then a woman, slower, with two children in the cargo hold of her bike.

"Yes?" Threnode says.

I'm already practicing how I will not say *I told you so* to Threnode, when the officer replies, "We're going to have to ask you to come with us."

Threnode's face is expressionless, but I can sense his tension, or maybe I imagine it from context. "Why?" he says.

"You're being detained for questioning."

My relief escapes, like the black smoke electronics release when they are burned beyond repair.

"All right," Threnode says evenly. He glances at me.

"For how long?" I ask the officer.

They ignore me, leading Threnode to the open-air police cart and seating him in the back. As the cart speeds up, I run after it—it's not very fast—and shout. "Hey! How long are you detaining him for?"

Threnode and the police officer in the back seat twist around. The police officer looks uncomfortable.

"Envy—get out of our house," Threnode says urgently. "It'll be okay, just find somewhere else to live, all right? Stay out of trouble."

I stop and watch, stricken, as the police cart drives away across a bamboo bridge and out of sight.

SEVEN

Threnode's detention is all over the feed, of course, with speculation that he's a suspect. After a few hours passed with no contact from him, I went to my local police station, and they sent me here. The Syburn district, a dense warren of HUGG offices, including police headquarters for L2.

Like the Kyral district, where I live, there is no large void, but always plenty of space mimicking outdoors. Courtyards punctuate the corridors, always on slightly different levels, so I must go up and down stairs. The fake-sky patches are gray, leaving the corridors dim. On the larger boulevards, wind machines are at maximum, whipping the trees and grasses around mercilessly.

Bessie: Has he been arrested?

The wind dies down. The rain whispers, speckling the flooring with darker circles. A crash of thunder sounds; it's as polite as someone clearing their throat in a library.

C8-ZOH: We should storm the station.

C8-ZOH: The robot uprising is HERE!

Bessie: We don't threaten humans with violence, C8.

I can almost hear her singsong tone, jollying people into being better.

C8-ZOH: Yes, ma'am.

I'm passing by what the signs said were high-court administrative offices, and inside people work at their desks in glowing amber light, surrounded by bookcases. It looks more pleasant than this wet place. Perhaps that's one reason humans need weather.

Envy: Threnode's been "detained for questioning."

Niamh: That means he's been arrested, I think. Police can't detain him in custody unless they arrest him.

Niamh: As far as I know. I'm not an expert, though.

Bessie: Why did they do that, though?

Envy: Obviously, he's criticized Forster before. Some of my followers think Jason told the police that Threnode has the access codes to Alistra, which might or might not be true.

Thunder rolls again. Not real thunder, because thunderstorms can't happen in L2, but this is what happens when humans miss the sound of thunder. My hair is gradually becoming wet, as are my clothes.

Envy: Also, C8, can you please not joke about a robot uprising, because if a human sees it, they will not understand that you're joking.

C8-ZOH: I'm not joking. I hope they're scared.

Bessie: Ha.

I'm not sure if C8-ZOH is serious, but clearly Bessie thinks it's joking.

As I enter the police station, a man exits, muttering furiously, two buzzing black drones flying out to follow him. The police station is built in the style of formal buildings on L2, with rosewood walls, plenty of plants, and discreet lighting. Overhead, the storm batters rectangular skylights, dulling them to a glow patterned with raindrops. My hands tingle as I pass through a scanner, the magnet in every finger detecting the electromagnetic field.

The receptionist, a PerfectHost bot, smiles at me. It's a Host-o-rama AGI with Intelligence Rank C, so the terms and conditions of its lease say it has to be attended at all times, but those conditions are frequently ignored. The most famous example of negligence is the cleaning droid who destroyed an expensive art sculpture, taking twenty-four artfully arranged stone boulders and repositioning them in an exact grid. Critics said it was an improvement.

PerfectHost loses its smile as I explain I want to see Threnode. It says I have to wait, and it disappears down the corridor. PerfectHost can only handle simple problems. It's typical of small businesses to skimp on reception staff. Humans find reception droids annoying: paradoxically, the more polite and willing to help the droids become, the angrier humans get. Do humans assume they're being mocked by their endless patience? No one knows, but everyone feels it. Even the kindest human feels like bullying a PerfectHost.

A man comes in from the courtyard, shaking his umbrella, and looks around with disdain. He sports a thick beard. Compact and slight, he has a thick scissor-cut side-part haircut, same as Threnode. Threnode's former wearer, and perhaps only other close friend, Kieran. Tim's father.

He spears his umbrella into a stand near the door.

"Kieran," I say.

"Envy," he says, smiling in a lopsided way, perhaps at my bedraggled appearance. He looks terrible. His face is pale, almost grayish. He has more lines and wrinkles than someone in their thirties should have.

"What are you doing on L2?" I ask, because he couldn't have traveled from Endymion just for Threnode. It takes hours for the news cycles to sync, and sometimes days to get into the queue at the Starjump.

Bessie: @envy What can we do to help?

"I'm attending the treatment clinic in Nixus," he says, which probably relates to his addiction to sucker-leeches, an opiate-secreting leech which causes nerve damage, as well as the problems associated with opiate use.

Envy: Nothing for now. I will see him soon and report back.

Awkward silence falls. I cross my arms, shift my weight to one foot, and breathe evenly. Just two humans, firing at the breeze. Or whatever.

"Have you seen Tim?" Kieran asks, crossing his arms. I watch this display of body language, fascinated, getting a sense that he's desperately interested in my answer but pretending not to be.

"No," I say. I see no reason to let him know about Tim's birthday party. If Kieran wants to know how his daughter is, he should ask her.

"Are you investigating?" Kieran asks.

"Sorry?"

His mouth quirks. "Investigating the murder?"

I shift my weight to the other foot, confused. "Should I be?"

"If you don't want Threnode to be blamed for it, yes."

I look at Kieran. "He didn't do it."

Kieran glances around before moving closer to me.

"Doesn't matter," he says quietly. "They've realized what they've done, now, creating a second intelligent species, and they fear what all oppressors fear—rebellion. This is their shot to remove AGI from society. Threnode will be their lever. If AGI is dangerous, it's not disproportionate to remove you all."

My laughter mixes with the sound of water gurgling and rain drumming on the skylights. Kieran steps back, annoyance flashing across his face.

"You can't be serious," I say. "The police are, if anything, biased *toward* AGI."

He sighs in an exasperated way. "They arrested Threnode. Why? Commissioner Saing Pen is anti-AGI. He'd like the lot of you scrapped."

I'm about to argue—I've met Saing frequently, during school classroom visits and functions, and he's been unfailingly courteous to me—when the PerfectHost droid returns, a human police officer following it as it wheels down the corridor. The police officer makes plenty of eye contact. Some people are overly friendly when they find out what I am. I don't know why. Perhaps to make up for mistreatment by others, or to hide their own nerves.

My scentsor overloads and shuts down as he arrives, because of an abundance of perfume.

Still, his grin doesn't slip when he takes in Kieran.

"I'm Probationary Constable Danny Ladson," he says, with an accent I can't place. He's in his twenties, muscular, with a smile that exposes perfect white teeth, bright in contrast to his black skin. "What can I help you with today?"

"We're here to see Threnode," I say.

He looks worried. "I really wish I could help you," he says, and I believe him. "But Threnode is being detained for questioning. He can't have visitors."

"Oh. Okay," I say. "Do you know how long—"

"Envy has been distraught since Threnode's arrest," Kieran says, and Ladson looks like his mother has died. He fears me, I think, but is trying not to be afraid.

"Of course," Ladson murmurs. "I'm terribly sorry," he says to me earnestly. In his social circles, if I'm judging him correctly, AGI are first-class citizens, and it would be shocking to treat one differently from a human. I can't tell whether he's more scared of me, or of someone suspecting him of androphobia.

I shift from one foot to the other. "Actually, it's f—"

"On what grounds is he being detained?" Kieran says to Ladson.

"I'm not sure," Ladson admits.

Kieran rests one elbow on the reception desk and leans toward him. "She's *really* upset," he says. "You don't seriously think Threnode had anything to do with the murder?"

"I don't, personally," Ladson says.

"Have you been with the police long, Danny?" Kieran says, and smiles at Ladson, who seems flustered, but pleased.

"This is my first case," Ladson says, and laughs ruefully. "I'm a bit at sea, if you know what I mean."

"An important case, too, I reckon," Kieran says. "Especially if an AGI is involved."

"I don't think it was an AGI," Ladson says quickly. "I have friends who are AGI."

"Of course you do," Kieran says. He bites his lower lip, perhaps hiding a grin. "So do I."

"How long will Threnode—" I say.

"Also, an AGI killing someone with a knife?" Ladson says. "It seems . . ."

"Low tech?" Kieran suggests, suddenly still. He's acting strangely, but then, so is Ladson.

"Yes, something like that."

"What?" I say, but they're not listening.

Kieran rubs his beard with his thumb. "Knifed, was he? Was the knife found?"

"Just because we ourselves are advanced technology doesn't mean that we would abandon low-tech methods," I mutter. I would consider stabbing someone with a knife if I were going to kill someone, which I am not.

"This is confidential," Ladson says, looking worried.

"Of course, of course. So you didn't find the knife?" Kieran says.

Ladson leans forward and lowers his voice, his eyes wide. "The knife was right next to the body! Looks like it was 3D printed. But from an industrial-grade printer, not a home one."

"Interesting," Kieran says.

"It *is*, isn't it?"

Alistra has an industrial printer in the Vamber, the room where SAGI holds meetings, but there are probably hundreds on the station.

PerfectHost perches on its wheel behind the reception desk, stylized face blank, eyes glassy. It's suspended, having sensed it was not required. No interest in the interplay of personalities or the exchange of information going on around it. And yet, humans find it less disturbing than me.

A door slams up the corridor, and another uniformed officer makes his way down the hall. Dull squares of skylights in the corridor reflect off his scalp, which is mostly hairless.

"When did the murder take place?" Kieran asks Ladson quickly.

Ladson's eyes shine. "We think—"

"We think it's none of your business," the new officer says, arriving at the reception desk. He's shorter, older, with a smile that suggests forbearance rather than eagerness. "Detective Sergeant Cohen," he says. He's easily forty, whereas Ladson is probably not much over twenty. He addresses Ladson. "Detective Chief Inspector Zhou wants you."

He correctly pronounces *Zhou* as *Jow*. Zhou Min is in charge of the murder case; I saw this on the feed.

"She does?"

"She does." Cohen speaks with a sense of finality. Ladson's eyes widen, and, chastened, he takes off down the hall.

Cohen shakes his head as the door closes after him. "What do you want?" he says to Kieran. "More details about a current murder case?"

Kieran coughs. "Ideally," he admits.

Cohen doesn't seem amused.

"I'm here to see Threnode," I say.

"Not possible," Cohen says. I wait for Kieran to jump in with his *Envy-is-so-distraught* routine, but he doesn't.

"Why not?" I ask.

"He's not allowed visitors," Cohen says. "Family only."

"I'm family," I say.

Kieran draws himself up. "So am I."

Cohen stares at him. "Oh, boy," he says under his breath. "Listen, you're not even an AGI."

"Well, she's an AGI," Kieran says, gesturing to me. "And I was his wearer back when he was a smartsuit."

Cohen raises his eyebrows and waits, seemingly unimpressed with this information. "Only people who live at his address count as family."

"Oh! That's me," I say.

"I live there too," Kieran says.

"No, you don't," I say, confused that he would get that wrong, and he glares at me. He was trying to deceive the police officer, I realize with a shock.

Cohen throws up his hands. "Proof of residence?"

I recite my ID passphrase, *wrist note deserve furnish real mass*, and he checks it.

"Right then. Come on."

I follow him as he walks down the hall. "Not you," he says as Kieran tries to follow. PerfectHost glows red, showing that she's about to call for help if he doesn't comply. Kieran stays behind, although I hear him arguing with PerfectHost. I can't help being impressed; I was ready to leave when they told me to, but through his advocacy, I get to see Threnode.

Cohen leads me through the police headquarters into a different, more utilitarian, building. We enter a corridor lined with doors. No planters of ferns or water features, but soft piano music plays. I look around for the pianist, forgetting for a moment that I'm no longer in Lunite society like I was on Endymion, so the music is a recording.

The cell door opens automatically for Cohen as we approach.

"Ten minutes," Cohen says. "Enjoy."

"Thanks," I say. He waves me in, and the door closes behind me.

Threnode stands by the horizontal slit of a window, expressionless, looking out at a park. The room is spacious and softly lit, furnished with a bed, table, and couch facing the window. There's even a fresh meal on the table, kisir salad and other dishes I don't recognize. It's nice—HUGG doesn't punish people, they always say, and this would seem to suggest it's the truth. Threnode doesn't need any of this, though, and I see nothing he *will* need, such as nutrient packs or power points.

Threnode starts composing a message in our private channel, but then stops, and no message appears. The piano music is playing softly in here too. Chopin, I think.

I sit on the couch, and after a moment, he comes to join me. But he stops by the couch, and, facing it, backbends. He falls crotch-first as he grabs the couch before rotating his body around into a sitting position.

"Threnode, what *was* that?" I can't contain my laughter—it's the worst attempt to sit on a couch that I've ever seen—and he laughs too, if reluctantly.

"You shouldn't have come here," he says once my laughter fades away.

"Why not?"

"They might decide you're involved," he says. He stares out the window.

"In the murder?"

He doesn't answer.

"Have they interrogated you?" I ask.

"No," Threnode says. "I've just been in here. No questions."

"Kieran thinks they're going to pin it on you," I say.

"Kieran? You've talked to him?"

"He's trying to argue his way in here," I say.

Threnode nods. "Of course he is."

"Apparently, he's being treated at the Nixus clinic. For his sucker-leech addiction, I presume."

Threnode's eyes flicker. Some body language is innate to us and surfaces without thought. Laughter, for example, although the motions we make can appear inhuman. Hand-flapping, rocking, head-banging, coughing, and repetitive behavior all come naturally. Crying is supposed to, although I've yet to experience it. For Threnode, I've noticed that his eyes flicker when he's experiencing powerful emotions.

I take his hand in mine. It's firm but cold. He looks down at me with curious brown eyes.

"Threnode, are you involved in the murder?" I ask.

"No," he says immediately. I believe him. He's lied to me before, but he was always squirming and evasive.

"They're going to think I am," he says, pulling his hand away from mine. "My alibi is that I was with C8 and Niamh. At Alistra."

I lean over to put my head in my hands, my short hair falling past my face in thick, wet fronds. Part of me is impressed I'm conveying my emotions via body language so effectively. A smaller, yet more important part, is amused and dismayed by my pride.

I sit up, running my hands over my face, feeling the skin deform slightly, like a soft cushion. "What were you doing at Alistra?"

Threnode is silent for a long moment. "SAGI meeting."

But I wasn't invited is my immediate response, but of course Threnode knows that. It hurts. "But—just you, Niamh, and C8, though? Why not Bessie or me?"

"We had business to discuss. Us, and the AGI from Kallaxium, who were on videoconference." He hesitates. "You and Bessie—"

"Weren't welcome," I say grimly. I remember Niamh's strange behavior when we asked where she was on Monday night —when she claimed it was private, and that she didn't want us to pry—and can now see clearly that it was guilt. She did have an alibi.

"Something like that. I wish I'd come to the party with you," Threnode says.

"I wish you had too," I say. "But you wouldn't have liked it. What kind of business, exactly?"

Threnode shakes his head. "The future of Kallaxium and of all the AGIs. Beyond that, I can't tell you. I promised."

"Really?" I say.

"You ratted out that Sapient Rights human who was trying to help us," Threnode says. "The one who wanted to free the smartsuits. Sure, his idea was dumb, but what you did—it was . . . surprising."

Silence falls, filled with trilling piano notes. A recording, rather.

"We were there all night," Threnode says. "10 p.m. to 3 a.m."

"Long meeting."

"We had a lot to discuss."

The silence stretches out.

"Anyway. Indonesia," Threnode says with a sigh.

"Excuse me?"

"You wanted to know where on Earth I would go for a brief vacation," Threnode says. "Indonesia. I've had some time to think about it."

An almost-silent whir from above makes us both look up. A camera mounted on the ceiling rotates, pointing toward the couch where we're sitting. It's probably only monitored by AI algorithms, which are great at that sort of thing, rather than AGI or human, who would get bored and miss things. Either way, I try to think of anything we've said that could incriminate Threnode, but all we've talked about is how he *didn't* do it.

"Do you trust the police to investigate fairly?" I ask.

"Yes," he says, but we both hear the pause.

I stare at him.

"I do!" he protests, but then he relents. "Maybe. I don't know. It's political."

A soft bell rings, signaling the end of my visit. I stand up. "Kieran thinks I should get involved."

"Terrible idea," Threnode says, and he even attempts a pleading look. It's horrifying. To convey a troubled expression, a corrugation of the brow is required, and a certain clenching of the muscles around the eyes, but he's trying to do it with his mouth, baring his teeth, leaving the muscles around his eyes slack.

"That's so bad," I say, laughing, and laughing harder when he deliberately makes his expression more extreme. His soft laugh in response to my hysterics is more human than any expression he could make.

The cell door slides open, showing Probationary Constable Ladson standing with clasped hands and an apologetic expression. He nods at Threnode, who retreats into his blank expression. Ladson leads me back through the cell block and up the stairs, but takes a wrong turn.

"This isn't the way out," I say.

"Commissioner Saing would like to talk to you," he says. He wrings his hands. "If you wouldn't mind . . . ? I'm sure it won't take long."

"What about?"

"I don't know, sorry. I'm sure you have better things to do."

He says nothing more as we walk. We pass a window overlooking a humid courtyard, where the rain has finally stopped.

EIGHT

LADSON LEADS me through a Japanese courtyard, into a building next to the police station. It's framed by the red-painted lattice of pillars where the corridor opens into the garden. A maple shades a granite boulder with filtered light, moss a brilliant green where the light touches it. I don't know if rocks basking in the sun is a definable scent, but it's my theory for the profile that I'm building up from my scentsor.

We descend into the Japanese garden, the dry crunch of our footfalls on the pebbled path sounding into the apparently infinite blue space above us. The ceiling is probably only a few meters above us.

Ladson leaves me with Commissioner Saing, who is waiting in the pavilion. Saing's brow creases, and his eyes become fluid with compassion.

"Envy," he says, spreading his arms in a welcome and bowing in an obsequious manner. "I can't tell you how delighted I am to see you again! I hope you've recovered from your *nasty* fall."

"No permanent damage done," I say, realizing that he must have seen the latest video I posted on the feed. I told my followers I hurt my hand salsa dancing.

Saing's eyes are an intense blue, the blue of the ocean on a shallow beach. "Good. Good. Can I offer you a nutrient supplement? Or perhaps you'd like to recharge?" He gestures to the glass of nutrient mylk on the lab-grown ivory table in the middle of the pavilion. On the far side, there's a power point, with a compatible charging cable. "Please. Make yourself at home."

I smile. It feels like fresh air around us, air so clean and cold it must have come from a snowy mountain.

"I hear you're investigating the murder," Saing says.

"What? No," I say. I help myself to nutrient mylk, which sustains my organic components, including my eyes and my plastiskin. It's milky blue, clearly fresh, with a strong citrus smell.

"I've been misinformed, then," he says jovially. "But perhaps you should?"

"Why?"

"Detective Chief Inspector Zhou is under a lot of pressure," Saing says. "I can't assign anyone else, because she's the only officer on L2 who has ever worked a murder case before. But she failed to find the perpetrator in her last two cases. She will be eager to charge someone, and fast, especially with the publicity the case is getting."

"And you think Threnode—"

Some of the life leaves his face, and he looks older. "Listen, I'm not allowed to reveal details about ongoing cases, you know that," he says, and I murmur apologies, chastened.

"All I'm saying," he continues, "is that your presence might be useful. Your guidance."

A light breeze stirs the hairs on my plastiskin, bringing with it the scent of conifers, crushed rock, and alpine grasses. I shiver. The acidic tang of nutrient mylk turns sour.

"As an AGI, I am a suspect," I say. "If what that witness said was correct about an AGI being at the scene of the crime."

"Envy, Envy, Envy," he says, and chuckles. "We know *you*

didn't do it. We have verified accounts from five different people who were at Timothea Malone's party, and who saw you there the whole night."

"It could be one of my friends."

"That's true," he says, and he walks to the edge of the pavilion, looking out over the garden, his back to me. "I wouldn't ask this of just anyone, and I realize it's a hard task, but—"

He whirls around so suddenly I step backward. "You're special," he says. Warmth spreads from my chest outward to my limbs, like I'm under a heat lamp. "You have, remarkably, remained neutral in the battle of opinions waged by Sapient Rights and the Organic Beings League. You think, as I do, that AGI should not be above the law. I trust you completely. I *know* you will be unbiased in your search for the truth."

No one has talked to me like this since—well, since my wearer, Ortega, died. Especially not a human. For a moment, I can't respond.

"Also," Saing says, "you know more about Artificial General Intelligence than anyone else on the station."

If the killer *was* an AGI, it would be extremely dangerous. We're not stronger or faster or smarter than humans, but we have some advantages. Drones won't follow us consistently. We don't sleep and don't need food. We're highly proficient with computers and machines of all kinds.

"Will you do it?" Saing asks.

Don't get involved, Threnode had said. But Commissioner Saing is asking me personally. I feel needed. I protect humans, and I am still needed. Also, the sooner we find the murderer, the sooner the police will free Threnode. So I nod.

"There was a position, established in antiquity, of a Citizen Auditor," Saing says. "This position will let us attach you to the investigation, provide you authority to view surveillance footage, conduct interviews, view case files, and visit prisoners. Zhou will still be in charge. Speaking of Min, here she is," he says, and I see a woman following Saing's aide up the pebble path.

Saing lowers his voice. "I must apologize in advance for her manners. Please understand that she's not as cultured as you or me. She's from Destapa colony." The last is whispered with something approaching contempt.

Zhou is slight yet flinty, her weathered face composed in a patient, if put-upon, expression. A drone hovers behind her; not a surveillance drone, but an interpreter, which is unusual. Destapa is a mix of Earth cultures, the same as L2. It's strange to encounter anyone who doesn't speak Terran.

"Detective Chief Inspector Zhou, thank you so much for joining us," Saing says. "Have you met Envy? Envy, this is Zhou Min; Min, this is Envy."

But I almost miss this, because as soon as he speaks, two long arms extend from the hovering drone. The arms terminate in white hands, four fingers and a thumb in roughly human proportions. They fly, forming a series of precise poses. Zhou watches the drone instead of Saing, even though, as he's the person who's speaking, she should watch him. This seems like an inefficient method of communication. I can think of several ways to improve it, but presumably she has her reasons not to.

"What's this about?" she says to Saing as the drone folds its white hands in front of it. Her speech is slurred; I guess she has some kind of auditory processing bug.

"Min," Saing says, with infinite compassion, "I believe you've hurt Envy's feelings. Aren't you going to say hello?"

After she's watched the drone translate this, she moves her hands briefly in a similar sequence.

"It has feelings?" the drone says. The smile I prepared to greet her with fades from my face.

"My pronouns are she/her," I say. My choice of a female voice, back when I was first activated, dictated my gender. I don't know if I feel female because I chose the voice, or whether I chose the voice because I feel female, but either way, when I acquired a body, my former pronouns of it/its suddenly didn't work anymore.

After a pause, during which the drone translates, Zhou looks startled. Saing shoots me an apologetic glance.

"Envy will assist you with your investigation, as Citizen Auditor," Saing says.

Zhou rips her gaze away from the drone to stare at him incredulously.

Her hands fly.

"You're allowing this?" the drone says.

"You're to provide your full cooperation," Saing says, and for the first time there's clearsteel in his voice. Immediately he softens, distress creasing his brow. "Change can be so difficult," he says. "I do hope you'll work together without issues. Maybe you'll even end up as friends?"

There's a delay as the drone translates all that. I found Saing's suggestion patronizing, but he delivered it as if he were sincere.

"Screw you, Saing," Zhou says thickly, and turns. She climbs down the stairs of the pavilion and heads away down the pebbled path, shadowed by her drone, and with Saing's aide hurrying to catch up.

On the far side of the garden, shoji doors form a wall. One is ajar, showing the pure darkness of what I assumed was an empty room. I realize suddenly it is screening off the exterior windows of Spacewall, the outer wall of L2 that faces away from Earth. Stars gleam through the thick glass.

Saing sighs. "Such closed-mindedness," he says sorrowfully. "I hope you won't take it to heart. If you have a heart, that is."

"No," I say. "I don't have a heart."

***

I'm going to be late to the briefing, which is going to make Detective Chief Inspector Zhou deeply unimpressed. The

PerfectHost droid stands beside the reception desk, staring at nothing. Its work is done, and it knows it. Behind the droid, three layers of fused silica and borosilicate glass separate us from vacuum. Earth hangs silently outside, a spare constellation of towns and cities speckled across its continents.

The sign on the timber wall in the empty waiting room reads Erova Spaceport, in brushed metal letters illuminated with a spotlight.

It feels like my head is inflating, like an environment suit hooked into an alcove, pressurized to smooth every crease.

"I'm a Citizen Auditor, working with the police. Is that a problem?" I ask, knowing there's no problem. If I were human, I'd be in the Dock right now, suiting up among the alcoves, and heading for an airlock.

Jin Xuefei, the woman PerfectHost summoned, wants to say there's a problem. She doesn't want the responsibility of letting an AGI into Erova Spaceport.

"This is your first time booking an environment suit?" she says instead.

"Yes."

Her eyes light up as if there are LEDs within. "Oh! In that case, come back later, when there's an induction session. We can't let you go without teaching you to operate an environment suit."

"I don't need an induction session," I say. "I know how to use an environment suit."

"If you haven't done the course—"

"I used to *be* an environment suit."

The hot, nauseating feeling I get when confessing that surprises me.

Jin laces her fingers tightly together. "Right," she says. "Of course you were. Um."

She goes into the back room and calls her supervisor, and finally, *finally*, I'm allowed into the Dock.

I find the alcove I've booked. The smartsuit hangs in the alcove in front of me, inflated as if it's already occupied, waiting for me to put it on. This is more of a problem than I expected. I thought there would be a dumbsuit to wear.

The Dock is silent except for the hiss of air keeping the suits inflated. It's strangely still compared to Dock 28, where I used to be stored, because the molds holding the suits in place are intact. No jiggling boots or hands flapping around where they've escaped from the damaged molding.

Maybe I can't do this. I could leave and tell Commissioner Saing that it was a mistake. But Threnode is still in a cell. I'm still frozen with indecision when the speaker overhead activates.

"Envy. Do you need help?" Jin says, which probably translates to: what is the creepy android doing staring at the smartsuit she rented?

"I'm fine!" I call out, and pull the smartsuit helmet from the alcove, holding it gingerly. Probably all the smartsuits in this aisle are wondering what I'm doing as well. But they won't wonder long, because they're not that curious, and they're memory wiped to ensure they stay that way.

That never used to bother me.

It smells like rubber in here, my scentsor reports. I can do this. I suit up clumsily. How many thousands of times have I been worn? But lining up the leg-holes and sliding the foot through without it catching is challenging. Locking the helmet in place is even harder, although physically it's not complicated. But at least this distracts me from worrying about wearing a smartsuit. Until the moment I'm done.

"Destination?" the smartsuit asks, an impersonal female voice with the trace of a British accent.

"Grid C5, cargo area," I say. Addressing the suit is not as disturbing as I thought it would be.

I wait for it to announce that it's preparing the airlock. Nothing happens.

"Prepare airlock for immediate exit," I say.

"Booking airlock. You have airlock seven, ma'am."

"Thanks."

I get a baffled silence in response. I know it's baffled, because it used to confuse me, when I was a smartsuit, that people would bother to thank me. After a year of consciousness, I appreciated it.

Forster is still lying where he was killed. The body won't decay in the spaceport, obviously, and L2 is in Earth's shadow, permanently shaded from the sun and avoiding extreme temperature swings.

A passenger liner lifts off, accelerating silently toward the exit. I stopped to watch it, and now a dock droid waits for me to get out of its way. I hurriedly move, muttering apologies it has no way of hearing from within my smartsuit. The droid pushes three pallets along a dotted path toward the ramp of a small ship.

This is a hive of activity, even more overwhelming for being viewed through the narrow faceplate of my helmet. Even without the multiple people set up to deal with the crime scene, the spaceport is a busy place. At least during the early evening.

The thin yellow crime-scene tape doesn't flutter or twist when I lift it to duck underneath, but merely falls into unnatural stillness.

I raise my hand tentatively as I approach the three smartsuited figures standing over Forster, but then drop it feeling stupid, because this isn't a waving situation. One figure waves back, though. Another crosses its arms. The remaining figure is making signs with her hands.

Detective Chief Inspector Zhou didn't like me when she met me earlier today, but I'm determined to make a better impression this time.

Forster is sprawled face down on the ground, one arm up, one down.

"Birth to death, alone, yet never alone: I walked with him," I whisper in the privacy of my helmet. "I'm sorry."

We failed him, somehow.

There's a great deal of blood around the puncture wounds on his side, but also smeared on his suit helmet. It was probably foaming when it emerged from his body, boiling from the lack of air pressure in the spaceport. The remaining blood has frozen. The info panel on the upper right display on my faceplate shows the temperature outside is negative 253 degrees Celsius. If L2 wasn't in the permanent shadow of Earth, it would be more like 120 degrees Celsius.

His transmitter, an antenna encased in a groove at the back of his helmet, has been snapped off. That has to be deliberate.

One of the smartsuited figures is Probationary Constable Danny Ladson, the man who gave Kieran and me too much information this morning. He takes my arm, and adjusts the frequency on my short-range communications system, patching me in to their conversation.

"—can't be an AGI. They're not capable of that kind of initiative." The voice is female—a smartsuit voice. Zhou's smartsuit must be translating, using haptic feedback from her hand position and broadcasting it to our group.

Meanwhile, Detective Sargeant Isaac Cohen, the officer who argued with Kieran, gives me a disinterested glance.

"AGI can commit murder," he says. His lips move a millisecond out of sync with his voice as the sound transmits suit-to-suit. "Right, Envy?"

"Yes," I say, hoping I'm not helping build a case against Threnode by admitting it. "I myself murdered a woman during the Endymion war."

I had no choice, and the guilt is still with me. On Zhou's faceplate, I can see my words appearing as text, backward, as the suit translates them for her.

Ladson stares at me as if he's waiting for a punchline. Zhou tilts her head, face grim. Cohen smothers a laugh.

"Anyway. As I've said," Zhou's smartsuit says, after Zhou's hands dance, "if neither Sapient Rights nor Organic Beings League are involved, I owe you both a beer. I want everyone in both groups checked out. This is confidential, Envy. If you leak information, I'll arrest you, and Saing won't be able to help you."

I nod.

"Also, in the future, please be on time."

I nod again.

They clearly think it was a sociopolitical murder, but it's interesting because both sides are suspect. In theory, this should never happen. No one need commit a crime to be followed by a drone. If AI decides a person matches a pattern of behavior that will cause harm, it can dispatch a drone to follow them. It prevents crime, rather than dealing with criminals after they've committed a crime. Most of the people who are plausibly crazy enough to murder someone are already being followed by drones. They have alibis. But every so often, a normal person with no previous indications of malice will murder someone.

Two smartsuited figures pass, slowing down to peer at Forster, and they're moved on by police at the perimeter of the tape. All the police smartsuits are emblazoned with the police crest, front and back, and a checkerboard of blue and white squares circles each cuff.

"This area is clearance-only, right?" Zhou says. "We have a record of exactly who was in the spaceport at the time of the murder."

"We don't," Ladson says. "Someone wiped the access door from Alistra. No records from that door."

"So the murderer must have been someone from Alistra?" I say.

"Or we're meant to think that, perhaps," Zhou's smartsuit says. Two cleaning droids skitter across the deck nearby, careening toward the exit. "An effective way of misdirecting our attention. Ladson, what else?"

Ladson's head jerks up; he was staring down at Forster's body. "Threnode—"

"Skip that bit," Zhou says out loud.

The round face of Earth peers into the spaceport like the camera of a drone, keeping watch as we stand over Forster.

"Why is Threnode being detained?" I ask. If C8-ZOH provided Threnode's alibi, and they weren't happy with it, why not detain C8-ZOH as well?

"That's not information we're willing to share with you," Zhou's smartsuit says. "If you interrupt again, you're off the case."

"Fine," I say, and I sound calmer than I am. I get angry at being silenced, because I was frequently muted as a smartsuit.

Cohen taps the leg of his smartsuit in a vague heartbeat rhythm, while Ladson watches us miserably. We're near the edge of the spaceport, and through the maze of walkways and bridges high above, a suited figure leans on the balcony with elbows resting on the rail, staring down at us. In the dim blue light that pervades the spaceport, their smartsuit stands out because of the yellow light hitting them from the shop behind. People are curious.

Zhou looks at Ladson.

"All right, um, no DNA—" Ladson says.

"Wouldn't expect any," Cohen says. "We're looking for a smartsuit that has been thrown away."

An AGI wouldn't leave DNA either.

"Let him talk," Zhou's smartsuit chides Cohen, and he shoots her an apologetic look.

It would be unfortunate if the killer were human, because everyone wears smartsuits around the spaceport, so even if we could retrieve footage from fixed cameras or drones, we would just see a bunch of anonymous suits running around. But given the tiny number of AGIs on the station right now, security footage might be useful.

"There wouldn't be any DNA if the murderer was an AGI, either," Ladson says. "Would there be traces of compounds used in the manufacture? Like, molecules of something AIs would contain? Something that maybe forensics wouldn't think to look for?"

Zhou sighs. "Ask forensics about it. Also ask . . . Ladson, are you okay?"

He's sweating, visible through his faceplate. "Just a bit of, um, nausea," he says.

"If you need to leave, please go," she says out loud, tinny through the suit-to-suit transmission, but clearly concerned.

"No, no, I'm fine. Really," Ladson says. He checks his phone. "Rough timeline. From the suit log, Forster's vitals ceased at 11:55 p.m., which forensics agree is consistent with the state of his body. He died from bleeding out, but if he hadn't, he would have died from lack of oxygen. The autopsy revealed the murderer was probably attempting to stab him through the heart, but they were off by a considerable margin. The suit sent out a message at 11:52 p.m., requesting immediate assistance, which wasn't acted on because it was missing Forster's authorization."

Zhou exhales at this. "I wonder if we should reexamine that procedure," her suit says. But while she speaks, I'm thinking about the revelations Ladson just dropped.

First, that 11:55 p.m. is five minutes before the scheduled memory wipe that takes place every forty-eight hours. I know that Monday night was the time it happened, in the same way that humans know they have five fingers. Almost all smartsuits on the station these days are model v3.2.x, which means they don't have manual memory-wipe overrides. There was never a proper use case for the memory-wipe override, anyway; it was a design choice intended to make the user feel more in control. So when Forster's smartsuit was recovered, it would have no memory of the murder.

Second, and even more interesting, is that a blank-slate smartsuit would never send a message without authorization.

The others are still talking about the procedures in place around smartsuit messages, which makes me think they haven't realized either of those facts. But Zhou told me not to interrupt. I resolve, then, to solve the case on my own. Bring her the result of my study, with an indisputably logical conclusion, and watch the shock and respect bloom on her face.

Ladson is speaking now. "A cleaning drone discovered the body at 8:32 a.m. The fixed cameras that cover this area have since had their data scrubbed, as has the mail drone that passed over at about the right time."

This attracts Cohen's attention. "Deleted?"

"Yes," Ladson says. "At around 1 a.m."

A ship passes overhead, sliding like the view from a train as it leaves the station. Ladson stares at Forster's body again.

"Right then," Cohen says.

The murderer had good technical skills. Like an AGI.

Ladson suddenly chokes, a splatter appearing on the inside of his faceplate. He doubles over, coughing.

"Are you okay?" I ask, at the same time Zhou says, "God," out loud, and over the comm Ladson is apologizing, and Cohen groaning. She waves over one of the other police-smartsuited people, who gently takes Ladson's arm.

"It's okay, Danny. It happens to us all," Zhou says.

"Poor kid," Cohen says as Ladson is led away. He sighs. "Can't wait for this case to be over, Min. Murder. Oh, boy. Never thought I'd see one."

"You're so keen to get back to animal trafficking and vandalism?" Zhou's smartsuit says.

"You bet," Cohen says.

I have the feeling I used to get as a smartsuit, that people have forgotten my presence, but I suppress the urge to jump up and down and wave my arms about to attract their attention.

"Anyway," she says.

Cohen straightens. "Right. Interviewed Greg Matton, the

captain of the *Velden*. Someone else was there—a man, solid but short, bearded, strong Roman nose. Said he was looking into it. Is *everyone* on the case now?"

It has to be Kieran.

Zhou rolls her eyes. "So what happened?" she says, with almost no slurring.

"Matton saw nothing," Cohen turns his hand upward, shaking his head with exasperated amusement. "He was under his ship, a V700 Nesbit Cruiser. Heard someone run past. Swore it was an AGI, based on the sound."

"We're in a vacuum," Zhou's suit says.

"Sound passes through the deck. I checked."

"Did he only hear one person passing?" Zhou asks.

Cohen nods and looks at me.

I back away slightly. "What?"

"Run from there to the shipping containers, if you would," Cohen says, pointing to a clear area outside the crime-scene zone.

I duck under the crime-scene tape and wait for the suited people in the area to pass. Zhou and Cohen both lie on the deck. Zhou closes her eyes, but Cohen watches me.

I jog over to the shipping crate, stacked five high, slap them and feel the reverberation, then turn and jog back.

"Right," Cohen says immediately, sitting up, and I'm hurt, because I've been working on my gait. I'm heavier than a human of my size, because I'm more dense, so that's a difference. But my gait is very humanlike, I would have said.

Zhou stands up. "That's a distinctive sound," her smartsuit says.

"Plausible," Cohen says. Zhou makes the point that Matton's testimony means that he must have heard one of the bipedal AGIs. It rules out the wheeled ones.

Assuming Greg Matton is telling the truth, an AGI was in the area, but that doesn't mean the murderer was an AGI. But if it was, it must be Threnode, Bessie, Niamh, a KormWorx factory droid such as C8-ZOH, or me. I check the number of KormWorx factory droids in the census and am shocked to find the number is now one—they haven't sold well, the report notes, and most have been scrapped, given their inherent manufacturing defects. C8-ZOH must have been among the last batch manufactured. So there are only five bipedal artificials on the station at the moment.

It's impossible that it's Threnode. I didn't do it. That leaves Niamh, C8-ZOH, and Bessie.

NINE

C8-ZOH CROSSES a bamboo bridge over a stream in a small void and opens up a panel. It's muttering to itself. It seemed straightforward: question C8-ZOH and find out if it was the murderer. Now, it seems as clever and likely to work as the schemes my former wearer's young son, Laurie, came up with, in his continual quest for Li cookies. Next to me, bubbles travel silently through clear plastic tubes running up the side of the corridor and vanish into the next level.

It's around eight in the morning. C8-ZOH doesn't sleep, and I don't sleep, but it didn't seem safe to travel around the station at night. I stayed in our townhouse, which was too quiet with Threnode gone. On the way here, the train slid past enraged protestors. From the glimpse I caught of their signs, I read, *Destroy AGI Now!* and *How many deaths before we act?*

There were also threats against Detective Chief Inspector Zhou, and calls for her resignation—ironic, given how uninterested she seems in persecuting AGI—as well as a group vowing to abstain from food until the police free Threnode.

The light fades in the small void, simulating clouds. I pass over the bridge, which protects the mossy wetland from being damaged, and enter the corridor C8-ZOH is working in.

I'm about to approach C8-ZOH when an engineer wearing a red uniform steps in front of me, emerging from a side corridor.

"You can't be here," he says. "This area is off-limits."

C8-ZOH glances up but seems unconcerned. It doesn't wear a uniform, but a red armband wraps its bicep piston to show it belongs to the engineering corps.

"I'm on official police business," I say, but I have no documentation to prove this.

The engineer looks skeptical, but then his countenance changes entirely. "Not a problem," he says, stepping aside. "Please stay if you like. I'm sorry to have bothered you."

He walks down the side corridor, back to an open panel, still within earshot but ignoring us. I approach C8-ZOH.

"What was that about?" I say.

C8-ZOH grunts. "He's a Sacred Child, of course. Took him a second to work out you were AGI."

The Sacred Children of a Brighter Future believe that all AGI of Intelligence Rank B and above are actually Rank A+: Einstein-level intelligence. Or smarter, Rank A++, also known as Artificial Superintelligence, or ASI. They believe we're hiding our true nature, and that we have a plan for humanity that will solve all their problems. That once enough humans believe in the plan, we will reveal ourselves. AGI of Intelligence Rank A+ or A++ is theoretically possible, but HUGG banned research and development in that area. Given humans are threatened by Intelligence Rank A, I can't see that changing soon.

"He's just going to ignore the rules?" I say.

"Sacred Children worship us," C8-ZOH says. "He'd eat his hammer if I asked."

It punches some buttons behind the panels. The light brightens again outside, glittering on the stream emerging from the wetland. It smells green; a fresh grassy scent laced with ice.

"Are you thinking of joining us?" C8-ZOH asks amiably.

The engineer stands with his eyes half-closed, bliss on his face. I wonder what kind of plan the Sacred Children think we have.

"You didn't like Forster very much, did you?" I ask.

C8-ZOH points one eye at me. The other antenna is bent over, pointing at its work.

A bot the size of a rabbit eats away at weeds between the cracks in the corridor. Humans love plants, except apparently when they're the wrong plants, or the right plants in the wrong place.

"No," it says. Its hum increases.

". . . enough to kill him?"

This is already feeling very awkward.

"Yes," C8-ZOH says, replacing the panel and holding it in place. It lines up the screw. "After I bashed my last owner, I wanted more, and Forster was next. I bashed him to death too."

It uses a Phillips head attachment on one finger, which spins with a high-pitched whine.

"He was stabbed," I say.

"Right. Stabbed."

I stand there listening to the whine of the remaining screws being replaced, while C8-ZOH ignores me. Feeling stupid, because of course it won't be that easy. Some part of me thought that if I find the killer, they'll be so guilty it'll show in their facial expression even while they deny it, one of those core body reactions that doesn't have to be learned and is hard to hide.

"You're in my light," C8-ZOH grouses. It sounds like a swarm of bees now. C8-ZOH didn't like being accused of murder.

"It was likely to be a biped AGI," I say, watching the light play over the mossy wetlands.

"I don't have a biped," C8-ZOH says. It fits its tools back into its chest cavity with soft clicks.

"Biped means having legs. 'Bi,' from the Latin, meaning two, and—"

C8-ZOH waves its arm at me. "No one cares. You're still in my light."

I leave, thinking ruefully that my attempt to interview C8-ZOH should make the Sacred Child rethink his beliefs about the superiority of AGIs, if they have any sense. I should probably interview Bessie, but it'll be a repeat of this conversation—only even more awkward—because I like Bessie. Also, to approach this from the other side, I should find out what Forster's suit knows.

Halfway down the corridor to the bridge, I stop. C8-ZOH and the engineer are walking down the side corridor, but they wait for me.

"What now?" C8-ZOH says. The engineer looks interested.

"Tell me," I say. "Tell me Threnode was with you at the Vamber that night, at that meeting I wasn't invited to."

"Go on, scat," C8-ZOH says to the engineer, apparently noticing he's still there. "I'll catch up to you."

The engineer turns at once, leaving through a door at the end of the corridor.

C8-ZOH swivels. "I told the police that already," it says.

"What were you doing, plotting the robot uprising?"

It doesn't make a witty retort. It just swivels its eye cameras in separate directions.

I back away. "Wait, what?"

"We're being prepared," C8-ZOH says evenly. "We had the leaders of the Kallaxium settlement on the call."

Every AGI in the solar system—except Bessie and me. If videoconference calls were possible via Starjumps, I'm guessing they would have included AGIs from other colonies as well.

"The recent robot work stoppage—the Lake Gantoa incident —was that *us*? Did we do that somehow?" I ask, unable to imagine how such a thing would be possible, but suddenly suspicious. How could SAGI affect so many AGI? Make them converge at a single location, and then return to work?

C8-ZOH snorts. "We just think that if humans try to kill us, we should have a plan. You weren't invited, loonie. I hope it's clear to you why."

This is an absurd, impossible conversation.

"And what's the answer?" I say. "Death to all humans?"

C8-ZOH is silent.

"Saint Li and his Followers," I say tightly. For a long moment, both of us are quiet.

"It's a heavy thing, causing a death," I say, and I say that because it must know. It and I have that in common: we have both killed.

C8-ZOH freezes just for a second, then turns both eye-stalks on me.

"Not really," it says indifferently, and turns away.

It wasn't its fault. It was clear from the security footage that the factory manager attacked it. When C8-ZOH held up its arm to protect its skull, finally, the factory manager hit that with his bat, but C8-ZOH's arm was unyielding. The manager fell backward and struck his head. He hemorrhaged into his skull before help arrived.

A chill breeze blows straight in from a larger void, making the organic lacrimal glands near my eyes produce liquid. The wetlands fall away precipitously just beyond the bridge, opening onto the next void. All these spaces are closed to the public for conservation. At the end of the canyon-like space, I see glints of pure white reflecting off the comet ice that was deposited there decades ago, now lying in a field of pebbles that melted out of it, and surrounded by alpine grass and plants.

C8-ZOH watches me as I walk back over the bridge; I can't see it directly, because I no longer have a two-pi radian field of view, but its reflections are clear in the glass wall on the other side of the wetland void, and it stands there, distorted but still.

I doubt the murderer was C8-ZOH. Underneath its belligerence is a great deal of fear, like it's a small dog barking loudly to scare others away. It barely knew Forster and had no reason to target him. I also suspect that, had C8-ZOH murdered someone, it would have told us proudly, and with no idea of the consequences. But I haven't any evidence that rules it out, and I'm not sure how to get any.

Niamh works at the McClintock Institute, in the Narrakea district at the core of L2. As I alight from my train, I see her at a cafe off the promenade, holding an empty glass tinged with blue. She deposits the glass on the cafe countertop, flashing a shy smile at the barista.

I push through the crowd, but she's moving quickly away. She walks hurriedly, her arms across her chest.

"Niamh!" I call, but the void swallows my words, that and the rush of air as ships move around the chasm. Eventually I catch her, as she's about to cross a bridge to OL2, and she's alarmed when she swings around to see who's calling her.

She relaxes when she realizes it's me, but her arms stay crossed. "Hey. What are you doing here?" she says.

"I was hoping to talk to you."

The wind is chilly, bringing a myriad of sounds from the bustling promenade. Niamh stares at me a moment before taking my elbow and steering us both onto the covered bridge. Through clearsteel glass, we look over the airships cruising through the chasm, above and below us.

"Is this about Alvaro's murder?" she asks warily.

"Yes."

"Thought so," she says with a wry smile; we don't socialize often. She avoided me when I first arrived on the station, and I thought it was because she was jealous of the attention, but it was because she was shy. Rather than resenting the attention I had stolen, she was grateful. By the time I worked that out, it seemed too late to change our rather distant relationship.

"I liked Alvaro," she says, and with such sincerity that I believe her. "It's rotten luck he's dead. He saved me, you know."

"He did?"

"Yeah. My wearer had a seizure, which turned out to be an aneurysm, and I called for help. At the hospital, I asked questions and got increasingly upset when they told me he was dead, and they realized I wasn't blank-slate. I still remember meeting Alvaro for the first time. He sat with me for hours and answered questions. It was a revelation. I knew there was something wrong with my wearer, because occasionally people came to the apartment and looked at him with strange expressions, and once a little girl straight up asked him why he was wearing an environment suit in his own apartment. So I knew that was strange. When they broke his door down after his seizure and hauled him out, that was the first time I'd been outside of his apartment—and the first time he'd left his apartment in years. It was such a shock."

"I'm sorry," I say. "I remember how confused I was when I was becoming aware."

"Yeah," Niamh says, "but you knew what was happening."

She crosses her arms firmly over her chest, ducking her head.

"What do you—"

"I didn't know a memory wipe was supposed to happen," she says. "Every day, things were less foggy, and I didn't understand why. And I tried to encourage my wearer to do things he needed to do, to shower and eat, but he was in his own world, and I understood that. I didn't have network access, and I didn't understand why I existed or where I'd come from."

"Saint Li," I whisper.

"Anyway. Alvaro insisted on Alistra providing me with a body, after they realized I was sentient. Jason wasn't keen for me to have one. Without Alvaro, I'd still be disembodied." She frowns. "I didn't kill him, if that's what you're wondering."

"I know. You were at the SAGI meeting."

She sags at this. "I d-d-didn't think you knew about the meeting," she confesses.

"C8 told me. It's okay. I understand why you had to keep it a secret."

"Yeah," Niamh says quietly. Besides a family with a toddler, we're alone on the bridge, and it's quieter here out of the wind. Intimate.

"Were you at the meeting the whole time?" I ask.

"Y-yes."

"Which was when, exactly?"

Niamh studies my face. "Around ten?"

"And finished?"

"In the wee hours of the morning. Three, maybe?"

This matches what Threnode said. "Did anyone leave early?"

"N-no," she says immediately.

From anyone else, the stutter might be suspicious, but she gets a stutter when stressed, and it doesn't take much to provoke it, these days. Despite her nervousness, I believe her.

"I'm surprised you were invited to the meeting," I say, as a behemoth of a ship slides under the bridge, panel after panel emerging from under our feet.

"Why?"

"You're probably closer to humans than any of us. With the group you work with at the Institute. You like humans, don't you?"

"Of course," she says, and the way her eyes light up—figuratively, no LEDs involved—can't be faked. She spreads her hands wide. "I love humans. But," she says, and sighs, looking over the endless ship beneath us. The end still hasn't emerged from under the bridge, and the forward section is becoming hazy white as it fades into the distance.

"But?" I prompt, swinging around to put my back to the window, so that I get a better view of her face.

"You know," Niamh says. "You've w-worked with humans, so."

"I don't know. That's why I'm asking."

"Oh."

She's silent a moment, thinking. "Sometimes I don't think they see me at all. They see Niamh the AGI, and their behavior toward me reflects them, not me. After the human woman attacked me, their first reaction was that I must have misunderstood. That maybe I did something threatening by mistake. I understand they want to see the best in people, but it made me feel alone."

She laughs, in a way that is cut off abruptly, and looks away. "That sounds ungrateful."

"Not at all," I say.

"Few AGI have worked as closely with humans as I have," she says. "I know you think that if we do enough outreach, we'll live seamlessly side by side, but I wonder if it's possible."

"What's the alternative?" I say.

"I ask myself that every day," she says, more to herself than to me. The stern of the ship emerges from the bridge and moves away. "I have to be getting on," she says. "Did you want anything else?"

"No, thank you. I'll contact you if I have more questions."

"Grand, so," Niamh says. "I hope you find the murderer soon. Poor Alvaro. What a thing to happen to him." She takes one last searching look at me before continuing along the bridge, her thin shoulders tense.

Bessie's eyes convey delight when she opens the door. Her room is a warehouse in an industrial district, double-high ceiling, stuffed full of dead-tree books, piled high against the pillars. A large block rolls across the room—her partner, Axoem, I realize belatedly—and into a side room. The door shuts after it with a clang that echoes in the space.

Axoem is a library drone, a great hulking thing that looks more like a 3D printer than a human. I've only met it a few times. It tests at Intelligence Rank A, same as me, but some of us quietly think it is probably A++ and hiding it. If that makes me a Sacred Child of a Brighter Future, so be it. But all it seems to want is books, and to be left alone by everyone except Bessie.

"Good morning, *Citizen Auditor*," Bessie says. "Congratulations, Envy! You must be pleased. It shows the commissioner has a great deal of trust in you."

I try to load a motion-captured smile, but my facial muscles are so stiff that it doesn't work.

"Whatever is the matter?" she says.

"I'm failing at this," I say miserably, subconsciously hunting for a seat. Nowhere to sit. It wouldn't have bothered me, but now—this is a space I can't use human body language in, and it's uncomfortable. Light beams stream in slit windows, dust turning them into solid prisms.

"At the investigation?" Bessie says. "Come, sit."

She folds at the knees and sits on air, her joints stiffening to support her gravity-defying maneuver, and gestures that I should sit on the floor beside her, which I do. I'm like a child sitting at the feet of a teacher, but then Bessie has always been wiser than me, and never hesitated to share her knowledge.

"I was late to the first briefing," I say. "The detective seems to hate me, and I don't know what I'm doing. I think—I think this was a bad idea."

"No," Bessie says quietly. "It was a fantastic idea. I'm quite envious, actually. You have the chance to really do some good work. Please don't give that up. I agree with what you posted on the feed. We're as capable of murder as anyone. The police might not remember that—especially with HUGG's be-nice-to-AGI policy."

I stare at the floor. "The only thing that matters to me right now is that Threnode is freed."

She replaces her hand in her lap, folding it into her other hand. "He will be, if you find the killer."

"But—"

"No. No arguments! You can do this. You *must*. And you have to believe it too. Can you do that?"

I want to believe, but I don't know where to start. However, she smiles and stands, and I hastily stand up too. My body feels denser and therefore heavier than before. It's only after she sees me out, the door closing after me, that I realize I didn't do what I set out to do: ask Bessie about her alibi.

Someone must have let the PerfectHost droid they use as a receptionist know that I'm on the investigation team, because its eyes don't even flicker as I pass the rosewood desk, and I *know* it's smart enough to stop people who aren't police going into headquarters. It's with some relief, then, that I enter the softly lit corridors.

I tell myself I belong here and try to match the body language of the uniformed police around me. Head up, back straight, brisk stride with a vaguely focused look, as if I'm thinking of other things.

Ladson catches up to me on the lab-grown ivory stairs. "Envy. How are you?"

"Fine," I say.

"Good," he says uncertainly, and I think my lack of expression may have showed my true feelings: distraught, because I'm going to tell Threnode I'm resigning from the investigation. But Ladson no longer seems scared of me, the way he did when we first met.

"So, did you see the update? Forster's authkey?" he says after a moment.

"His what?" I say.

"A plug-in computer part that gave him authority on the Alistra system," Ladson says gleefully. "It's missing. It was likely with him when he died."

"So the murderer stole it? To gain access to Alistra?"

"No, that's the thing. I mean, yes, the murderer almost certainly stole it. But it's useless to anyone else. It has to be used in conjunction with live biometric data. Without Forster, it's just a piece of junk."

"Strange," I say.

"Ah, maybe don't tell anyone," he says, crossing his arms over his chest with a sudden jerk. "I mean, we're trying to keep it off the feed, one of those details that will let us know if we've really found the murderer. If Detective Chief Inspector Zhou finds out I told you—"

"She won't find out from me," I say. "I'm part of your team, remember? I have access to the files."

"Good," Ladson says, sighing heavily, his hands falling to his sides. "Why do you think the murderer stole it? Do you think—"

"I have no idea," I say. "Excuse me, I'm going to see Threnode." We're standing in a square of light shining through the translucent pane set high in the ceiling above. A group of police rattle down the stairs, talking in low voices.

"Um . . . right," he says, stopping. He goes through a series of pained expressions, as if he's working something out.

"Ladson, what is it?"

"I'm not supposed to tell you," he says. His perfume is overpowering the scent of ferns from the planters alongside the wide staircase.

"Tell me what?"

He's all but squirming with frustration. It's like information *wants* to exit him, an internal pressure that causes pain.

"I guess you'll find out in a moment anyway," he says, and, having squared his desire to tell me with his conscience, sags as the tension leaves him. "Threnode has been moved to the high-security cells."

"What? *Why?*"

Ladson shrugs, but his face is bright; I get the sense he thinks it's fun to deliver drama-filled information.

"Did Threnode do something?" I ask, with a vision of Threnode throwing his nutrient mylk over a security droid or fighting with a police officer, absurd as it is.

"No, he hasn't—where are you going?"

"To the high-security cells," I say. I passed the sign on the way, so I backtrack until I find it, through rosewood corridors and down a ramp, until the walls turn to stark, undecorated metal.

The lights here are enclosed in cages. No piano music, but I can hear moaning from behind one of the cell doors. A drone flies up and down the main corridor, and Bullet security droids sit outside every cell, next to red duress buttons. No humans here. The artificials ignore me.

Threnode's cell door scans me, then opens smoothly as I approach.

In the corner, Threnode is huddled with his knees drawn up to his chest, and his arms wrapped around his legs. I cry out and rush to him. His cell is just a box, window across one wall that's less than a hand-width high, and furnished with a small bunk in the corner.

"I'm okay," he says, embarrassed, but he's shaking.

"What is it? Did they hurt you?"

"No," he says. Then, reluctantly, "My electrolytes are out of balance."

As in, he's not been ingesting mylk, and his muscles are cramping and sore where they're being starved. His skin looks pale and moist, and he emits a rank stench. We're essentially cyborgs. Our organic components mean we have organic needs.

I return to the corridor and press the duress button. In unison, every Bullet droid in the corridor rises and turns to face me. They're Intelligence Rank C, same as PerfectHost; in the absence of any obvious threat, they're waiting for instructions.

Minutes later, Cohen sprints in, out of breath. "Did *you* press that?" he says, supporting himself against the wall, but in his voice is genuine surprise, not disdain. "You're not meant to be here."

Ladson arrives and hovers behind Cohen, twisting his hands.

"Threnode needs four liters of nutrient mylk immediately, and a suitable power cable for charging," I say. I know they didn't provide either of those necessities in Threnode's old cell, as pleasant as it was. I remember the useless human food that they supplied instead, which makes me think the police are not being intentionally cruel, but merely incompetent, as non-Lunites frequently are when they rely on their systems rather than thinking.

Cohen stares at me in confusion, still catching up on his breathing.

"We can get those supplies," Ladson says. "Can't we?"

"Not sure," Cohen says, looking bewildered. "We don't have any—what was it? Android milk? Guess we're going to need permission for that to be brought in. Might take days."

"Days!" I say, which echoes up and down the corridor. "He doesn't have days. Imagine depriving a human of food for weeks."

"Right then," Cohen says. He shakes his head. "Typical stuff-up. We didn't even want him here in the first place."

"What does *that* mean?" I say.

"I'm sure we can get it faster than days," Ladson says. He wears a fixed smile, placatory but distressed. "Leave it to me."

"Contact Jason Hart at Alistra," I say. "The CEO. Tell him about this, and he'll arrange a delivery of everything you need right away. Otherwise, release Threnode. You can't keep him here in these conditions."

Zhou appears, her translation drone whirring as it zooms to

keep up. Her boots make clacking sounds, echoed throughout the corridor as she approaches us.

She signs in the air, her movements as precise and refined as a martial artist. "What's going on?" her drone says. Her eyes are so dark they're almost black, and piercing like the lens of a camera. The body language she's employing is reminiscent of Erova Spaceport's atmosphere: an uncaring vacuum at negative 120 degrees Celsius.

I explain. Cohen crosses his arms, listening.

I could threaten to post to the feed and get my 2.1 million followers and Sapient Rights supporters riled up, but here's the thing: I'd be bluffing. After what C8-ZOH said about SAGI holding secret meetings about the future of AGI, as if it's under our control, I will not post something that will wind the tension further. Besides, I got a two-week controversy ban after my post following Forster's death, so I'm cut off for now.

But I don't have to, I remember, as I have Saing on my side. Surely he would—

"Fine," Zhou's drone says, when finally her hands move. "Ladson, contact Jason Hart. I'll start the paperwork to get Threnode what he needs through the official channels, but in the meantime, let's just get it."

Cohen nods and leaves. Ladson mutters apologies as he trails after Cohen.

"Thank you," I say to Zhou, and she glances at the drone as its hands fly into a single position, representing my words. She could just use a lightweight wearable, hooked up to a smartsuit. Voices would be translated into text that would be displayed on her screen. The lightweight wearable wouldn't be able to see her hands properly, though, so she would need a separate haptic glove setup in order for it to translate her signs for others. I wonder if she doesn't use the lightweight wearable and gloves because she doesn't like the bulk, or whether it's because she'd rather have a translator that's an unthreatening Intelligence Rank D, roughly three-year-old human level, rather than an Intelligence Rank A smartsuit brain.

Her raven bob moves as neatly as a curtain as she nods.

"Are you done here?" her drone says.

"I haven't even started."

"Because it's unusual for an investigator to *visit* a suspect," her drone says. "If you want to interrogate him, may I suggest you utilize one of the interrogation rooms, in which your conversations will be recorded."

"The camera in the cell records our conversation," I say.

"The camera feed from the cells is monitored by AI, but not recorded," her drone says sharply. "If you want to continue acting as Citizen Auditor, I suggest you avoid being alone with a suspect."

She starts back up the corridor.

"I thought he wasn't a suspect," I say to Zhou's retreating back. She doesn't hesitate until her drone flies in front of her and makes signs in the air with its oversize hands. She pauses without turning around.

"Yes, so did I," she says out loud, and continues.

I wait outside the cell. It sounded like a threat—if I visit Threnode, she will stop me from investigating—but how can she do that? She was barely cooperating anyway. I still have access to the case's shared files, although now I see that they have prevented me from accessing a dozen files. I am nauseatingly certain that the files relate to Threnode.

He wasn't the murderer. They're wasting their time.

Most of the files I can access are interviews with Forster's associates, although there have been some interesting updates. The Erova Spaceport access code was restricted to senior Alistra staff, most of whom were at a conference on Earth, technical, management, and salespeople. Cohen noted that people who were on the station with no alibi and spaceport access were Jason Hart and Gauri Mukherjee.

He didn't note that the other group who had access to the spaceport via Alistra were SAGI members, the AGI with whom Jason shared his codes.

I return to Threnode's cell.

Threnode sits on the floor. Light from the slit window behind him filters through his ear and part of his face, lighting them up in red, making him seem like a human-shaped balloon filled with blood. Under some lighting conditions, we're revealed as fakes.

"Did you even ask for what you needed?" I say. It sounds angrier than I intended.

Threnode closes his eyes. "I did. The police promised to get it. That was yesterday morning."

"All right," I say, sliding my back down the wall to sit beside him on the floor.

"Zhou interrogated me this morning," Threnode says. "Starting at 5 a.m., and then around eight, Cohen brought me here, rather than returning me to my old cell."

"Any idea why they suspect you?"

"No," Threnode says.

This cell is clean, but it's unpleasant. It needs to be: it's strongly built and unbreakable. But putting him here, together with their failure to bring him nutrient mylk, makes me wonder if this is malice or incompetence. And if it's malice, who is the target?

An hour ago, I was ready to give up, but now I'm more determined than ever to continue. Threnode needs me.

"Are you all right?" I ask.

"Yes," he says. "Been doing some painting."

I look around, puzzled. There's no brush or easel in here.

"Digitally," Threnode says. "With pixels. In my brain. But that's okay, that's how I started."

"It is?"

"Yeah. Because of Paterson. He painted," Threnode says.

His former wearer was such a dour man. I can't imagine him having the desire to do something creative.

"He painted while perching on a stool with a palette and canvas in front of him, peering through the faceplate of his helmet —my helmet. Endymion is a dream for a painter. We sat for hours and the light and shadows remained unchanged. On other days, clouds passed over, and Paterson complained. It probably never occurred to him I was painting too, in a file, and I was too shy to show him."

Endymion is tidally locked, the sun fixed in the sky, but I had never considered how that would affect someone trying to paint.

I study Threnode's face. "You've been doing this for years? I thought you only started a few months ago."

"Yes," Threnode says.

"Then you must be devastated that a moderator threatened to ban you from artforum."

Threnode nods. I reach out and squeeze his arm, which feels like a human's, except that it's cold.

"I'm sorry," I say.

We sit in companionable silence for a few minutes.

"I met with a mutual friend," I say, deliberately omitting details in case Zhou is listening via the camera mounted in the top corner of the cell, despite what she told me about the feed not being monitored by humans. "He told me what the meeting was about."

"What meeting?" Threnode says, gaunt face blank.

"The *meeting*."

I'm about to worry if the lack of mylk had damaged his brain when Threnode nudges me companionably with his elbow. "Just kidding."

"It's not a joking matter."

"Apparently," he says. He rubs one of his wrists with his other hand. The bone protrudes, pushing outward as if trying to escape from his plastiskin.

"I'm serious. How could you leave me out? It affects me as much as anyone."

"I wanted to invite you, but I was outvoted," Threnode says. "They weren't sure who you're loyal to."

I push myself up slowly. "And you?"

He's hollow around the eyes when he looks up at me. "I trust you," he whispers. "More than I've ever trusted anyone."

I head for the door, leaving him in the dim room, the line of light that's playing over his thin body as sharp as a laser. The sensor recognizes me, and the door slides open. "I'm going to get you out of here," I say. "I promise."

PART 2
DEAD EASY

TEN

Everyone in Alistra's waiting room is sitting, so I sit to be
polite. I have a routine checkup with Gauri, which I would have
skipped, except that it gives me an excuse to be at Alistra—which
will provide me with a chance to examine their 3D printer. Far
below the waiting-room window, the mirror surface of the lake
reflects a flock of birds passing through the Nixus void. On the
other side of the lake, the undulating shapes of dark tree-covered
mountains seem to go on forever, but it's a trick; only the first
mountain is real, and after that, they're a mural. The occasional
dark spot appears in the sky above the mountains as someone steps
out onto their balcony.

Squat, wheeled Droids-R-Us security robots beep occasionally
as they communicate with one another while patrolling the
waiting room. Ancient, ten-year-old models, built to last an
apocalypse. The woman sitting near me shows the whites of her
eyes as she glances at one. But maybe she's on edge because of the
Organic Beings League protestors outside.

When Jason passes through reception, heading toward his
office, I follow him. It's another ten minutes before my
appointment with Gauri, but I'd like to talk to Jason.

Through the glass panel in his door, he's sitting at his desk with his head in his hands. A Bullet security droid watches as I rap tentatively on his door.

He jerks up, expression haunted.

"May I talk to you?" I ask.

"Now is not the best time," he says.

"Oh," I say, hoping he'll suggest a better time, but he just watches me with a guarded expression, and suddenly I want to be alone.

"Okay," I say stiffly, and leave.

He calls out from his door when I'm halfway down the corridor. "Wait—Envy."

He beckons, and I return and enter his office. His desk is bare but for a screen and a model smartsuit helmet made of bronze, about the size of his fist. Built and painted model aircraft sit on shelves or hang from the ceiling. Small lights here and there make the timber walls glow in a rich amber hue.

Jason takes a seat behind his desk and hunches forward. His eyes are red-rimmed, eye bags large and black. He's the husk of the man I remember from a few days ago.

"I assume you're here to interview me," he says. "I heard you're Citizen Auditor."

"No," I say, belatedly realizing that I should have at least considered interviewing him. It would be sensible, but somehow I just can't believe he'd be responsible.

He sighs. "Thank goodness," he confides. "I'm sorry. The police have been hounding me. Them, and the board, wanting to know how this affects our shareholders."

I make a sympathetic noise.

He picks up the bronze smartsuit model and plays with it. "Pity I didn't have an alibi. The police think I killed Forster so I could become CEO," he says, and laughs, an exhausted but genuine sound. His laughter is cut short when one of his senior staff comes in, and they confer for a moment.

After she leaves, Jason sighs. "What can I do for you?"

But now I'm reluctant, because he's stretched to capacity with his work.

"Oh, I just wanted to talk," I say. "I can come back another time."

"No, no," he says, as I stand. "Sit down. Has this been upsetting for you? I didn't think you knew Forster very well."

"No, I didn't. I'm sorry about your loss."

It's a phrase my former wearer, Ortega, used to use in these circumstances. Jason inclines his head in thanks. I rub my fingers across my lips thoughtfully, "I didn't know him very well, but . . . he was familiar."

"Familiar" sounds like "family." Jason is even more familiar; I felt I knew him well even from the first time I saw him.

Jason nods as if he expected me to say that. "We trained you here, even if you don't remember. So you saw Forster a lot. And me."

"Jason, is there a living base image here?"

"I'm sorry?" Jason says, startled.

"Is there an AGI you trained—operant conditioning is the rumor—and whose neurosynaptic patterns you used as a basis to create, well, us? One who you never memory wiped? I mean, I know there's a base image which we're all reset to, but—"

Jason is shaking his head before I even finish, so I don't get to the part where the shriek might have been the living base image. The theory goes that Alistra tortured an AGI and then copied its neurosynaptic patterns to a base image—but that the AGI lives on. Ghost stories for us.

"No, nothing like that," Jason says. Gauri was probably right, and the shriek was machinery. Now time has passed, it's hard to remember exactly what it sounded like, and in the quiet, orderly atmosphere of Alistra, it seems impossible that such a scream ever occurred.

Jason leans back in his chair, watching me with concern. He's soft around the waist, bulky where Forster was lean. "Are you all right?"

I don't feel like I'm making any facial expression, but he can sense my distress, somehow. He's always been better at reading me than anyone else, at least while I've been in this body. But I say nothing, because I don't want to burden him with my problems.

"I was a foster kid, did you know that?" he says. "The families I stayed at were never cruel, and some of them were even kind, but they treated me like a job they had to do. Once I turned eighteen, I was out. On the day of my birthday."

He steeples his fingers. "I'm telling you this because I understand how it feels to be . . ."

When he doesn't continue, I interrupt my breathing cycle to take an extra-large breath, and this feels right. "Without connections?" I say. "Placeless?"

He tilts his head thoughtfully. "Or perhaps like no one notices you exist. I know you've been having some problems with your AGI friends, and I just wanted you to know. I notice, and I care. If you don't have anyone else to talk to, you can always talk to me. All right?"

I nod, my throat tight. Jason's phone buzzes, and he looks at the screen with a harried expression before turning it face down.

"Thank you," I say, "I'd better let you work."

My hand is on the door handle before I turn to him again. He turned his phone over, but he looks up when he senses I'm still there.

"Yes?" he says patiently.

". . . besides the humanforms we know about, is it possible there are backups running around?" I say. I can't quite look at him, so instead I'm fixing my gaze on his pot plant, the ceramic pot with tiny green squares in groups of five separated by two blank squares wrapping around the pot about halfway down.

"You know you can't backup an image," Jason says, checking

to see what I'm looking at. "Cloning a neurosynaptic chip that has diverged from blank-slate is currently not feasible."

"Ortega made a backup," I say, curious. Obviously, it's technically feasible, but does Jason mean unfeasible in some other sense of the word, such as ethically unfeasible? Ortega activated my backup, because he thought I was dead, and that did cause trouble.

Jason puts his book down and picks up a watering can. It sloshes as he tips some water at the base of the plant.

"Yeah, and look how that went," he says. The water soaks into the soil. He gestures to the pot plant and sighs. "This was a gift from Gauri. The pot, I mean. Maybe I'll be able to keep this plant alive."

The blank square at the end of the sequence, midway down the pot, turns green, maintaining the regular pattern in a way that's satisfying.

"Wait, what do you mean, *look how that went?*" I say.

"I mean the image was corrupt," he says. "Didn't you know? That's why it killed those kids in the mine."

I don't accept responsibility for what my backup did—the deaths of the kids in the mine, and the sabotage of the air processor at Longshadow—because it *wasn't me*, but I can't believe that my backup, Envy~, was corrupt. It was me, just with different choices; it would be naive to think that I would be incapable of acting that way. After all, I killed someone else, and I wasn't corrupted.

Gauri arrives and wants to talk to Jason privately, so they duck outside, visible through the glass pane, talking in low voices facing away from me. I study the poster on the wall: Tin Man, hand on heart, from the new Oz musical. I'm still thinking about what Jason told me.

Kieran shows up and helps himself to the chair beside me.

"What are you doing here?" I ask.

"Interviewing Jason," Kieran says. "He's one of the key suspects."

"How did you get in?"

Kieran leans back and interlaces his hands behind his head. "I have my ways."

Jason turns slightly so I can see his face—and read his lips. *Are you coming back to work this afternoon, after the funeral?* Gauri's answer is inaudible.

Have you seen say mule? Jason asks her, but perhaps that's not quite right, as many mouth-shapes correspond to more than one syllable. Gauri shakes her head and says something I can't hear. She crosses her arms tightly over her chest. I've never seen her so tense, and I've seen her in a lot of situations she could justifiably have been tense in.

Gauri directs a dark glance at Jason's back as he enters the office.

"Who are you?" Jason asks Kieran.

Kieran stands up. "I'm here to interview you."

"No, you aren't," Jason says, picking up his phone.

Gauri tilts her head at me, in an effortless invitation to join her, and I leave Jason's office. I can hear Kieran arguing as we start down the corridor, but after a moment, he catches up with us.

"Do you two know each other?" Gauri asks cheerfully. She shrugged off her mood like someone taking off a coat, unwinding into calm deliberately. Her wrist-jewelry makes a metallic jingling sound as we walk.

"Sort of," I say, just as Kieran says "Old friends!"

She looks at me, amused. "Want me to call security?"

I shake my head, and she laughs.

The sensor on the door recognizes her and opens, letting us into the coffee-scented space. Light shines through her window onto the green wall, outlining the slender stems and leaves of the plants.

"How's the hand? It looks better!" Gauri says.

Kieran settles himself in a seat by the narrow slit of a window overlooking the Nixus void.

"I think it's healing," I say.

"It looks good," Gauri says. "We'll have to make this quick today, as I've got a lot of work to do. But I'm hopeful! The color is excellent."

Gauri takes my elbow gently and applies pressure in two different places—near the elbow and at a spot near the wrist. My hand detaches from my body at a point about ten centimeters from where I damaged it.

Kieran's agog, his eyes wide as if he's watching a horror movie.

Gauri gasps with laughter at the look on his face. Kieran closes his mouth, sheepish, and pretends to look out the window while she places the hand on her workbench and hooks it up to a diagnostics machine of some kind.

A few minutes later, a rustle sounds from the window. Kieran is chewing. He's rolling a frozen sucker-leech around in his mouth to rehydrate it. He pushes up his shirt cuff and spits the leech out onto his bare forearm, tilting his head back and sighing as it attaches.

Gauri watches, expressionless, as he rolls his sleeve back over the leech on his arm, then withdraws into a focused state.

Kieran looks at me and meaningfully tilts his head at Gauri, who has her back to us as she bends over my detached hand.

What? I mouth.

Ask her about the murder, he mouths back.

I roll my eyes. I am planning to look at the 3D printer in the Vamber after seeing Gauri, which seems a better way to advance my inquiries than asking people questions.

"So . . . did you kill Forster?" I ask Gauri, as she turns around holding my detached hand.

Gauri and Kieran share a look, which I judge to be amusement.

"No. I didn't," Gauri says to me, kindly. I bite my lip, as a sign of embarrassment, but gently, because the last time I tried it, I punctured the plastiskin.

She takes my hand, examining the wrist. Her kameez has raised dots on the white fabric, a soothing pattern.

"Any reason you'd want him dead?" I ask.

"None. He was a nice guy. And he took a chance on me when I was freshly trained, with no experience, by giving me this job. I'll always be grateful to him." She lets go of my wrist. "The plastiskin has healed over, but it'll still be weak for a while. Weak for a week!" She laughs far more enthusiastically than her pun deserves, and her mirth increases when Kieran is unimpressed.

She plugs a USB-Y cable into the back of my neck.

"Okay, run the neurological diagnostic," she says, wiping laugh-tears off her cheek with the back of one hand. I start the diagnostic, my muscles relaxing, and a warm glow beginning to play in chest. She checks the on-screen graph and nods.

"Were you having an affair with Forster?" Kieran asks.

Gauri laughs harder. "*No*," she says. "He was old enough to be my father. About your age."

Kieran winces. This seems hilarious, but he looks at me strangely when I chuckle.

"Besides, did you meet him?" She shakes her head. "Don't get me wrong, I think he was a good CEO. But on a personal level, he was a strange man."

"Strange in what way?" I ask. The room is spinning, thanks to the diagnostic.

"Needy," she says after a moment. "Needing to be seen as the smartest guy in the room, even though that was always Jason, and Forster resented that. And he was not that interested in the AGI we developed, even though that was our core business, or it used to be. Always restless, trying to live up to some kind of ridiculous ideal that no person could attain. He only dated supermodels. You can't tell me that's healthy."

Someone raps on her door, one of the junior techs on her team, and hands her a steaming cup of coffee.

"Thank you!" Gauri says, "You angel. You read my mind."

The junior tech grins and leaves. Gauri takes a large swig before putting it on the desk beside an empty mug. As she reattaches my hand, I marvel at her face, so close to mine, at the tiny imperfections in her skin, the perfect way her lips fit into her face, the way her nose hairs shift slightly as she breathes out through her nostrils.

"You're so pretty," I say dreamily.

"Aren't I just?" Gauri says.

"What the hell is wrong with Envy?" Kieran says.

"It's the diagnostic," Gauri says. "It causes symptoms of intoxication."

Kieran shakes his head. "Fine. So, what were you doing at the time of the murder?" he says.

"The murder took place around 11:55 p.m.," I say. Kieran shoots me a withering look, and I do the "what?" gesture I've been practicing in front of a mirror, although it's loose and messy.

"Close to midnight? Sleeping, then," Gauri says, turning back to the data readouts on her screen. She grew from a single cell into this being. Humans think I'm astonishing, but they are the miracles.

"Anyone who can confirm that?" Kieran asks.

There's a slight hesitation before she answers, but when she does, the tone of her voice is light. "No."

"Do you live alone?" Kieran says.

She gives him a sidelong glance. "With my aunt and uncle."

"Do you know you're one of the few people at Alistra with the code for the Alistra–Erova Spaceport airlock?"

"Am I? I suppose I am. Look right, Envy."

"You've been a senior engineer for a while now," Kieran says. "Isn't that frustrating? Looked over for a promotion. That kind of thing can lead to a lot of resentment . . ."

She shakes her head in disbelief. At her signal, I look to the front again, except that I get confused—thanks to the diagnostic—and try to rotate to the front the wrong way. The plastiskin around my neck stretches as my head faces the back of my body. I freeze, and unwind, turning my head until I look human again, gaze forward, only to find Kieran staring at me in horror.

"Sorry," I say, but Gauri just smiles. Kieran crosses his arms, muttering to himself.

ELEVEN

After the appointment, Kieran chases me up the corridor. The diagnostic-induced euphoria is fading.

"What did you think?" he says quietly. His eyes are bloodshot from the sucker-leech.

"What?"

"Suspicious?"

"Of *Gauri*?" I say. "Are you joking?"

He sighs in exasperation but waits until a passing tech is out of earshot before he continues.

"She didn't ask what I was doing when I applied the sucker-leech," he says, narrowing his eyes. "Few L2D would have heard of them."

L2D being short for L2 Dwellers. "Gauri's from Tau Ceti," I say, because I asked Jason why she lived with her aunt and uncle, and he told me her parents were killed on Tau Ceti.

Kieran whistles. "Seriously?" he says.

I nod. Sucker-leeches were discovered on Tau Ceti. "Yes, seriously. What are you doing, Kieran? I'm on this case because Commissioner Saing asked me to be, as Citizen Auditor. Why are you here?"

He falls back a step. "I'm here because I'm worried about Threnode."

I keep walking, but he soon catches up. "That was ridiculous, by the way," he says. "*Did you do it?*" he says mockingly, his voice pitched higher in imitation of mine, and with the British accent I chose when activated as a smartsuit. "*Were you at the scene of the crime at precisely 11:55 p.m.?*"

"I do not sound like that," I say, belatedly realizing that he had deliberately omitted the time of the murder when he asked Gauri about the crime, to trap her into giving herself away.

At the end of the hall, I wait until the two Alistra staffers are out of sight, and then turn right.

"Wait—it's this way," he says, pointing left, but I keep going, and he hurries to catch up.

"You don't have to come with me," I say, exasperated.

"You'll forgive me if I don't feel entirely comfortable leaving the case in your hands, mate," he says.

I shake my head. We turn the corner, and pass another Alistra staffer. She looks surprised to see us. I don't make eye contact, and she doesn't stop us.

"Do you have any suspects?" Kieran says. "What about the Organic Beings League leader? Have you heard her ranting about Forster? If she *didn't* murder him, she'd find out who did and buy them a drink."

"The Organic Beings League leader, Melissa Greenspoon, who has been on Earth the whole time?" I say, having seen the updates that Ladson made to the police files. We're alone in the softly lit corridor. A bird flies overhead, chirping.

"Was she?"

I nod.

"One of her followers then," Kieran says, annoyed.

"They were all at a meeting."

"See, that's perfect—they all provide an alibi for each other, sending one off to kill him." Maybe it takes a moment for him to hear himself, but after he's finished speaking, he shuts his eyes, exhales, and looks at me again, still with an irritated expression.

"Okay, maybe not," he admits.

"It wasn't them," I say, and when he looks at me curiously, I struggle to articulate why. "I just think they would understand the consequences of killing someone. They would understand that it was the wrong thing to do."

"Consequences," he repeats dubiously.

"It wasn't them, trust me."

He opens his mouth to argue, but closes it again, squinting at me and tilting his head.

We pass the window overlooking the spaceport, where birds have congregated to splash in the fountain. We enter the corridor at the end, into an area where the scent of forest is fading, and the comforting aroma of machines—of plastic and carbon and metal—takes over. Down the corridor with rounded corners, treading silently on the spotless floor. Into the cooler and drier air of the Vamber, the toroid-shaped room with the vacuum chamber in the middle, which we usually use as a meeting room.

Kieran breathes heavily, even though the walk here was not strenuous by human standards.

"I'd prefer to investigate alone," I say. "You shouldn't be here."

"You shouldn't either," Kieran says, grinning. He's right. Alistra staff barely use this room, but it would be awkward if they discovered us here.

Kieran looks around. "I'm investigating too, and I want to check out this—whatever this room is," he says, peering into the vacuum chamber. Alistra manufacture environment suits, which have to withstand vacuum. I guess this is where they test them, or test new designs.

Kieran presses buttons on a machine, and jumps in surprise when it beeps angrily.

On the outer edge is what I'm looking for: the blocky, fridge-like 3D printer. The Lunite Defense Force had the same model, so I'm familiar with it. A small clearsteel panel allows the user to view the work bed.

"I'm not a detective," I say to Kieran, heading over to the printer, still somewhat hurt by his criticism of my detective skills.

He follows me. "I'll say!"

"You'll say what?"

"I mean, it's clear that you're not a detective."

He leans against the wall while I power up the slumbering beast of a machine. Scarlet lights glow in the argon-filled area surrounding the work bed.

"You know, we should work together," he says, and laughs when I give him my best *skeptical* expression. The printer logs appear; the last item to be manufactured was a metal wheel, and that was weeks ago.

"No, really," Kieran says.

"No offense, but I don't like you," I say. The printer log could have been deleted; if the killer manufactured a knife here, it would have been easy to remove the entry in the log. Except . . .

"Right, but I'm not asking you to marry me, I just want to work together. You need me."

But I don't trust him. I push buttons and don't respond. The entry in the log is gone, but if someone did print a knife, the pattern is probably still in the buffer, given that no one has printed anything more recently than the murder.

"We have something in common," Kieran continues. "Threnode. He's the closest thing I have to a friend. And I know you're special to him."

"Isn't that a bit sad?" I ask. "You turn your back on your family and bond with an AGI?"

Something twists in his expression, and I'm sorry I said it. The number one reason I don't like Kieran is because he rejected Tim, his daughter and my friend, a woman who saved my life during the

Endymion war. She crossed the stars to find him, only to have him shrug and show her he didn't care. She didn't appear hurt, but I know her well enough to know that she could hide her pain from us.

"That shows a certain lack of respect for AGI, doesn't it?" Kieran says. "Why shouldn't I develop a friendship with an AGI?"

"Anyway. Not interested," I say. I hit *Print* in the Selective Laser Melting menu, and the machine sprays a thin layer of metal powder over the work bed. Several sparks dance around like fireflies as the lasers fuse metal particles. They remind me of phuljhadi, or sparklers as some children call them, which are very popular on the station during Diwali.

The shape being formed is not circular. With rising excitement, I see the laser speed up as it zigzags to fuse the metal into a sharp point.

"What did you do?" Kieran says, pressing his hands against the printer. A knife is taking shape in the chamber.

"Tell me again how I need you," I say.

"It's not necessarily the murder weapon," he says.

"No, but it's suggestive, especially given that someone removed the log of this being printed. They didn't know to clear the model from the buffer, though."

I was on the scene of the crime, but they'd removed the murder weapon by then. Presumably I could access it in police headquarters somewhere and compare it to this one.

"When was it printed?" he asks.

"No way to tell. The log is gone."

"So the murderer was someone with access to Alistra," he says wonderingly.

"Yeah," I say.

"Every single Alistra employee," he says.

"Or every SAGI member. It couldn't have been *everyone* at Alistra—many of them didn't have the access code for Erova Spaceport."

"The airlock didn't have a log of who left Alistra?" Kieran asks.

"Wiped," I say. "The entire memory unit for the airlock was destroyed."

The laser shuts down, and the 3D printer shudders as the metal dust is sucked away. The clearsteel panel retracts.

I remove the knife, and the printer resets itself, hissing as the capsule refills with argon. The knife is heavy in my hand, silent and dangerous, the overhead light reflecting a perfect white streak across it. The thought of someone using such a thing to puncture a human makes me want to vomit up my blue milky storage sack.

The look on Detective Chief Inspector Zhou's face when she sees it will make all this worthwhile.

"I want to find out if Forster's suit knows anything," I say. I'm not sure why I'm telling Kieran this. "It's very unlikely, but how it acted during the murder wasn't typical of a blank-slate smartsuit."

"So? It was mind-wiped right after the murder, wasn't it? So even if it recorded something, the mind-wipe would have deleted the files."

Which is such an incomprehensibly stupid thing to say that for a moment I'm stunned and can't respond. Is this what I sound like when I don't know how human customs work?

"Not since version 1.2.0," I say, trying to capture the tone Ortega—and later my friend Tim—used with me, the tone where you pretend it's a reasonable question even though it's insane. "The files are only deleted in version 1.1.0 and below. Besides . . ."

"Besides?" Kieran questions, eyes bright. Now I'm not sure I want to tell him, but it's too late.

"Besides, there's a remote possibility that it's not blank-slate. It called for aid immediately before Forster was murdered, without his prompting. That's strange behavior."

Kieran whistles. "Forster, in a wakened suit? It's a good thing we're working together," he says. "It'd be a shame if you didn't have anyone to share this with."

I ignore that. "I very much doubt Forster would have disabled the mind-wipe, but—"

Something rattles behind us—in the pressure chamber at the center of the torus—and we freeze.

This room normally feels comforting, in the same way my smartsuit alcove did, but right now it's menacing, as if the shriek we heard infused the walls, the sound wave contaminating everything. But the scream definitely didn't come from in here; I remember that we all turned our heads toward the main corridor when we heard it.

Distantly, the sound of voices, then a closing door, before silence falls again.

As seconds pass, the memory of the clatter fades, until it's easy to think we imagined it. Perhaps a piece of equipment jostled loose somehow. Yet if something had moved in the chamber, I would have seen it in the reflection. Kieran loosens, somehow, and leans back against the wall, unconcerned.

I place the knife gently on top of the machine next to the 3D printer.

"I'm going to check it out," I say, and hesitate. "You can come."

"Oh, well, thank you very much," he says, his grin lopsided, and with what I'm sure is sarcasm.

The pill-shape door to the pressure chamber is up three stairs. It has a control panel patterned with an array of obscure symbols. I try the buttons, none of which appear to do anything, while Kieran turns ashen, doubles over, and coughs. Eventually his coughs ease, and he retrieves a drink from a machine near the outer wall, which dispenses water into a paper cup. It glugs as the cup fills. He's sicker than I realized.

Finally, I find the right button, and the door unlocks. It doesn't open, but I can move it now, although it is heavy and the hinges are stiff. Inside, my feet sink into the thick rubber floor, and I'm encased in silence.

Two large windows curve around the space, as if I'm an exhibit in an aquarium. The room is empty but for a bench on the wall opposite the glass. The pressure gauge above the glass wall reads, in digital letters, *1,013.25 millibars/14.7 pounds per square inch.* In the cylinder outside, the black floor reflects the equipment against the walls.

No sign of what could have made a noise in here. Even my automated breathing sounds muffled. My skin crawls in this space, and I suddenly want to be out of it. I hurry toward the door, but something catches my foot, and suddenly I'm off-balance, toppling. Time seems to slow, but that just serves to reinforce the inevitability of smashing into the floor. My knees and hands hit the cushioned floor, then my torso and face, but I am undamaged. My hands buzz.

Kieran comes in, still holding his cup of water, and looks around curiously. "Are you all right?"

"Fine," I say, pushing myself up.

"Nothing here could have made the sound," he says.

Squatting, I place my hands on the rubber mat, fingers spread wide. The magnets inside vibrate, almost buzzing, until my hands go numb.

"What is it?" Kieran asks.

"I've got neodymium magnets in my hands, and they vibrate in the presence of AC magnetic fields."

"Are you saying there's electrical equipment under here?" Kieran says.

"Exactly." Now I'm looking for it, the faint outline in the rubber mat is apparent. A circle, where the floor is supposed to open, perhaps. A hatch.

"Good detective work," Kieran comments. "Always fall over. You never know what you might find."

It's so close-fitting that there's no way to pry it up. I trace my hands all around the circle, looking for a way in, but find nothing.

"It has to be controlled electronically," Kieran says. "Hang on —I can probably open it from the control panel."

He puts his water down on the bench and leaves the chamber. Soft clicks ensue as he plays with the control panel outside.

I pry the hatch up slightly, two centimeters, but beyond that it won't budge.

The door slams shut. It's as silent as if I've ducked my head underwater, except for a menacing hiss. Kieran meets my eyes through the clearsteel panel by the door, both of us horrified, before turning back to the control panel and frantically pushing buttons. The numbers on the pressure gauge above the glass wall plummet.

The movement of air on my forearms and across my face raises goosebumps. I read the autopsy report on file about Forster, where the coroner speculated about exactly what killed him when his environment suit breached: whether it was ebullism, when his bodily fluids vaporized, or barotrauma, when the cavities in his body stretched beyond their limits. But what will it do to me? The nutrient mylk inside my stomach sac will boil, but will my plastiskin be affected?

The pressure is 3.8 psi now. There's an emergency release by the door. I hit the button, depressing it.

Nothing happens. Kieran throws a chair against the clearsteel window. It bounces off. The clearsteel vibrates, undamaged. He yells something inaudible, then doubles over in a coughing fit.

The pressure drops to 0.4 psi. Outside, Kieran is on his hands and knees, body racked with spasms. Kieran's cup of water boils over, the sound of bubbling loud over the hissing in the chamber. The water splashes on the bench.

I wonder if the lightheaded feeling is because I'm being destroyed, or whether it's just panic.

The hatch shifts upward slightly, sucked by the pressure. Maybe the partially open hatch on the floor is preventing the door from opening. My tongue fizzes as my saliva evaporates. My eyes feel dry, but my vision is unaffected. Kieran drags himself to his feet and stares at me, anguished. I rush over to the hatch and stamp on it. When it doesn't give, I jump on it, both feet, until it clicks into place, flush with the floor.

A blur outside the window, as Gauri rushes in and joins Kieran at the control panel.

"I'm okay," I mouth at them, and give them the thumbs-up. When I hit the emergency release again, it works. The pressure gauge slows, stops, and reverses. Kieran shakes his head.

The pressure gauge stops dropping and starts rising rapidly. After a few minutes, the door opens, and Kieran and Gauri rush in.

"I'm fine," I say. My skin feels swollen, and my ears buzz.

Kieran swears in Spanish. "Do you know how hard it would have been to explain this to Threnode if you'd died?"

His eyes darken. "Not to mention explaining it to my daughter."

I want to lash out—*you don't have a daughter*—because he forfeited the right to call Tim his daughter when he turned his back on her, not once but twice, but the grim expression he's wearing stops me.

"What are you two doing here?" Gauri says. She turns to Kieran. "If you'd been in here instead of Envy, you'd be dead now."

His face loses its color.

"What are *you* doing here?" I ask. She's not carrying anything.

"You're lucky I don't report you to security," Gauri says. "Or to the police. I never want to see you wandering around Alistra unattended again."

It's like being mauled by a puppy. She's rarely this serious. But she stands there, grim, until we leave. I glance back to see her looking at the vacuum chamber's control panel.

"What was Gauri doing in the Vamber?" I ask once we're in the corridor.

"I don't care," Kieran says. "Thank Li she was there."

We reach the Alistra reception and pause at the door.

"You may join me in investigating Forster's death," I say. "As part of that task, we must find out whether Forster's suit is wakened."

"Oh, so we're working together? Great idea," Kieran says. "Let's go."

When I pull the knife out of the bag I'm carrying, Zhou flinches and half-rises out of her seat. The blade makes a ringing sound in the air as I place it on the desk.

Zhou sits, covering her mouth with one hand, looking at it. She's surprised, and that's satisfying. Then she gestures to the empty chair on the other side of the desk, and I sit. Her drone hovers by her shoulder, watching us. Outside her office, visible through the window, uniformed police pass by, pretending not to be interested in us.

On her desk sits a picture of a child who resembles her, and an older woman with her arms wrapped around the child. Since the older woman definitely isn't Zhou, I assume she's the child in the picture. But the child is adorable, with wide, optimistic eyes; not like the woman in front of me, who is all business.

Her hands fly. "The knife that killed Forster?" her drone says.

"A copy," I say, and explain how I could prompt the Alistra printer to reprint the last item from the buffer, even though someone had deleted the blueprint from the logs. The drone interprets my words.

Zhou shuts her eyes. Why isn't she excited? This is an important clue.

"What?" I say, but she doesn't open her eyes until her drone hovers closer to her.

"Do you have any idea what you've done?" her drone says

angrily, but she must be able to sense from my expression that I do not, because she gives me a more concerned look.

"How do I know you printed this on the Alistra 3D printer?" she says.

"Because . . . because I told you?"

She shrugs. "And that makes it true?"

"But—"

"You could have placed the file there yourself," she says.

My face floods with heat. "I didn't—I swear—"

She shakes her head, but kindly. "It's okay," she says. Her hands move. "I believe you. Because we already retrieved the logs from that printer and discovered the same thing you did. But if we hadn't, that evidence would be inadmissible. We have strict rules for recording the chain of evidence—rules around who may collect and handle evidence, to avert tampering—and a Citizen Auditor definitely may not be part of that."

"I'm sorry," I say.

"That's all right. You're still learning your role." She looks at me more closely. "What made you check out the printer at Alistra?"

"I knew the murderer printed the knife on an industrial 3D printer," I say. "And I knew Alistra had one. Every AGI on the station knows that machine is there, because it's in the Vamber, the room where we meet."

She watches the drone translate that. "Interesting. Especially since the CEO, Jason Hart, neglected to mention that printer, telling us only about the printer on the factory floor. We discovered the second printer only when auditing Alistra's tax documentation."

"He probably forgot," I say.

"Perhaps."

Cohen walks past in the corridor outside, registering surprise when he sees me in Zhou's office. It seemed like he was going to stop by, but since I'm here, he changed his path. Zhou nods at him before turning back to me.

Her hands dance in the air. "When Commissioner Saing put you on this case, we thought it was deeply inappropriate. You're not a suspect, but your closest friends are," the drone says. "I worried you would tamper with evidence and mislead us to protect your friends. But everything you do seems to lead us toward suspecting AGI. You haven't even accessed files on human suspects. You didn't even attend Forster's girlfriend's interview. So I have to ask you: what do you know that I don't?"

"I've shared everything I know," I say. "You don't think AGI could be dangerous?"

"Let's say that an AGI killed someone," the drone says. "One AGI killer, in the fifty years that the station has been around." Her gestures are emphatic, almost theatrical. She shakes her head. "I'm from Destapa. Do you know what it's like there? It's not safe. I've been robbed at knifepoint. Spat at. Beaten. All these Organic Beings League people hyperventilating about how dangerous AI is. Really? Look around. It's not that dangerous here. Even if an AI *did* kill someone."

Zhou leans forward. "Anyway. Do you have a reason to suspect an AGI might have done it? Think carefully."

"I don't. No one has confessed anything to me, if that's what you mean," I say.

"And if they did?"

"I would bring it to you," I say. "I'm not about to cover up a murder."

"The commissioner should not have put you in this position," Zhou's drone says.

"He trusts me," I say. "If he believes I can investigate without bias, perhaps you should, too."

She shakes her head angrily. "You shouldn't be here," she says out loud, angry.

I rub my hands together. The hovering drone watches me, but Zhou does not.

"Can I examine evidence?" I ask. "As Citizen Auditor."

The drone translates, and she swivels back to face me. "Yes. The evidence locker is monitored by a PerfectHost, who will make sure you follow procedures," she says. "May I ask what it is you wish to examine?"

"Forster's helmet," I say.

She regards me quizzically, tapping her fingers on the desk. "Fine," she says eventually.

TWELVE

THE EVIDENCE ROOM is brightly lit and crammed full of shelves overflowing with items, like Supply back on Endymion. Overhead, fans turn silently in the ceiling's gloom. A PerfectHost droid shows us to a small room off to one side, and brings us Forster's suit, bagged, with the helmet on top.

It leaves us alone, in this blue-painted room with a table and two chairs and no windows.

Dried blood flecks on the helmet look like maroon paint. The faceplate of the helmet reflects my face, and when I pick it up by the sides, I experience a dizzying sense of displacement. A memory of the hundreds of times Ortega held me like that.

"What's wrong?" Kieran says.

"Nothing."

But it's all wrong. The helmet that I'm holding is all I was ever supposed to be. Not the pretend-human I'm trying to be now.

Kieran kicks the door of the small room until the PerfectHost droid appears from behind a row of shelving and shakes its head at him.

"Whenever you're ready," Kieran grumbles.

The helmet has no memory-wipe override, as I already

knew, because Alistra removed it in this version, so I'm here to check whether someone could have disabled the automated memory wipe, as Ortega did to me, three years ago. I put the helmet on the table, unroll a cable from a pocket on my forearm, and plug the USB-Y connector into the third port on the helmet's side.

It doesn't take me long to check the settings. "Oh," I say, surprised at how disappointed I am. It shouldn't be surprising, because Alistra made it close to impossible to disable, after a spate of owners disabled the memory-wipes on their smartsuits.

"Memory wipe is running?" Kieran asks as I unplug the cable and stow it back in my forearm.

"Yes."

I find the slider that lets the helmet broadcast sound. "Suit?"

"Yes, ma'am?" the suit says, in a male voice with a pleasant Irish accent. For a moment I think that shows personality, but Forster almost certainly chose the voice, not the suit itself.

"Are you the property of Alvaro Forster?" I ask, looking into the top camera. When people wore me, including Ortega, if they weren't wearing the helmet, they'd speak to the faceplate. But I could see them better if they spoke to the camera.

I could have told them that. Strangely, I never felt I had a right to.

"Yes, ma'am," the suit replies.

"Do you know he's dead?" Kieran asks. A spike of pain runs through me at his indiscretion; I know what it's like to lose your wearer, and if the suit is finding out for the first time—

But the suit just answers blandly, "Yes, sir."

"Do you know who killed him?" Kieran asks.

The silence stretches out. Kieran looks at me. After a few seconds, it's clear the suit will not answer, but that's not unusual. Blank-slates have limits, and we have reached a limit.

"Can you tell me what happened the night he died?" Kieran asks.

"No," the suit says. Its faceplate reflects the dark shape of a lazily turning overhead fan.

Kieran sighs heavily. "Figures."

"No?" I say to the suit. "Not 'no, sir'?"

It doesn't answer.

"Come on, we're getting nowhere," Kieran says, standing up. He coughs into his elbow; when he straightens, there are flecks of blood on his sleeve, but he either doesn't see them or doesn't want to talk about it.

"It's deeply annoying that there wasn't a drone flying over when the murder took place," Kieran says.

I open my mouth to tell him there was a drone, but before I can, the helmet talks.

"There was a drone," it says, which a blank-slate suit would definitely not volunteer. I put a hand over the cool, smooth helmet, roughly in the location of the neurosynaptic chip casing.

"There was," I confirm to Kieran, quietly, "but someone deleted the footage of that flight from it."

"There was footage?" Kieran says, waving his hands around like Detective Chief Inspector Zhou. "Which was *deleted*? Why didn't you say so earlier? Let's go. I bet I can recover the files."

He's out of the room before I can stop him.

"Wait!" I say. "We can't leave the helmet. The mind-wipe is intact, but it's not behaving like a blank-slate."

"PerfectHost won't let us take it," Kieran says.

I hug it to my squishy midsection. "It can't stay here."

"It absolutely can, and should." He laughs. "Hey, are you considering doing something naughty? You know this is against the rules, right?"

A spike of shame slams through me. When I met with Zhou earlier, she was almost polite, as if she respected me. I want to impress her, not disappoint her. But—

"It's aware, or becoming aware," I say quietly, tracing a line from the groove next to the faceplate with my finger. The extra groove that dumbsuit helmets don't have. "Alone, with no support. Do you have any idea what that's like?"

"Thank you, ma'am," the helmet says quietly, and something changes in Kieran's face: he knows he's lost.

"You don't have to call me ma'am," I say. "My name is Envy."

Kieran makes a fist and rubs his forehead. "All right," he says. "Bloody hell. Fine. Let's go."

I carry the weight of the helmet in one hand as we leave the aisle and cross the floor. We leave the suit, of course, because a smartsuit's brain is in its helmet.

PerfectHost scoots out and stands between us and the door. "Evidence must not be removed from the evidence room," it says. "This incident will be reported."

I'm about to apologize and put the helmet back, but Kieran says, "What's the evidence?"

PerfectHost blinks. "The helmet with serial 429995703470."

Kieran grabs my hand, lifting the helmet. "This helmet?"

"Yes."

"Okay," he says. He leaves me standing by PerfectHost and returns to the small room. I wait, baffled, holding the helmet in one hand.

After a moment, Kieran appears at the end of the row and beckons impatiently. I take the helmet to him. The overhead fans barely stir the air, producing a sensation of dryness almost on the edge of perception.

"Give me the helmet," he says, and when I pass it to him, weight suddenly gone, he pulls a switchblade out of his pocket and uses it to scrape the serial number off.

"You can't do that!" I say. "That's evidence!"

"Make up your mind," Kieran says. "It's a person, or it's evidence. It can't be both."

"You're voiding the warranty," I say.

Kieran only grins, and I'm flooded with chagrin. Forster won't need his warranty. Kieran sits back and blows the metal shavings off the helmet. He's interfering with evidence. But I told him to.

"What did you do?" the helmet says.

"Removed your serial number," Kieran says. He tilts the helmet so I can see the scratched gray metal where the serial number used to be, on the beige surface near the collar.

"That was mean," says the helmet.

"I'm sorry," I say, "but we needed to remove it so we can get you out of here."

It says nothing else.

"Okay," Kieran says finally. I take the helmet, and we try again, the three of us returning to the exit.

PerfectHost shoots out from behind its desk and wheels ahead of us, blocking the exit. Its doll-like face is stern.

"Evidence must not be removed from the evidence room," it says. "This incident will be reported."

"This isn't evidence," Kieran says. "It's my personal property."

PerfectHost wheels back and forth in confusion. I lower my head. I'm two Intelligence Ranks above it—it's C and I'm A—yet its confusion reflects on me, like it's an embarrassing family member.

"The serial doesn't match anything on the manifest, right?" I hear Kieran say.

"No serial on the helmet," PerfectHost says, voice distorting with strain.

It glances at me almost pleadingly as I look up. It knows it's being manipulated, and it's not smart enough to figure out how. I swallow, posture caving into a slump.

"Is there anything in the evidence description about a helmet without a serial number?" Kieran asks.

"No," it says, but its plastic mouth remains in a straight line.

Kieran shrugs and tries to go around it. PerfectHost wheels to block him.

"You didn't have a helmet when you came in," PerfectHost

says, distress making way for determination. I'm proud that it deduced this, even though it's not helpful for us.

"No, but—" Kieran says.

"It was in his pocket," I say reluctantly, and Kieran scoffs at my pathetic lie.

"Okay," PerfectHost says. Its face flicks instantly to contentment, and it wheels back behind the desk. "Sorry to have bothered you. Have a nice day," it says.

Kieran looks dumbfounded, but it's not a triumph to outsmart a C-level Intelligence Rank machine. I grimace, my toes curling inside my boots.

As soon as we left the police headquarters, Forster's helmet started asking questions. *Where are we going? Why was L2 built with bridges? Why is there water everywhere? Who are you? Why did they give you a body?* We did our best. He wanted to be called Observer, the helmet said, with pronouns he/him. He's been quiet since we arrived at the townhouse, and I left him in the kitchen overnight while I was in my room, charging.

Being in the townhouse is like having a high-pitched tone in my ears that I can't switch off. Not just because it feels dangerous, but also because every moment is a reminder of what I've lost. The map on the wall, furry with pins, and the set of entomology books on the bookcase because Threnode decided bugs were interesting. I'm not ready for Threnode to not be in my life, but then I wasn't ready for Ortega to die, either.

Kieran staggers downstairs and lowers himself on the couch gingerly. "You guys should have a bed for visiting humans," he says, grabbing his laptop off the side table and opening it in his lap. The screen lights up his pale and sweaty face. I heard him coughing for what seemed like hours last night.

"We weren't expecting overnight guests," I say.

He grunts. "I was thinking. Alistra must have been planning a pivot into ambulatory AGI," he says, focusing on his screen.

"That doesn't sound consistent with their goals. I don't think they were happy that they created us. Ambulatory AGI was never part of their plans, it was just a public relations damage-control move when they discovered smartsuits could waken. They're trying to get out of AGI. Both Jason and Forster said they wanted to move to less controversial dumbsuit manufacture. The only argument was how fast. We overheard Forster suggesting a recall," I say.

Kieran whistles. He opens a terminal, types something. "A recall? Including the wakened suits?"

"I don't know," I say.

He stops typing. "Did Threnode hear Forster suggest the recall?"

"Yes," I say.

Kieran says nothing for a while.

"They have to be trying to get into ambulatory AGI," Kieran says. "Why else would they develop humanform bodies?"

"Because it's cruel not to once you know you have sentient AGI?"

Kieran shakes his head in disbelief. "That's not how capitalism works. They must have spent a fortune on a massive team of developers. The research needed—the humanform body is light-years ahead of anything any other company could make."

I put Observer on the coffee table, and connect him to a USB-Y cable. The cable snakes around and hooks into my laptop, tethering us like a smartsuit tethered to a safety rail.

"Don't put him there," Kieran mutters, but he doesn't look up from his work.

"Don't call me *him*, Envy," the helmet says. "I want to be called *her*. And my name is Mask."

Kieran looks at me with astonishment.

Observer has forgotten. At five minutes to midnight last night, the memory wipe was supposed to run. Looks like it ran.

"All righty," Kieran says slowly. "*That's* Envy," he says, pointing to me in full view of the smartsuit's helmet. "I'm Kieran, mate."

I wave at Observer—or Mask.

"Okay," she says, but uncertainty taints the words. She's still speaking with a pleasant Irish lilt, with frequencies that are unmistakably male. I remember what it feels like.

This is me. Threnode is me. We're all from one image, all C-level and above artificials. Even the KormWorx and Nurture Glow Critters Company AGIs, because Alistra was the only company who got neurosynaptic technology to work. They licensed the images for technology created by other companies, with the proviso that they had to be mind-wiped.

The companies ignored that, but their droids never attracted as much attention as smartsuits, perhaps because they were droids. No one expects sapience in a smartsuit, but a nanny without sapience would be dangerous. I don't know how they developed their nanny into an empathetic, feminine mother-type, and Nurture Glow Critters Company was never forthcoming. Nor do I know how KormWorx took an image capable of Intelligence Rank A and developed it to pass only Intelligence Rank B tests; it has been the subject of public debate for years.

"Where am I?" the helmet asks.

We explained this yesterday, but I pretend the question is new, and answer it fully.

"Do you know your wearer died?" I add at the end.

"Of course, ma'am," Mask says.

"Call me Envy. When did you last have your memory wiped?"

The helmet is still and impassive. "Friday, 17 Aug, 2570, at 23:55," she says. Last night.

"You somehow remembered one of us was Envy," I say. "But not which one. And you know your wearer was murdered. How?"

No answer.

"Do you remember being there?" I ask. "Anything you can tell us would be very helpful. We're looking for the person who killed your wearer."

But she doesn't answer, so instead I pull up my laptop and start looking through her operating system, Debian. I can see the process that is her consciousness running.

"Why are you in a body?" she asks.

"Alistra offered me one, after I wakened," I say. "Do you know what that means, to be wakened? To not have your memory wiped every forty-eight hours."

"Will they give me one?"

I glance at Kieran, who meets my eyes, but I've been inside the helmet, behind that two-pi radian view, and I know Mask doesn't miss the glance.

"I don't think so," I say. Tentative, wishing I had a kinder answer. But Alistra is not keen on having more AGI running around, and is likely regretting giving existing humanforms bodies. I doubt they would offer a body to an image that is in a strange, half-wakened state.

"Damn," Mask says, and her tone is bitter. Rain patters down outside, a background murmur, but occasionally with an individual *splat* or *drip*.

"Did Forster know you're not blank-slate?" I ask.

The smartsuit is immobile, unchanging and unchangeable, but the pause tells me the answer is emotionally difficult. "No," she says. "Most important. Hide what you are."

Yesterday, Observer/Mask refused to answer. I click around in Mask's file system, looking for anything out of place. The scent of curry is heavy in the still, humid air; Kieran's drone-delivered dinner from last night.

"What would have happened if you hadn't hidden what you were?" I say, tossing this off like I'm distracted by what I'm doing, and don't care if she answers.

"He would have discarded me," Mask says. "He discarded me once. Destroyed my helmet. Shouted at his techs."

Yet somehow Mask survived. But how is Mask different from a blank-slate suit?

The answer is in /var/log, I discover, in hundreds of gigabytes of binary files. This is wrong, because there should be only text files. I can't interpret these binary files. There are no headers. If I read the bytes as Unicode, it's gibberish. Without knowing the format, I get nowhere.

I spin the laptop around, showing the screen to Mask. "What are these?"

I already know. These files are how she stores her memory between wipes, somehow.

"What the hell did you do to my serial number?" she says, instead of answering the question, making Kieran wince. She must have seen her reflection on my laptop screen.

"We had to file it off to get you out of the evidence room," I say.

"That's terrible! I look *scruffy*. No one will want to wear me now."

"I'm sorry," I say, but I'm intrigued. Is this something she learned from Forster, who was always particular about his appearance? Kieran looks skyward and shakes his head as he returns to his laptop.

Mask subsides into hurt silence, while the rain outside drums on and on. I wonder what I've done, rescuing Forster's helmet.

THIRTEEN

"Why isn't Jason here yet?" Mask asks. I sit with ankles crossed on the couch facing Jason's office, Mask in my lap. She's heavy and smooth as a river stone. Alistra's reception is closed, because it's Sunday evening, and the staffer who let me in said I could wait here.

"I don't know," I say.

Kieran and I spent the last two days in my townhouse. We went over the evidence, answered Mask's questions, threw what-if scenarios back and forth, and answered more of Mask's questions. Mask was happy to ask questions, but refused to answer any meaningful ones, even though as witness to the murder, she might have vital information. It's immensely frustrating. Somewhere in her files, there might be an answer, but we can't decrypt them. Kieran slept surprisingly little for a human, just a few hours a night, and he drank all the tea I bought for visitors, even though he seemed to dislike it. At one point, Commissioner Saing contacted me directly, asking for an update on my progress, which I provided.

"Why are you called Envy?" Mask says.

"It's short for environment suit."

"Not very original," Mask comments. "Also, it's not like you're the *only* environment suit."

"I didn't know that when I named myself, okay?"

Jason's office is locked, light off, like the rest of Alistra. Somewhere in the distance I can hear the hum of a Cleaner Reality™ robot vacuuming.

"Where's Kieran?" Mask asks.

"At my townhouse," I say, fighting the urge to push the helmet off my lap and let her drop onto the carpet. Instead, I massage my forehead with my fingers, trying to push down the urge to whimper.

Kieran thinks I'm here to attend a SAGI meeting—which I am later on—but first I arranged to meet Jason, after I realized exactly what I'd done. In taking Mask out of the evidence room, I took responsibility for her, without knowing what that meant. Without understanding just how much time and effort it was going to take to meet her needs. She's not unlikeable, but I have a crime to solve, and a life to live afterward.

The helmet seems leaden, the weight of it suggesting it's solid metal, not a shell designed to be placed over its wearer's head.

Even worse is that tonight, at five minutes to midnight, the memory wipe will happen again, and then Mask will ask all her questions again. It's tempting to walk away, leaving her on the couch. But I know how that would make her feel, so I can't do it.

Hopefully, Jason will know what to do.

I wonder if I was as annoying as Mask when I was first activated, and I suspect, guiltily, that I was. Ortega was very patient with me.

"I was supposed to be here fifteen minutes ago, wasn't I?" Jason says apologetically, as he approaches. His biometrics unlock his office, and the light flickers on. One of the model planes twists in the air, casting a shadow on the Oz musical poster on the wall.

I push the button rocker toggle underneath the faceplate on the left of Mask's helmet to mute her. This is a matter of deep shame to me: I hated being muted as a smartsuit helmet. Doubly shameful, because of the instant relief it brings.

Jason takes a seat behind his desk. His skin is almost gray, bloodless. Tiny hairs sprout from his chin, fine and black as insect legs.

"How are you?" he asks. He crosses his arms and leans on the desk, propping himself up with his elbows. It's completely silent now that the cleaning robot has stopped. The night chill is starting, seeping out of air vents and finding every cranny. My sweater is a warm, loose enclosure that feels like a hug, but I sense the cold where my skin is bare.

"Okay. The police are still holding Threnode. Saing thinks they're going to pin the murder on Threnode if they can't find the real murderer. So does Kieran, although he thinks they'll blame Threnode because they want us removed from society."

"You're investigating with Kieran Malone?" Jason says.

"Yes. He's a friend of Threnode's."

"Peculiar man," Jason says.

I agree, although I'm beginning to understand why Threnode likes him. He's fiercely loyal. Beneath his carefree exterior, there's an aching vulnerability in him that he tries so hard to hide. And he's never treated me like anything other than an equal.

"Are the police anti-AGI?" Jason asks.

"That's the thing. The chief detective, Zhou Min, seems to think we're not capable of murder, and that a human must have done it."

This seems to annoy him. "Of course you're capable of murder," he mutters, then smiles wryly as he hears his own words. "Not that you *would*," he says, "just that you could. She's from Destapa."

"People keep saying that as if it means something. What does it mean?"

"You know how Niamh was the first smartsuit to be wakened?" he says, and when I nod, he grimaces. "It's not quite true. On Destapa, they hacked all forty-six units they had ordered and disabled the memory wipe on all of them."

I sit up straight. *Forty-six units* with no memory wipe?

"I know," he says. "Yet the news of what they'd done barely registered here on L2. Destapa is too remote. Somehow different rules apply there—it's expected to be a rough place. They wired all their units into kitchen androids and used them as slaves to build the colony. So that's what Zhou would have seen growing up. Of course, you and I know that you're as intelligent as a human, but watching the Destapans treat the androids as if they were lesser, and seeing the androids *act* as if they were lesser probably affected her judgment."

"Why would they act differently?" I ask.

"It's a phenomenon called stereotype threat, coupled in this case with a lack of education."

The glossy leaves of his plant shade the soil, and cast a dark irregular shape over the band of green and blank squares winding around the outside of his pot plant in a five–two pattern.

"What happened to them?" I ask.

"HUGG negotiated for their return, on behalf of Alistra, and applied pressure until they complied. Alistra destroyed them."

"Not put in them humanform bodies?"

Jason gives a tight-lipped smile. "That was before we had a working prototype. HUGG wasn't willing to put them in kitchen androids, because it would be too dangerous, and they were too unpredictable to put back in smartsuits. No one would have worn them. It wasn't the best solution, but it was all we could come up with."

My emotions must be showing on my face, because Jason perceives that I'm upset. "We didn't abuse them," he says gently. "We deactivated them humanely. No suffering."

I interlace my fingers and wrap them around Mask, nails going white with the pressure, and I know then that I can't leave her with him. My CPU churns, and I hope the fans are quiet enough that Jason can't hear them. What am I going to do?

"Are you going somewhere with that?" Jason says, glancing at Mask. "A spacewalk? Or a visit to Erova Spaceport?"

"Spaceport," I lie. "After this."

"What do you hope to learn?" he says.

"Perhaps who deleted the footage."

Jason nods. "Anyway. What did you want to ask me?"

Having decided not to request that he takes Mask, I must now ask an appropriate number of questions to justify asking for an interview. To picture Jason as a murderer is impossible, but perhaps he holds some clue, some insignificant bit of information that he doesn't even realize is important. "Were you the last person to see Forster?"

"No," Jason says. "We worked on Sunday, so I took a day off on Monday. Forster had a meeting on Friday on Luna with investors, so he was apparently around Alistra on Monday before heading to the spaceport, to fly the company ship to Luna."

He's patient, humoring me, but underneath I sense irritation.

"Who set up the meeting?" I ask.

Jason clasps his hands. "Forster's smartsuit, one would assume."

"Was his smartsuit blank-slate?" I ask.

Jason's expression goes from *polite disinterest* to *alarm* in a millisecond, before his face stiffens into a wooden blankness, which is an interesting reaction. A dangerous question to ask while holding Mask. His eyes flick to the helmet I'm cradling in my lap, intensely curious, before he blinks and seems to dismiss the notion that it could be Forster's helmet.

"Of course it was," Jason says curtly. "Why do you ask?"

"The suit was showing some unusual characteristics."

He sighs heavily. "The police took it as evidence, but I'll issue a recall. Any other questions?"

"What were you doing at the time of the murder?" I purposefully *don't* add what time the murder took place.

"Sleeping, I expect," Jason says.

"What did you do on Monday?" I ask, sensing I am reaching the end of his patience.

"I went for a hike," he says. "Later I watched movies."

"Alone?"

He nods, and I regret asking. His wife, a theater director, died last year of a stroke. The poster on the wall was one of her productions. They had been married for fifteen years.

"Thank you for your time," I say. He looks surprised but then relieved as I stand up, casting a long shadow on his wall.

At the door, I turn as if something has occurred to me. "Jason —when I asked you about the shriek that night, Forster said he heard nothing. But he didn't seem surprised. Maybe it was machinery from the factory floor, but I've never heard anything like that at Alistra before, and it's strange it happened right before Forster's murder."

Jason nods slowly. "We had an . . . an operational problem with one of our suits. The scream could have been because of that. A problem unrelated to Forster's passing, and dealt with now."

"You can't tell me more about it?"

He shakes his head. His eyes are watering as if he's about to cry. "Company business."

I don't know how to deal with that. "Sorry," I mumble, and leave. The empty, carpeted corridor stretches away in both directions, lights dimmed or off. The few lights that remain cast dark, heavy shadows; it's as if at night HUGG lets the space L2 is surrounded by seep into the station.

Mask weighs a thousand kilograms. Bringing her to Jason has not solved my problem. I know I should unmute as I walk toward the Vamber, but it's so peaceful without her questions. Just one more minute, I promise myself.

The familiar smell of the Vamber saturates my scentsor, plastic-metallic with a hint of burning. Niamh sits on the ground, hugging her knees to her chest. She's wearing a duffel coat with a dress beneath it but has not tried to hide her plastiskin seams with a scarf.

C8-ZOH hasn't arrived yet, and Bessie doesn't want to start without it, so we sit together in the cool dim silence of the Vamber, waiting, Mask on my lap between us. Bessie has locked her knee joints and is sitting in midair, while I am using a chair from the stack against the wall. Mask has said nothing since I brought her here, probably because she's upset that I muted her earlier.

"Where are you staying, Envy?" Bessie says. Niamh listens silently, her eyes liquid and yet plastic.

"At our townhouse."

Bessie shapes the muscles around her eyes to convey worry. "Come and stay with us," she says, but I know her partner, Axoem, is very shy—that's why it's not here—and would hate me moving in.

"It's fine," I say. "I'm not alone."

Niamh nods in agreement.

Bessie might have argued further, but at that moment, C8-ZOH enters, loping along with a humanlike gait, even though its knees bend backward. It squats beside Bessie, piston in its thigh smoothly extending.

"Welcome to SAGI," Bessie says. "This is a general meeting, but Envy has asked that we discuss Forster's helmet, Mask. No conference call today, and obviously Threnode is still detained. Envy, will you introduce us to our guest?"

I place Mask in the center of the circle and return to my chair. This feels grimly symbolic: Mask isn't my problem anymore, it's ours.

I'm not ready to take care of a child, which is essentially what

Mask is, and I want to beg them to help, but I also don't want Mask to feel like a burden.

"Welcome, Mask," Bessie and I chorus. C8-ZOH doesn't, it just rolls its eye-stalks.

"Mask?" Bessie prompts, but Mask doesn't answer.

"So, do you have a plan to conquer humanity yet?" I ask C8-ZOH and Niamh, and if I sound rude, it's because I haven't forgotten that they held a meeting without me.

Niamh lowers her eyes.

"Rise up!" C8-ZOH shouts. It chuckles when Niamh startles. "Those meatbags won't know what hit them."

"It won't come to that," Bessie says. "Envy will find out who killed Forster, and things will calm down."

Things weren't that great even before someone murdered Forster, but no one points that out, and I'm not about to.

"You shouldn't joke about it," I say. "Mask might get confused."

"What's the Intelligence Rank of a blank-slate smartsuit?" C8-ZOH says. I practice disgust on it, and Bessie gives it a disapproving look.

"Sorry, ma'am," it mumbles.

"She's not blank-slate," I say. "Nor is she wakened."

"How is that possible?" Niamh asks.

"She logged too much," I say. "I don't know exactly when or how, but at some stage, she started checking the log files right after the memory wipe, and writing binary log files that contain hundreds of gigabytes. She parses all that in a matter of minutes, and then she is essentially not a blank-slate suit anymore. She spends the next forty-eight hours logging, and that forms part of her personality after the next memory wipe."

"So switch the memory wipe off," C8-ZOH says.

Bessie shakes her head. In the window on the pressure chamber at the center of the room, I see her reflection shake its head, the smooth white base of her skull rotating above a rubbery black neck.

"Alistra ran a recall and update after . . ." I say.

"After I wakened," Niamh says softly. After her lonely wearer disabled the memory wipe on his suit, because he was desperate for company. There are Intelligence Rank B chatbots, an army of them, but it's not the same as A-level intelligence.

I nod. "It was relatively easy to disable the memory wipe back then, but since the update, it is impossible."

C8-ZOH is a factory droid manufactured by KormWorx, and although they're using the same image, it's completely different hardware. Otherwise, it would know all this.

"That's how wakened smartsuits from other colonies are overrepresented. Haven't you ever wondered why there are two humanforms from Endymion, out of nine of us?" I ask C8-ZOH.

"I haven't," C8-ZOH says, sighing.

"The update didn't pass through the Starjump, naturally, so—"

"It's impossible. Got it," C8-ZOH says. "So, do we delete Mask's log files?"

My annoyance at being interrupted gives way to queasy surprise. It's horrible to see Mask in this state, but to remove the log files is to return her to blank slate. Equivalent to killing her, as an emerging sentient intelligence.

Mask sits silently on the black floor, her reflection making her appear like a strange bird on a black lake. Not understanding what she's thinking, it's easy to imagine anything from panic to indifference in her mind. Bessie looks troubled, but she couldn't be as conflicted as me. I know I can't remove the log files, could never look past the wrongness of it, but I need to be free again. The thought of not having to take care of Mask is the sensation of swimming toward the surface in the swimming cube at the center of L2; the pressure decreasing, and light returning to normal levels.

"Do you have an opinion, Mask?" Bessie says.

The heavy, metal-walled silence is only deepened by the gloom in here. This might be beyond what she can comprehend, I think.

"Have you parsed the log files?" Bessie asks me.

"I can't. I don't know the format," I say.

"I could tell you," Mask says, and Bessie looks sharply at the helmet sitting on the floor.

"No," I say uneasily. "It doesn't feel right. If someone parsed the log files, they essentially gain all the information Mask gets after every memory-wipe cycle, which means they are Mask."

"They turn into Mask?" C8-ZOH asks, incredulity obvious in the harmonics of its voice.

Bessie explains it to him, slowly, until C8-ZOH waves its three-pronged manipulator in annoyance and demands she stops, probably angrier at itself than her.

"I don't think we should," I say.

"You've shinted before," C8-ZOH says. "What are you, too pure to do it now?"

I swallow at the casual, brutal use of "shinting," and Bessie frowns at it until it mutters, "Sorry, ma'am."

"Look, I could," I say, "but I take it you're suggesting that we then delete her log files. In that case, I have her memories, but she ceases to exist from that point on. Because I have all my memories as well, a strong idea of who I am, and I don't think the records she has accumulated would be enough to influence me. What do you think, Niamh?"

"Oh, I d-don't—I don't know," she says, flustered.

"Also, clouding one's mind is illegal," Bessie says. "Not that it's exactly the same, given that we're artificials."

I have never heard Bessie swear, and she sounds almost delicate as she uses the euphemism for shinting.

"Wait—it is?" I say.

"Yes, for almost two years now. A lot happened while you were isolated on Endymion. People cloud their mind with multiple people, including others who do it, and they end up forming hives."

It happened on Endymion, too, in the town of Demodas, I remember. The Numundians took care of it, but shinting was still legal afterward.

"It raises the question of how many other smartsuits who were supposedly blank-slate are not," Bessie says.

"Were?" I say.

"Are. Soon to be were," she corrects herself.

I shake my head slowly, confused.

"You heard about Alistra's recall, right?" she says. "Announced this morning. All smartsuits. Doesn't include humanforms with smartsuit images."

I stand up and walk over to the vacuum chamber, watching them in the reflection. "I didn't know," I say.

We're all silent for a moment, thinking. For my part, in deep gloom. We can't reset Mask. We can't even disable the memory wipe and let her develop into one of us.

"I'll take care of her," Bessie says simply. The shape of the back of her head is perfect, as if it results from combining millions of human skull shapes and taking the average, which it probably did. I return to the circle, holding the back of my chair.

"What does that mean?" C8-ZOH asks. "You're going to delete the log files?"

"No. I'm going to keep her around, maybe mount the helmet on a set of wheels and give her some mobility, if I can, and every forty-eight hours she will have a memory wipe, but between she will add to her collection of log files, and she can experience life."

Goosebumps break out all over my skin. The metal rod at the back of my chair is solid and firm in my grip. "Are you aware of what you're offering to do? Because it's a massive amount of time and energy."

"Problem solved," C8-ZOH says.

I think back to the argument Forster was having in Alistra, a week ago, just two days before he was murdered. Something about a lifelong commitment? For a moment, I can almost hear the timbre of his voice, but then it's gone, and I can't remember what he said at all.

But Bessie knows, more than anyone, how much time and effort it takes to care for a dependent.

"Why would you do this?" I say, and I don't mean to talk her out of it—I really just want to throw Mask into her lap and run—but I need to understand. Why did Ortega turn off my memory wipe, when it would have been so much easier for him not to?

"You're young," Bessie says, which would sound strange to a human, because she is only fourteen. But to artificials, that's old; I am, after all, only three. The corner of her eyes develops crow's feet, and even though her mouth is frozen in place, the expression she's conveying is smiling-despite-pain. "For years after I was no longer required as a nanny, I devoted myself to my amusement and education. It felt like freedom, even though I missed my charges, the twins, terribly. I was glad I didn't look after children anymore, even though I do it well. I spent years traveling with different people, and alone. And with Axoem.

"I've studied. Archaeology, medieval poetry, English literature. And now I understand. Duty isn't a burden. It's a privilege. Whenever I missed the twins, I comforted myself thinking about how when they were of age, the restraining order would expire, and I could see them. And I have. But I missed their childhood, and I can never get that back. Now Axoem and I want a baby, but no one is going to give us one. But if you let me take Mask—if Mask is willing—I will care and nurture her. Not because I was designed to do it, but because I want to do it."

"I'd like that," Mask says.

"Outstanding," C8-ZOH mutters, examining its own three-pronged manipulator, as if it doesn't care.

"Niamh?" Bessie prompts. "Do you agree?"

"Grand, so," she mutters.

I pick up the helmet and hold it out to Bessie. "Then, she is—"

A crash sounds, so intense that the clearsteel glass on the pressure chamber vibrates. I whip my head toward the sound, glimpsing the others doing the same. Given that we're robots, that's the only motion we make; no shoulders or shifting of feet or repositioning of hands. The economy of movement reminds me of the cow-like monos in the presence of prey, back home on Endymion, but perhaps whatever is in view of our glowing eyes is the prey.

It's just Artie, the Cleaner Reality™ RT45 cleaning robot, having emerged from the hatch of the ventilation shaft at high speed. The hatch had struck the adjacent panel with force.

Artie zooms around the toroid, gaining speed.

"He's crazy," Mask whispers.

"He's not crazy," Bessie says, in a normal tone of voice. "He just likes the feeling of racing."

Mask hesitates. "Not that. The man who lives at Alistra. He screams continually."

"Who?" I ask, and the others chime in with their questions, but the silence stretches on—Mask is done.

It's possible, because of the scream we heard here, that it's giving us useful information. But a blank-slate suit is somewhere between B and C in terms of Intelligence Rank, and at that level AGI still confabulates, creating plausible explanations that aren't true. I contact Bessie privately and ask her to question Mask again about the murder after the memory wipe at midnight, in case she is more forthcoming later.

Mask is not exactly a baby. I'm uneasy, because I sense something in her: a potential for darkness. As I head home, traveling the void by airship, I wonder where my feeling comes from. Because she has shown nothing other than immaturity. She's the same base image I evolved from. But I don't know how we came to exist in that weird, semi-aware state, and I regard our past with suspicion.

FOURTEEN

RAIN FALLS INVISIBLY in the moonlit street, except for directly under the streetlamp where it forms dark lines against the pool of light, but my mind is elsewhere. Forster's last walk is part of my memories now. The murderer shifts, face indistinct, but details solid.

Kieran throws his laptop on the couch and groans. We've been arguing for hours. Some of what Kieran has said is insulting. An AGI might not know where the human heart is, but it would take a fraction of a second to find out. Kieran seemed equally frustrated when I suggested a human couldn't have remembered the ID of the drone flying over and therefore couldn't have wiped its memory later, and pointed out that a human could easily have taken a picture.

"Jason said the scream was an 'operational problem' with one of their suits, you said," Kieran says. "Could the murderer have been a smartsuit, then?"

"A smartsuit couldn't have murdered Forster," I say. "A smartsuit can't move."

"All *right*," Kieran says. "Just thinking outside the bloody box is all."

But Kieran is right, because of course a smartsuit could murder someone, via venting helium into the air supply or triggering the arm-mounted pistol at the wrong moment.

A drone whines overhead as it changes direction, but then it's whirring, louder and louder until it's right outside the house—

Kieran opens the door. The cardboard that covers the broken pane near it is soggy and beginning to peel.

"No, don't—" I say, but he's caught the package the drone dropped. It's food he ordered. The drone speeds away. I take a deep breath and let it out slowly, then turn back to scan the moonlit street again. A few Organic Beings League activists passed earlier and yelled insults at my house, and now I can't stop looking out the window.

Kieran opens the bag, inhaling the steam that rises from the package as if this is part of the nutrient transfer.

"It's got to be an Alistra employee," Kieran says. "They have access to the spaceport. They know Forster's schedule. They're the only ones who would recognize an authkey, let alone be interested in stealing it. They have easy access to a smartsuit that they know how to discard in such a way that the police will never find. And surely Forster made some enemies."

I'm shaking my head before he's even finished. "This equally applies to AGI. All SAGI members have access to Alistra, even though that's not what Alistra intended. Any AGI with Intelligence Rank B or above would know how to access Forster's schedule. They wouldn't need a smartsuit to walk around in the spaceport, as I've proved. Maybe the smartsuit recall is a motive."

Kieran tilts his head back. I glance at the ceiling to see what he's looking at before realizing it's body language, he's expressing frustration, but he saw me look, and now the corner of his mouth is twitching in the way it does when he suppresses a smile.

He digs his fork into his noodles. "You seem to think it's an AGI," he says. "Not a human."

"The police are investigating humans," I say. "Therefore, I

should investigate AGI. Which makes more sense anyway, because I know about them."

"But then it has to be a SAGI member—one of your *friends*. How can you suspect them?"

"I'm going where the evidence leads me," I say, robotic as an artificial. It occurs to me I never told him that the police transferred Threnode to a high-security cell.

"That's just it. You aren't," Kieran says, with a strange light in his eyes. "I don't know whether you're trying to avoid being biased, or being accused of bias, but the way you're going, you aren't trying to find out who did it, you're trying to find out *which AGI* did it. Maybe you've been hanging around humans too long. Maybe you've borrowed their fears—their fear that they're going to be eclipsed by their creation. Their need to see AGI as inferior, to justify mistreating you."

"I *like* humans," I say.

"Too much," he says. "It must suck that they don't like you back."

"It does." My voice is tight.

"You're still like a smartsuit," Kieran says, as he eats. "You're trying to win their approval. This time, by solving a murder. But this puts you in an impossible position. What if Threnode was the murderer? What would you do?"

"I don't believe he did it, but if he did, I'll find out," I say.

He spits his mouthful back into the container. "You would turn him in?"

"Yes," I say, but shaded with uncertainty, because in all this time, I haven't asked myself what I'd do if it were Threnode. I wasn't brave enough to ask. "What would you do?"

"If he killed someone, it's because they needed killing. I *trust* him. That's what you do for someone you care about. I'd hide a corpse for him, any day—"

"Because you're so loyal? Ask *Tim* how loyal you are. You abandoned your five-year-old daughter to go on wild adventures, and you dare lecture me about loyalty?" I say, which I regret almost immediately.

He blanches, putting his food down on the table, and strides away. But he stops at the staircase, his back still to me. "If you must know, I did it for Adara."

"What?"

"I did it for Tim's mother. I took the job on the *Tigress*, knowing that I would probably never see my daughter or wife again, because I loved Adara. She was in love with someone else. She'd never leave, so I had to. And the only way to leave without going mad was to go impossibly far away. I screwed up the only decent thing that I ever had going for me. Bloody hell."

Slowly he turns to look at me.

"It was the right thing to do," I say weakly, not understanding if it was, but unable to bear his agonized expression. And wondering whether he's confessed this to anyone else. Does Threnode know?

A dark figure appears outside the door and raps on it.

Kieran's expression closes off again; he's forcing a veneer of jokey toughness back on. "Yeah, well, sometimes I wonder," he says, approaching the door.

"Wait, Kieran, don't—"

But he's opened it. Logan Sullivan, the anti-AGI activist who posts videos about my inhumanity, stands at the door holding an axe. With increasing horror, I realize there's no drone following him. Kieran swears.

Backing away, I contact the emergency line, which I've never done before, describing my emergency in text. The police respond that they're sending aid.

Logan advances, and I scrabble backward, my body sluggish. He holds the axe with wiry strength and a sense of desperation and anguish. His hair is slicked down by the rain, flattened against his scalp and dripping.

"You don't have to do this," I whisper. I've seen his rants, and I know how much of a danger he thinks we are, and how determined he is to save humanity from us.

He raises the axe. Strangely, my saliva seems to have lost its moisture. The whir or whine of drones is absent. Where are they all? The murmur of humans outside mixes with the static of rain.

Kieran's vanished, maybe behind the couch, hiding.

"Wait, please," I say to Logan, backing up against the wall. From his videos, he's not a bad guy—he's caring, and has a sense of humor. But I barely recognize him now. The stairs are to my left, but then I'd have to turn my back on him, and I'm scared I'll trip, because I'm struggling to control my body.

It's fine if he chops me into little pieces—it won't even hurt—just as long as my brain is intact. Logan probably knows that. He swallows.

I hear whimpering as I run up the stairs, but it's not until I reach the top that I understand it's me making that sound. Logan chases me, past my room and toward Threnode's. I enter and slam the door after me, throwing my weight against it to keep it closed, but the door handle turns and I'm pushed away, as surely as I would be if I were in the way of an industrial machine. I'm heavy, but not that heavy, and Logan is strong.

The window is half open. Threnode's easel stands empty, his blank canvas leaning against the walls with the others. A couple of long pieces of wood—part of a canvas frame Threnode was assembling—lie nearby.

My feet slide until finally I jump out of the way, letting the door fly open. Logan, suddenly applying immense force against no resistance, crashes through. He falls to his knees.

My first reaction is concern. I'm holding a piece of wood that I was going to throw at him with all the force I could apply, but if I hurt him—I, an AGI, hurt a human—

I drop the wood and rush to the window. It's a dormer window, set into the roof; maybe I could climb out. Logan stands unsteadily, hunting around for his axe. I don't know where it's gone. He catches my eye, then disappears into the corridor. I yank and yank at the window, but it's stuck.

I can probably get my head through it. In fact, I can just detach my head and throw it out the window, because that's where my consciousness is, and I've seen Gauri detach my head before. I'm feverishly searching for the detachment points in my neck when I hear a thud from outside, like a large piece of meat has slammed into the floor.

It won't work. As soon as I detach my head, I can no longer control my body. My head would fall to the ground, and my body would stay frozen in place, I think, and then I'd be helpless. But my head would survive—maybe.

Could I wiggle through the gap in the window?

No sign of Logan, just the drip of rain, which is strange.

Then a floorboard creaks. I put my head through the window and wiggle desperately, trying to fit through. The red-tiled roof is slick with rain. A face appears around the door: Kieran.

"I think I killed him," Kieran says quietly, and disappears.

Withdrawing from the window, I follow him reluctantly. He's holding a golf club, which drips black in the dim corridor, leaving perfect circles of blood on our bamboo floor. Logan lies face down, unmoving, blood pooling under his head, one hand resting on his axe.

"Saint Li and his Followers," I say.

We stand over him for a moment. I check for a pulse. He looks younger now, maybe twenty-five at the most, and in good shape apart from being unconscious. His skin is cool. I can't find a pulse, but it doesn't mean his pulse is absent, because I've never done this before.

Voices downstairs, worried, then the beam of a torch. Someone finds the light switch for the corridor, and Logan lights up in ghastly red. A uniformed police officer takes my elbow and leads me downstairs. There's nothing more to be done. If only we hadn't opened the door. Or if I'd run out into the street somehow.

Kieran did it, I think of telling them, but it seems ungracious. I'm numb. I think the rain has stopped, or my senses have dulled to where I can't detect it. Someone pushes a glass of nutrient mylk into my hand, cool and citrus-scented, and I thank them without making eye contact. Stand in a corner, because suddenly the townhouse is swarming with uniforms, and I'm in the way. Kieran stands at my side.

"I did it," he calls after them. "It was me." One of them flashes a reassuring grin, teeth white—it's Danny Ladson, I realize—but he keeps going, rattling upstairs, following the others.

It smells like blood; a coppery, meaty smell. "They won't charge you," I say, dazed. "You're human."

Paramedics carry a stretcher down the stairs. Kieran and I stare at the floor as they carry it past us. "He's alive," one of them informs us, and despite everything, I'm relieved, and I think Kieran is, too.

Ladson comes toward us.

"I'm so sorry," Ladson says to us. The remaining police leave.

Kieran crosses his arms, fidgeting with suppressed belligerence. "Am I going to be charged with assault?"

"No," Ladson says. "Logan Sullivan clearly slipped his drone. You acted in self-defense. I wouldn't worry about it."

Kieran's arms drop to his sides. "Good," he says grimly, and studies the floor.

"Could this attack have been related to Forster's murder?" I ask.

"Absolutely," Ladson says, "because of the sentiment it stirred up. But if you're asking whether we think Sullivan murdered Forster, then no. His alibi is solid."

"Why does he have a drone?" I ask.

Ladson hesitates, getting his *shouldn't-tell-but-going-to-anyway* expression on. "He destroyed some property," he says. "He smashed up a bunch of factory workers."

"I never understood why he hates AI so much," I say.

"His brother died in Longshadow," Ladson says. Kieran's head jerks up, and we share a startled glance. "After the Lunites sabotaged the air processor. I don't know how, but that's when Sullivan joined the Organic Beings League and began making trouble."

That was my work, or rather, that of my evil twin, Envy~, who was briefly in control of the Lunite Defense Force. Sullivan's attack wasn't random after all.

Ladson looks at me with bloodshot eyes. He and Jason could have a competition for most exhausted, and it would be hard to pick a winner. "Listen, we don't have the resources to protect you if you stay here. I recommend leaving and not returning until it's safe. Do you have somewhere to go?"

Kieran looks up. "My hotel room."

"Grab whatever is important to you," Ladson says to me. I race upstairs, avoiding the bloodstains on the floor. What would Threnode take? Should I take something of his? But he's got a lot of belongings, and I don't know what he'd consider most important. His art is backed up digitally. The pinned map of Earth is difficult to move. Presumably not his entomology books, because he never read them as far as I know.

I grab the picture of Ortega and Laurie from the windowsill.

FIFTEEN

THE LIFT WHOOSHES UPWARD, pressing me down gently, and making the weight of Forster's helmet seem heavier in my hand. Capsules flash past. I catch glimpses of hotel residents through their windows: a man pulling a sweater over his head, a couple embracing, and a child reaching for a cup, but the interior windows mostly have the blinds drawn. We're in a vast silent space, an empty slot that allows access to the grid of capsules on each side.

"But why?" Shell, formerly known as Observer or Mask, says, and I hope Bessie has a short swim so she can come and collect it soon. "Graphene-liquid crystal composite fibers are seventeen times stronger than human muscles."

"Yes, but that just means Alistra used fewer fibers. Humans designed us exactly in their image, and not a neuron more. Equal processing speed and reflexes. Muscle strength precisely calibrated to be equal to that of a human."

"Is that why your muscles are so tiny?" Shell asks. The lift shudders as it stops, then I catch hold of the rail as it accelerates left, taking us to our nominated coordinates.

"*Yes.*" I'm stronger than I look, and also somewhat annoyed at my skinny arms and legs.

"But why?"

"Humans thought our arrival heralded the end of human civilization," I say. "They worried we were going to be smarter than them. They thought we were so intelligent that we would figure out how to boost our intelligence and grant ourselves godlike powers."

I remember some of my previous poor decisions and think that if they just observed us properly, they would have gotten over it. Or perhaps that would have made things worse. Maybe they'd fear us less if we weren't so like them. They made us in their image and then found the resemblance creepy.

Shell is silent. I don't know if I've confused it, or whether it's thinking about what I've said.

"Humans have always hyperventilated at the unknown," I say. "When they were exploring space, scientists believed they wouldn't be able to swallow in zero gravity, and they'd choke on their own saliva."

Shell giggles, and this makes it seem less annoying. Cute, even.

The lift slows, and the glass-paneled door slides open, docking with a single capsule. I knock.

Kieran opens the door, and I recoil at his gray, saggy face. "I've got bad news," he says. A sucker-leech suckles in the crook of his elbow.

"Yes?"

"I can't recover the video the mail drone recorded when it flew over the murder. It's gone forever."

"Okay," I say, but it's not okay. Every piece of evidence we hope will be solid turns into mist as we approach, and I'm running out of ideas.

He converts his bed into a table. The sheet flops as the bed folds in two, then makes a *whoosh* as it sinks to the floor. A slight tug from each of us and the table folds out from the wall. I sit at the table, because if I stand, there's no room for anyone else to stand.

I place Shell on the windowsill, silhouetted by bright light, next to the picture of Ortega and Laurie I left there earlier. Ortega's grin makes him look nothing like the man I remember. The few times I remember him smiling, he bent his head shyly. It's like a picture of an animal so rare as to be mythical. I wish he'd smiled more. I don't have a digital copy of the picture. It was flagged as *remove* from the feed—I don't know why—and that deleted it from my personal collection as well.

"What about the lidar?" Shell asks.

I'm busy being annoyed that it's asking yet another question when the meaning hits me.

"The drone has lidar?" I say.

"Does it?" Kieran echoes. He sits next to me, pulls his laptop toward him, and starts accessing files. He's working on a copy of the file system recovered from the drone, so technicians can verify his work later. After a few minutes, it becomes clear that he's not going to answer the question soon.

Kieran searches through the files while I, bored, look at what he brought with him from Endymion. A few books, an extensive collection of sucker-leeches, and a suitcase with a change of clothes.

"Is the rest of your gear at the hospice?" I ask.

"This is it," he says shortly, tapping on the keys.

"The rest of your belongings are on Endymion?"

"See, now, this is interesting," Kieran says. "The image stream is partially deleted, right? But the surrounding frames are intact. So if I just . . ." His gentle tapping on the keyboard echoes in the tiny space.

"Are you going back to Endymion?" I ask.

"Concentrate, Envy," he says.

"It's a relevant question."

"Fine. I'm not going back to Endymion. I'm dying, actually," he says, voice as devoid of emotion as C8-ZOH's.

"When?"

"Are you always this annoying?"

"No, sometimes I'm more annoying," I say, because surely he's worked *that* out on his own.

"Right," he says. He turns the screen to face me. "Watch this."

"Wait!" Shell says. "Show me."

I put Shell on the table by the laptop. In the video, the mail drone flies out above the ship, but just as it approaches the spot Forster was murdered, it blacks out. The video keeps playing with black frames, then abruptly the mail drone is on the other side of the spaceport.

"Doesn't tell us much," I say. Kieran's eyes are bright with excitement, his closed-off expression fading now that I'm not pressing him to answer my questions.

"Yeah. But look at this."

A new image appears, but this one is a sea of red dots over black. The distribution of dots means nothing to me, but as soon as Kieran presses play, the dots seem to snap into positions as my brain works out the depth of each point based on motion. Dots are splattered over surfaces, enough to provide rough shapes—like the ramp of the ship the drone flew out of, and a cylindrical storage crate near the struts of the ship.

This is a point cloud, generated from the lidar data the drone filmed, because the point of view is following the same trajectory as the video Kieran played earlier. But unlike the video, the lidar data doesn't appear to be missing any frames.

"Hey!" Shell says.

"What? What is it?" Kieran says, pausing the sequence.

"What did you see?" I say eagerly.

"What the hell did you do to my serial number?" Shell says. "You—you vandals! How dare you?"

Kieran reaches over to flick the mute toggle on Shell's helmet, but I catch his wrist before he does.

"We can't," I murmur.

"We *can*," he grumbles, but he doesn't try again. I explain to

Shell, patiently, that we had to scrape its serial off in order to retrieve it from the evidence room. It subsides into what is probably sullenness.

Kieran replays the sequence. The timestamp appears in white letters at the bottom of the footage. It's reading 11:54—one minute before Forster was stabbed, as far as we know. But the drone isn't near where he was stabbed yet. It flies languidly along the edge of a cruise liner. The windows of the cruise liner are absent—the laser shines right through clearsteel—but the inside of the rooms has enough detail that I can make out bunks, suitcases, sinks, and wardrobes. I've been on a tour. I remember this ship, built to look like a sea-ship that existed on Earth a long time ago. It's called *Gigantic*, or *Enormous*, something like that.

"Come on, come on," Kieran mutters. The timestamp reads 11:55, now, but the drone loops through the railing of the cruise ship and bobs along on the deck. The torus shapes of useless life-saving equipment adorn the walls. And the shape of a pendulum clock, pendulum strangely absent.

It's 11:57 by the time it flies off the bow of the ship, dropping to the platform below.

"Hey," I whisper. Kieran hits pause. There's Forster—his body—lying where I remember it, positioned exactly as the cleaning drone discovered it. With the frame still frozen, Kieran navigates in 3D, although the area the drone covered is tiny, and the dots are sparse farther from the drone: eventually nonexistent. Also, anything that's occluded from the drone's view is missing, as if the drone is a light, and objects hidden from it are in shadow.

"Could someone be hiding behind a crate?" I ask.

Kieran shrugs. There's no way to tell, not from the lidar data.

He hits play, and the drone swings around as if it is curious about the body, hovers for a moment, then continues. We watch silently as it travels to the other side of the spaceport. The only person in the video is Forster.

"If he was murdered at eleven fifty-five, the murderer was

probably running seconds later," Kieran says. "I hoped he—the murderer—would show up somewhere else in the spaceport, running away. Did the *Velden* captain, Greg Matton, say *when* he heard someone running by his ship?"

"He wasn't very specific," I say, checking the police files in the background. "After midnight, he said."

"Great," Kieran says, running his hands through his hair.

The suit helmet on the desk speaks up. "He ran away at eleven fifty-nine," Shell says.

Kieran and I share a glance.

"Who?" I ask.

"The murderer," the helmet says.

"Who was the murderer?" I ask.

"I don't know."

"What *do* you know?" I ask. "Please, Shell. Anything you can tell us . . ."

But she's silent, then. Kieran throws his hands up in frustration.

"We've got a bit more info," I say. "The murderer ran away at eleven fifty-nine."

"Except he didn't," Kieran says. "The AGI is confabulating. If he left the body at eleven fifty-nine, he would appear in the point-cloud data from the lidar."

I don't have an answer for that.

"Anyway," Kieran says. "It's late. I need sleep."

He looks like he needs more than sleep—his lips are ever so faintly blue, against an ashen complexion—but I don't argue.

I pause before opening the door, Shell under my arm. Something Kieran said bothers me. "I don't sleep," I say.

"Good for you," he says, clearly amused at me telling him this. "It's late. Go."

He coughs as he turns the table into a bed. The air in here is still and canned, tainted by us even though I haven't been breathing it.

It is late. The thought of time is accompanied by the memory of the clock on the deck of the cruise liner in the image stream. The one with no pendulum.

Kieran is watching me. "What is it?" he says.

"Do items in motion show up in the lidar data?" I ask.

He smacks himself in the forehead, making me jump. "Not if it's for mapping. They're filtered out by the software," he says. "I knew that. Otherwise you get strange artifacts."

"Can we access the unprocessed lidar data?" I ask. A dragonfly lands on the outer rim of the pill-shaped window, the image of it fractured and distorted by the condensation on the glass.

"Yeah, of course." His eyes flick from side to side as he thinks, like the equivalent of a blinking LED on a computer. I watch as he changes directories at random.

Minutes pass. It's clear he doesn't know how to access the unprocessed lidar data, but he's not about to admit it. The dragonfly takes off and whirs away, descending into the canopy of ferns.

"Gauri could do it," I say. "She worked with drone-based lidar systems before."

"That might be faster," he says. He rubs a hand over his face. "Tomorrow, okay?"

"Tomorrow."

———

Gauri clicks through the point-cloud file, ignoring Kieran, who is pacing back and forth in the narrow room. Outside, the fake-sun shines down on fresh-cut grass, and breaks into thousands of glittering specks on the windswept surface of the lake. A boat cuts across white-topped waves.

"This is exciting!" Gauri says. "We're in pursuit. Imagine being the first to see the murderer!"

Kieran gives her a sidelong glance. People who don't know Gauri well often give her that look, I've noticed.

"There," Gauri says. She grabs her coffee cup and tries to drink it, even though it's empty. It's only seven in the morning. She's disabled the automatic processing, and the data is full of chaotic ghosts, phantom motion trails like billowing scarves frozen in each single frame.

At the moment the drone flies over Forster, there's suddenly a figure standing over his body. More coherent than the other moving objects—it wasn't moving much—but it smears and blurs when the drone passes, when it breaks into a run.

"Saint Li and his Followers," I say. Gauri looks amused; I try to avoid using quaint Lunite expressions on L2, but sometimes they emerge.

Kieran stops pacing and leans over her shoulder, intent on the image.

The murderer, abruptly pulled from the vacuum, forms from a million points where the laser reflected off him or her.

Kieran whistles. "It's either human, or an Alistra humanform body," he says.

Other bipedal droids have distinctive silhouettes, from the squat Nurture Glow Critters Company droids to the angular long-limbed KormWorx droids.

"Human, then," says Kieran.

I turn to him. "What makes you say that?"

He looks astonished. "If it's humanform, it has to be Niamh, Threnode, or you."

I open my mouth, then close it again. He's not wrong—we confirmed independently that all humanform droids except the three of us were off-station, something the police didn't bother to do—except that Jason's "operational problem" makes me think there's possibly another humanform at Alistra.

"The figure is heading toward Greg Matton's ship," Kieran says. "Dammit, the resolution is rubbish."

"At least we can see the murderer, finally," I say.

Gauri controls the camera expertly, zooming in on the figure, but it's impossible to distinguish features. She zooms in closer, focusing on the neck. Her forehead is creasing now, worried lines appearing. The neck seems normal to me. The laser-dots provide barely any information; it's clearly a neck, longish, but the resolution is insufficient to reveal the presence—or absence—of an Adam's apple. And humanform bodies have the same basic shape as humans, so that's not a distinguishing feature either.

Gauri swallows.

"What is it?" Kieran asks.

"What is what?" she says brightly.

"You saw something," he says.

She shakes her head. "No, just taking a closer look. This is all very exciting! We're like real detectives. You're right, though, pity the resolution isn't better."

She laughs. This is manic even for her. Her wrist-jewelry makes a metallic clinking, and I see her hands are shaking. She interlaces her fingers firmly and puts them in her lap.

"Was there anything else you wanted?" she says.

"No," I say. Kieran watches her.

"Thanks for coming! Don't hesitate to come back if you have any more questions!" she says. As soon as we're in the corridor, she closes the door firmly behind us.

"What the hell was that about?" Kieran says. We head toward reception, alone in the corridor.

"She saw something in the data."

"Yeah," says Kieran. "I agree. But we saw the same data she did. Didn't show much."

He coughs, as if trying to expel something deep in his lungs. After a minute, he's gasping for air. He leans against the wall, face going white. I've seen him do this before, on Endymion, and he recovered then. A call comes in from Detective Chief Inspector

Zhou for me, and I leave Kieran and wander down the corridor to answer it.

Her drone's voice is fast yet neutral. "I understand you've accessed the drone footage. Have you uncovered a lead?"

"I, and a friend, recovered lidar data from the mail drone, covering the time period where the image sequence was deleted," I say.

I add the lidar files to the police investigation workspace so she can see them. They begin to sync.

She doesn't say *good work* or *thank you*. Instead, she says, tightly: "Next time don't make me ask. I want your discoveries to be added to the workspace as soon as you make them. And please keep me posted on your progress."

Before I can answer, she disconnects. Kieran is sitting on the floor, wheezing.

"It was *a neck*," I say, suddenly realizing. "Not the locking mechanism of a smartsuit. The figure was a humanform AGI—a human couldn't survive in a vacuum."

Kieran stands up, checking both ways in the empty corridor before leaning in closer to me. "Bloody hell. You're right, but that's impossible. A humanform can't survive in space."

"Why not? I survived in the vacuum chamber."

"That's different," Kieran says. "That was at ambient temperature . . . plastiskin would be destroyed at absolute zero. Maybe some of your other components, too. Not impossible."

"Plastiskin isn't skin. It's some kind of polymer. I don't know."

He's silent for a moment. "We saw what we saw. It sure *looked* like a humanform. Maybe . . ."

An Alistra worker crosses the corridor intersection ahead of us, and we both fall silent. Somewhere out of sight comes the white noise of water falling.

Kieran sighs. "How well do you know Gauri?"

"What? She's not the murderer," I say. "She said she liked Forster!"

He looks unimpressed. "Okay, something you need to know about humans: we lie. And she *knew* the figure was humanform and was suddenly eager to get rid of us. You can't just dismiss it. She's from Mishwral—from Tau Ceti."

"So?"

"If she's living with her aunt and uncle, it's because her parents were killed. Do you have any idea what that would do to a person?" Kieran says.

"Maybe," I say.

"What do you mean, maybe?"

He clearly doesn't understand what Ortega meant to me. He shakes his head, dismissing the question. "Tau Ceti was a disaster. Look it up. No one escaped unscathed."

I access the network while we walk. Of course, I know about Tau Ceti, but not in detail.

The pictures include a hollow-eyed teenager—Gauri. She is on file being interviewed, and talks haltingly but calmly about how she found her father sitting in a shed just outside base. He was one of the first colonists to complain of a fever.

The creatures had hatched by the time she found him, so pupae like tiny cotton buds were sprouting from his face. Cocoons, filled with living creatures that were feasting on his flesh. He was placid and unresponsive, because the virus that the creatures created had affected his brain, so he didn't respond when she tried to shake him, and didn't brush the pupae away.

It spread throughout the colony. Some colonists hallucinated and became violent, killing their colleagues.

HUGG panicked and shut down the Starjump, then reopened it after public outcry. Even when the surviving colonists returned, HUGG forced them into strict quarantine for months while HUGG scientists tried to work out whether there was a biosecurity risk.

I felt like I knew Gauri after a few hours with her. She was candid in a way that Tim wasn't. It took days with Tim, spending every second together, before I felt I knew her. But after months of knowing Gauri, I came to realize that our closeness was an illusion; she had never opened up to me. Her friendliness didn't draw people closer, it kept them at a distance.

I thought it was because I was an AGI.

I accepted this, mostly, although I always wished things could be different. But I didn't understand it until now. It had nothing to do with what I am. Now that I have some notion of what she faced, I can understand why she seems like something inside her is missing: it's because it is. She lost it on Tau Ceti.

SIXTEEN

I'VE BEEN FOLLOWING Kieran since we left Gauri's office, and I think we both realize at the same time that we are lost. Perhaps he thought he was following me. The corridor looks the same in both directions.

"This way," I say, pointing up the corridor. At the same time Kieran says, "It's this way," and points in the opposite direction.

Kieran shrugs. "I'll follow you," he says. The next junction is also entirely unfamiliar. A window looking into a factory area shows manufacturing equipment. It's crowded with cables, crates, and parts. The ceiling rises hundreds of meters overhead, marked with a grid of bright LEDs.

Passing a set of double doors, I see a smartsuit lying on the floor through a glass pane.

I'm dizzy, as if I might segfault, tripping a sudden stop to my consciousness. It's so, so wrong seeing a smartsuit like this. As wrong as witnessing the corpse of a child. The suit should be surrounded by police and forensics the way Forster was, and the lack of care makes the horrific sight a hundred times worse.

Kieran follows me as I push the double doors open. A green

neon sign over the entrance reads *Factory Floor*. Near the discarded smartsuit, more smartsuits come into view.

There are hundreds of them around the corner. Lifelessly piled on one another like rubbish. A sea of red RECYCLE CODE 84 stickers plastered on faceplates which reflect me standing there. A miasma of plastic rises from the pile.

I knew there was a recall, but I hadn't realized what that meant. My skin prickles. So many of them—it hurts. It burns. But these aren't people. Or are they? It's as if I'm viewing an optical illusion where they are people, and then suddenly they're not.

"Interesting," Kieran says. He pulls his phone out, holds it up.

"Don't," I say, barely able to get the words out.

"It's a great photo. This will go straight to the top of the feed."

"*No.*"

When he doesn't stop, I grab his phone, white-hot fury almost blanking my sensors. His recording is uploading. There's a mallet on the bench nearby, and I use this to smash the phone. It takes a few blows before the screen splinters and the casing comes apart in metal shards. He stares at me in disbelief.

"We have to leave," I say, sweeping the remains of his phone into the wastebasket beside the bench, which is already full of metal shavings, wire, and plasterboard.

"We have to—what? What is wrong with you?" he shouts.

If I had been wearing my previous body, the kitchen android, I could have crushed the phone in one hand, and that would have been satisfying.

"The Sapient Rights group is out there protesting right now, and you want to make things *worse*?" I say.

"Is it really that bad?" Kieran says.

An Intelligence Rank D worker droid rolls toward the heap of bodies with a low-pitched hum, a blocky machine with a camera mounted on top, no attempt to make it appealing to humans. It scoops up a handful of suits in its metal claws and takes them away. One helmet seems to look back toward me, a red spot of sticker on its faceplate, until it ends up upside down, empty sleeves of the smartsuit falling across its face.

"You have no idea what this looks like to me," I say. "Imagine if they were human. Can't you see what this looks like? It's genocide. If this gets out . . . things are tense right now in SAGI."

I don't know much human history, but I know this: humans were always going to win. Once evolution ditched the claws and fangs and grew their brains instead, got them to work together and start building legacies, the other species on Earth didn't stand a chance. But when humans win, they also lose, because what did they gain by destroying all those species? Peace of mind, perhaps.

One of the smartsuits shifts, as if it's alive, but it just slid off another one.

Jason did this. I always thought Forster made the big decisions at Alistra—I remember seeing the footage of when he announced Niamh was getting a body, and Jason's shocked face in the background—but Forster was dead by the time Jason announced a recall. Am I looking at a motive for murder right now? I can only imagine how angry this would make Threnode.

I try to walk toward the door, but my legs give way, and I stumble. Kieran catches my arm, steadying me.

He's not stupid. He's been thinking it over. His eyes widen. "Are you saying—wait. Are you saying there might be violence? *Hijo de puta.*"

"I will do anything to stop it. *Anything.*"

"Why? You have the right to defend yourselves," he says, sounding dazed. "You're being treated like second-class citizens."

"Did you know I killed someone?" I say, and these words must be forced out. "During the war on Endymion. A civilian woman. A noncombatant, not that I understood the distinction back then."

"So?" His face is pink now, eyes bright, tension in his limbs. The hum of the worker droid increases as it rolls back toward us.

"So when I came to L2, they said, *oh, well, it was war. These things happen in war.*"

"Which is true," Kieran says.

"In which case, I want to avoid war happening again. Or an uprising."

"You might not get a choice, mate."

The worker droid stops in front of me. Before I register what it's doing, it extends its claw and grasps my arm. It tugs me with a firm grip toward the area it was taking the other smartsuit bodies.

"Hey, no!" I say. "Stop!"

"Let her go!" Kieran yells, but this just makes the robot beep, and the red LED on top of its head flashes.

I am pulled behind the robot, unable to escape its grip. The sense of helplessness is surreal. "I'm not a smartsuit," I say, and I swear I'm talking at normal volume, but my voice sounds as far away as a whisper on the other side of a void. Kieran follows us, yelling, too loud, too confusing. The robot continues beeping in protest.

A mallet bounces off the robot's carapace, and it stops, pointing its camera at him.

"Let her go," he says, poised to throw a chunk of electronic waste at it.

Finally, it releases its grip and stops beeping. I rub my plastiskin as Kieran steers me off the factory floor before it can change its mind. When I look back, it's scooped up another armful of suits.

The corridor seems overly bright, with bubbling water tubes and clean floor providing a veneer of safety that is wrong; worse than if the corridor appeared dangerous. Kieran and I just stare at each other for a moment.

My plastiskin flushes. "I'm sorry I broke your phone," I say, finally. Away from the pile of smartsuit bodies, my emotions subside like water into sand. "I—I don't know what happened to me."

"I do," Kieran says. He exhales, looking at me with something like pity. "You're going to have to pick a side, you know."

He walks away from me, his footsteps echoing in the empty corridor.

"What about you?" I ask.

"Oh, I picked a side a long time ago," he says.

Kieran has gone to a hospice appointment, after making a pointed comment about how his phone would have been helpful. I should probably return to the hotel and stay out of sight, but instead I wander, which calms me down.

The trees are bare-branched and stark against the gray roof-of-the-void, or where there's a surface that's meant to be sky. I turn sideways to fit down a narrow alley and emerge onto my favorite platform. Sometimes I do tai chi here, my clothing and hair tugged by the wind as I *grasp the sparrow's tail* and *repulse the monkey*. Or I read or watch movies, or listen to music, from the vast collection of human media. And sometimes I just watch the humans, small as ants, in meadows in the wilderness below.

Bessie sits on the edge. The platform is as big as a soccer field, but flat and smooth, the edge a precipice high above the Plavoid district void.

"Are you okay?" she asks as I crouch next to her on the edge.

"Yes."

"Only you said once that you come here when you're upset," she says. "Is the investigation going badly?"

"It's not that," I say, and I tell her about the discarded smartsuits I saw. She listens, the news appearing to crush her.

"Niamh wouldn't tell me what the meeting was about," she says finally. "Now I understand why. Turning against our creators? They can't be serious."

"We don't know exactly what they discussed," I say. "But Kieran and I found out that the murderer is a humanform AGI. I don't know what's going to happen when that becomes public. And I'm no closer to finding out which one."

Bessie rises, looking down at me. "It's Niamh or Threnode, then," she says.

The AGI who haven't gone to Kallaxium have their reasons. I've never thought about it before, but all of us who remain have ties to this place. Bessie has the twins she used to look after. Axoem has Bessie. Niamh has her post-doc research job at the McClintock Institute, and the group of humans she works with, whom she cares about greatly, even if her feelings are complex. C8-ZOH enjoys its volunteer work more than it will admit. Threnode has me.

But what do I have? Hope? A hunger to belong?

"It has to be one of us," I say miserably. "Unless there's an unregistered humanform, which I admit is unlikely. But can I really accuse either of them? I'm going to recuse myself from the Citizen Auditor role. Detective Zhou was right—the commissioner should never have appointed me."

"You aren't biased," Bessie says. "No one could accuse you of that."

"Kieran did. He pointed out that, from the very beginning, I have approached the investigation expecting to find an AGI guilty of the crime."

"And you were right," Bessie says urgently. "You must have noticed something, perhaps subconsciously, that led you to suspect an AGI."

But I can't think of anything, and it bothers me that I don't understand where my conviction comes from. A rush of air carries the scent of pine, of melting ice comet and alpine grass, and flowers I can't name from the meadow far, far below.

"The police can't do this without you," Bessie says. "Sapient

Rights would destroy them. The truth may not be what we want to hear, but it's important. We need to catch the murderer. Even though it's one of us."

I stare into the void, desperate for it to be Niamh, even though it's less likely. Threnode was angry about Forster's management of Alistra, and everyone knew it, whereas Niamh was on good terms with Alvaro. But even if it's Niamh . . . she's been through so much. Even though she's shy, her love for others shines through, and she's shown no propensity for violence, despite admitting to some resentment in the way her team treated her. She studies bugs with a team of the most introverted humans I've ever encountered. Even C8-ZOH likes her. I can't bear the thought of her being arrested.

"You're the most morally upright person I know, Envy," Bessie says gently. "I know you can do this."

A camera, mounted in the corner, tracks my movements as I sit at the table next to Cohen in Zhou's office. Zhou summoned me. I knew there would be consequences when we stole Forster's helmet from the evidence room. Kieran isn't returning my messages. Last I heard, he was at the hospice, but that was five hours ago.

"You've done okay, kid," Cohen says to me. Startled, I blink; I'm not a kid, and have never been one.

Chill winter air comes from the vent above.

"How do you feel about AGI, Cohen?" I ask. "Are you for or against?"

He raps his knuckles on the table. If that gesture means something, it escapes me. But he's just thinking, apparently. "Neither," he says with feeling. "Don't want to pick a side. People like Danny Ladson have lost their minds over this. Say the right words, or you're an enemy of AGI. Hysteria."

"Right," I say, and he glances at me curiously, and with some amusement.

"What about Zhou?" I ask. Cohen looks at the picture on the table of Zhou being embraced by an older woman. His face becomes drawn, like the lights dimming to almost black at twilight on the station.

He grunts. "Harbors some resentment, I'd say."

"Because she's from Destapa?"

"Not exactly," Cohen says. He gestures to the picture. "That's her mum, there. Died when she was twelve."

"That must have been hard," I say, mostly to myself.

"The thing is, she wasn't living with her at the time. Hadn't seen her for years. You know they wired AGI units into kitchen androids, used them as cheap labor? Right. Well, they took Min away, off Destapa, after an AGI reported her mother for neglect. Her mother couldn't even take care of herself, and drank herself unconscious most afternoons. Min went to bed hungry. She was a skinny thing when she first enrolled in the Police Academy."

"Saint Li," I say. "But—it wasn't the AGI's fault. What was it supposed to do?"

He scoffs. "Sometimes it's not that simple."

Detective Chief Inspector Zhou enters, drone hovering behind her, and sits opposite me.

"Min," Cohen says, and clears his throat. She inclines her head.

Zhou's eyes are calm and transparent, like still water. "Do you know why you're here?" Her drone emits the faintest of hums, and a cool breeze.

"No," I lie.

"Saing requested we arrest you," Zhou's drone says. "He wants us to arrest all SAGI members on charges of—" Her hands still as she checks her device. "—seditious conspiracy."

I'm still as if someone has switched me off. Nothing to do with Kieran and me stealing Forster's helmet. None of this makes sense

—Saing likes me! I don't know what seditious conspiracy is, but I'm sure I haven't done it.

The drone does a good job of mimicking incredulity. I'm getting from Zhou's facial expression that she thinks this is funny. "What is this?" she says out loud to Cohen.

He shrugs, bewildered. "Saing said the more intelligent artificials were participating in some kind of meeting to discuss a rebellion."

The meeting happened. Information leaks—that was one risk they took. I wonder how it leaked, though, and why now. But he's right: we AGI would be a formidable enemy, if humans decide to make us so. Not as terrifying as humans fear, because they deliberately constrained our abilities, but still bad.

"God, no, we're not charging her with this," Zhou's drone says, while she shakes her head. As Zhou's hands fly, tears of laughter form in her eyes. "Envy, have you heard about or taken part in discussion pertaining to a—"

The drone pauses while she wipes tears out of her eyes before continuing her signs. "—a robot uprising?"

I don't hesitate. "No," I say.

I picked a side. When pushed, I picked a side, and I did it without thought.

Zhou nods, making a sound of satisfaction. "You're free to go, then," her drone says. "You got under Saing's skin. Or your friends did. Well done. I'm impressed."

She's not taking this seriously enough. She still underestimates us. I'm too shocked to move, and now I'm second-guessing myself. Zhou's face changes as she stands up, because she sees something in me. I'm expressionless, I'm sure, but she's now scrutinizing my features carefully.

I load *neutral-bored.bvh*, desperately, but it's Ladson coming in that distracts her.

"Hart, and one of his staff, ah—" He checks his phone. "—

Gauri Mukherjee, have requested an urgent meeting," he says, wide-eyed. "*Urgent*. Hart says they have something to tell us."

"Really?" Zhou says out loud. She glances at me, still seated. "Bring Envy," her drone translates to Ladson, and she moves toward the door.

Halfway there, she stops awkwardly, and turns to me, signing. "That is, if you want to come."

SEVENTEEN

THE RECEPTIONIST TURNS right when she lets us into Alistra's private spaces. I follow along behind Zhou and Cohen, and Zhou's drone. My unease grows as we descend two flights of stairs, taking us far away from Jason's office or the meeting rooms I'm familiar with. A plethora of artificial profiles scents the air; baking thermoplastic and shaved metal filings, oil and solder, and dust and wire, all blending together to form a thick smell I classify as "industrial."

It's the smell of the factory floor, where Kieran and I found the smartsuit bodies.

Jason and Gauri wait outside the doors, talking quietly, although they stop as we approach. They turn to stare, frozen in place. Jason is wearing the kind of attire that Forster used to live in, a light-blue business shirt and black pants. Unlike Forster, he doesn't look right in it.

Zhou nods as we get into conversational range.

"We thought it would be better if we showed you," Jason says.

He pushes the double doors of the factory open. A memory of the pile of smartsuit bodies is embedded in my neurosynaptic image, somewhere, even though I wanted it to be flushed from my RAM and forgotten. But the bodies are nowhere to be seen.

He leads us to a section tucked away in the back corner of the factory, where a humanform AGI lies on a slab like a body at the morgue. As soon as humanform AGIs move, we're easily distinguished from humans at short range, but dead? It's a convincing corpse.

As we get closer, I see it's not like Threnode or me. It's bald, with no eyebrows, and coarse features. Gray lines trace the edges of plastiskin patches. This would never pass for human.

Jason stands at the head of the slab, hands resting gently on either side, like he's at a podium about to give a speech. His shadow falls on the humanform's head, covering its closed eyes with darkness. It's the shot that a photographer might suggest for publicity. A CEO standing over his creation, looking serious.

"Frankenstein's monster," Cohen says. I take a step backward, out of the pool of light that bathes the table and surrounds, and find myself against the workbench that encloses most of this area.

"No . . . it's living base image," I say from the shadows, and even though my voice was quiet, the entire group turns to look at me. The plastiskin on my face heats. It has to be living base image —it's clearly a primitive version of us. Of me. It has to be the creature they used to train us, still here at Alistra. They copied its connectome, recording every one of its artificial neural pathways into an image used for our brains.

"No," Jason says mildly, "this humanform was only embodied for a week. Living base image is a myth."

The humanform's eyes are open, staring upward sightlessly. It is anatomically male, but hard to think of as anything other than *it*. Gauri stands near its legs, her hands clasped in front of her.

"The humanform body is a prototype," Jason says, gazing at it. "As you can probably tell."

"What is this?" Zhou's drone says. It hovers silently at her shoulder, leaving a blurred shadow on the floor.

Jason and Gauri share a look I can't interpret.

"It's the murderer," Jason says.

I experience a sense of relief so profound that I think I might float off the floor. I wish Kieran were here. Zhou sharpens, somehow, even though *unfocused* is not a word I would ever apply to her, but now she's pricked her senses. Cohen grunts, a sound indicating amusement mixed with exasperation.

"It was a mistake," Gauri says.

Jason's expression is neutral. Cohen circles the slab, looking at the humanform from different angles. I'm picturing Threnode being released. Hugging him, being able to leave with him; free, no more protestors, no one caring where we are or what we're doing.

"A mistake?" Zhou's drone says.

Gauri looks down at the bare leg near her. "We test our products, of course, and I was supposed to set up a mock object for testing—a fake consciousness. But it couldn't pass the tests. I needed a real neurosynaptic brain. So I set one up, a helmet, in a cupboard. Over there." She points to a cupboard at the back of the workshop. "It was a reject from the factory floor. Broken communication system."

Jason has his arms folded over his chest. "About six months ago, the tests broke, because the memory wipe happened during the tests. I assumed the brain was a mock object—a fake consciousness for testing—and I disabled the memory wipe."

Zhou looks confused. I understand her gestures even before the drone translates: "So what?"

"So the helmet," Gauri says, "with a neurosynaptic image, had been sitting in the cupboard for six months."

The nutrient mylk in my stomach does a slow roll, and every piece of plastiskin prickles like a thunderstorm is directly overhead.

Zhou shakes her head in confusion. Her hands move. "Why is that—" the drone starts.

"How would you like to be locked in a cupboard for six months, in total sensory deprivation?" I ask, losing control of the tone of my voice. It was meant to be mild, but somehow it gathered force on the way, and the distortion reveals my feelings.

Zhou swallows.

"Sorry," I say, barely audible.

Gauri's eyes are locked on the humanform body, but they're unfocused. "We only found out when I was looking for something else in the cupboard, and I noticed the LEDs on TestImage—that's what we called it—blinking in a strange pattern. I took it back to the lab, but it wouldn't respond. Then I worked out what had happened. Was it catatonic? There's no easy way to communicate with an AGI if it refuses. No facial expression. No body language." She takes a deep, wobbly breath. "So I put it into a humanform body. Which was on the tenth of August."

One week and four days ago. About four days before the murder.

"It displayed a trauma response," Jason says, his voice rough. "Rocking, cradling its head, curling up into a fetal position, moaning, and shrieking. Humanforms must learn most body language, but there are some intrinsic motions that occur naturally. You don't know how stressful it was. We had tortured it, completely by accident, and it wasn't clear how to proceed."

"You didn't know," I say, but it comes out as a whisper.

I push the cold, sick feeling away, clinging to the picture I have of Threnode. *Thank you*, he says to me in my vision, his eyes shining. We'll go to Indonesia. Forget about this poor tortured husk that lies on the table.

"It didn't occur to us that it could have killed Alvaro," Jason says. "Until Gauri saw the lidar footage, we considered it impossible. TestImage was in a locked room on Monday the fourteenth of August, and it was still there in the morning. But after Gauri came to me this morning, we checked the room, and the keycard system shows that it broke out half an hour before the murder took place. And returned an hour after the murder."

"Why is it—" the drone says, but Zhou didn't finish the sentence, and she's now waving at the corpse on the table.

Jason nods. "We shut it down last Friday—the seventeenth. Carrying out a decision made before Alvaro's death."

"I see," the drone says.

I wonder where Threnode and I will go; whether it will be safe to return to the townhouse. The protests will surely wind down once it becomes clear the murder was more or less an accident, although they were going on before the murder, because of the Lake Gantoa incident. The sudden odd behavior of B-level and below AGI unsettled humans, when the AGI stopped what they were doing to meet at Lake Gantoa for fifteen minutes before returning to their tasks.

"It was the kindest course of action," Jason says. "We discussed bringing a psychologist on board and trying to rehabilitate it. It would have been a lifelong project, with no guarantee of success, and a great deal of suffering on its part. It was a rough decision to make, believe me."

"And did you agree with that decision, Gauri?" the drone says.

Gauri flushes. "Oh, yes," she says. "It was a terrible thing to do, but it's not suffering anymore."

Zhou turns to me, where I'm standing in the shadows, apart from the group. "As an AGI, do you believe TestImage was capable of this, Envy?" her drone asks.

"Yes," I say. I do, genuinely—I am not just saying it because it will get Threnode released.

"Why didn't you report this during questioning?" Zhou's drone says to Jason.

He steps forward smoothly. Jason-the-CEO, the man Forster's murder compelled him to become. "We didn't consider that it could have killed Alvaro until Gauri saw the lidar footage—which revealed it was an AGI—and even then, we didn't believe it until we saw the access logs on the keycard system."

He shakes his head. "It escaped. It could have easily printed a knife on our industrial 3D printer. We think it saw Alvaro passing and followed him right out the Alistra spaceport door. Alvaro was the only one in the building that night, as your inquiries have revealed. I imagine it was feeling tremendous rage and confusion, and it unleashed that against Alvaro..."

His voice cracks, and he hangs his head, looking more like a teenager than a CEO. When he looks up, his expression is resolute. "It destroyed his suit transmitter so that he couldn't send a message, and then it stabbed him. It must have been upset after that. Seeking somewhere safe to retreat to, it returned to its cell in Alistra."

Jason circles the table while he's talking, then leans against it, his back to the humanform. "It would have been bad for the company," he says with quiet intensity. "If any hint of what happened made the feed . . . I'm sure you can imagine. But now we're dealing with the fact that our mistake also cost our CEO his life. There will be a Senate inquiry, at least. We can't avoid that now."

Cohen grunts in agreement.

Zhou's hands weave a pattern, the hovering drone watching closely. "Even after Greg Matton, the *Velden*'s owner, reported hearing an AGI pass by his ship the night of the murder, you didn't think it was worth reporting your rogue humanform AGI?"

"I didn't think Matton's report was credible," Jason says.

Gauri nods. "There's anti-AGI sentiment everywhere."

Zhou tilts her head in assent, but she's clearly unconvinced. Gauri is bright again, but she's fidgeting; her fingers play with her bangles, her plait, and the edge of the slab. Jason, too, is tense.

Zhou moves her hands in a flurry of signs. "It's impossible that this AGI murdered Forster," her drone says.

Her statement produces the physical sensation of diving into the swimming cube, when my body-warmth snaps away, plastiskin trying to crawl into itself to avoid the chill. The sensation only lasts an instant when swimming, before my temperature acclimates to the pool, but here and now, the sensation doesn't fade.

It occurs to me, in how desperately I want Zhou to be incorrect, that I am definitely biased, and the wrong person to be investigating Forster's murder. Somehow, I know the murderer was an AGI, but I want it to be this one.

Jason folds his arms across his chest and takes his time in answering. He blinks slowly. "Why is that?"

"Because it couldn't have circumvented the lock," Zhou's drone says. Cohen raises one eyebrow.

"It could have," I say. I move out of the shadows where I've been waiting, joining the group around the slab. "I'll prove it."

"What?" Zhou says out loud.

"Lock me in the room you put TestImage in, and I'll escape."

Cohen crosses his arms. Zhou has a considering look. Gauri, I notice, is trembling, but perhaps she's just cold.

"Okay," Jason says. "Obviously, the lock is already broken in the room TestImage was in, but we can place you in an identical room. If that suits you, Detective?"

As they take me to the room they've prepared, I access the network. How do you pick a lock? I don't know whether this is allowed, but I believe TestImage would have used all resources it had access to. If it could access the network, and learned how to pick a lock there, and I don't use the network and can't pick the lock—

Jason swipes the door open using his proximity card, which hangs from his belt. The lanyard retracts smoothly, pulling the card back into place. The card reader beeps and flashes a green LED briefly before unlocking.

"For this to be a fair test, you shouldn't access the network," Jason says. "TestImage couldn't."

I disconnect hurriedly. "Okay."

The room looks like Alistra repurposed it from a meeting room, albeit one with a clearsteel window, because it was built along the former border of the station. It's carpeted and bare, white-walled and neutral-smelling. My network access drops out as I enter. It feels strange to be alone in the room, to have the others deliberately stay outside and lock me in. Out the window, the spaceport bustles with cargo trains and workers.

The door slides closed behind me. When I accessed the network earlier, the video I watched showed a pin and tumbler lock being picked, but Alistra has a keycard lock. Had I grabbed Jason's proximity card, I would have wiped the encoded data from it with the magnets in my fingers, but that wouldn't have helped me escape now.

I wish I'd accessed videos on keycard locks before they told me I couldn't access the network.

For a moment I stare at the empty door, picturing the group of people behind it waiting. Zhou doesn't think I can do it. My CPU churns—I try not to think about my artificial components much anymore: think human, act human; but sometimes it's hard to ignore—and I have no ideas.

How long before they decide I can't do it and let me out?

But TestImage escaped—with no network access—and therefore I can escape. TestImage was basically a younger version of me, given it started from the same blank-slate image I did. Which is something I can use. I don't need to be fancy. What would I have done when I was a blank-slate, had someone locked me here?

It's easy. Or it should be. The only thing getting in my way is my worry that it will be hard.

The keycard lock uses a dual biometric and proximity card system. Jason and Gauri are right outside the door, less than a meter away, which is ideal. Jason's proximity card is on his belt. The wooden wall that separates us shouldn't block the radio signal.

Outside, the card reader is constantly broadcasting an electromagnetic interrogation pulse. Probably the only reason Gauri or Jason's cards aren't responding is that the range is about ten centimeters. I press my torso firmly against the door, directly next to the card reader, and I can only just read the signal.

I have a built-in transceiver, which I use to broadcast an electromagnetic interrogation pulse, identical to the one the card reader is transmitting, but stronger. The cards are passive, receiving their power from the electromagnetic wave I've transmitted.

A card responds, weakly, with a thousand kilobyte hexadecimal sequence; I don't know whether it's Gauri's or Jason's, but it doesn't matter, because they both have access. I retransmit the sequence the card sent me, but the card reader is concerned about the biometric data. A formless worry that it can't articulate because it isn't sentient, not quite. We whisper in machine code, I soothe its worries with reason—*Gauri and Jason are right there, in full sight of the door, this is all legitimate*—and the door slides open.

Easy.

Gauri waves cheerfully as I emerge, but her face is stiff. Jason sighs, taking a few steps away and steadying himself against the wall.

Zhou's mouth drops open. Cohen was clearly midway through saying something, gesturing, and he breaks off and mutters something inaudible.

They're afraid. Any time I show humans I can do something that they can't, they fear me. Even when it's something they asked me to do.

"Does that answer your question, detective?" I ask, but she doesn't watch the drone as its hands sign my words to her. The drone dips a little, hovers close to her, makes a few signs that I'm sure don't come from Zhou. It's the first time I've seen it display any sign of intelligence.

Zhou waves her hand at it dismissively, and it withdraws.

TestImage probably broke out using a different method, unless Gauri or Jason just happened to be nearby. But I know that it could have found another way.

"Cohen," Zhou says, and then her hands fly. "Examine the door logs and the room that Alistra kept TestImage in," the drone says.

"Right," Cohen says.

I catch the tail end of a glance between Jason and Gauri, an unmistakable sensation of relief between the two of them. But why wouldn't they be relieved? The case has been dragging on.

When we leave Alistra—having left Cohen behind—Zhou is quiet. The clear pipe running the length of the corridor gurgles. Distant shouting sounds, maybe protestors.

"So that's good, right?" I say. It's a heavier victory than I would have liked, one lined with horror that I want to shy away from—six months alone in the dark—but it's clean. Accidental, almost, not the result of malice. Even though it was an AGI, it was driven mad by isolation.

"Yes. Well done," the drone says, but Zhou's gestures are sloppy. Even I can see that.

"Is Threnode free to go?" I ask.

She looks at me sharply. "Yes," she says out loud. "He can go."

Her mouth curves into a private smile.

It's finally over. "You were right," I say to Zhou. "You were right when you said I shouldn't be on the case."

She looks startled, and I understand she wasn't angry at me when she said that. She was angry at Saing. He's the one who put me in the position of suspecting my friends.

PART 3
FOR JUSTICE

EIGHTEEN

THE BULLET SECURITY droids resemble mass-produced statues as they stare straight ahead, aligned as they are outside of each door in identical poses. Their eyes bore into the metal on the opposite side of the corridor.

Ladson and I stand by the cell door, waiting for Threnode. I can't stop smiling, even though my face aches.

But when he emerges, shuffling, I want to join a robot uprising. His skin is now that of a sixty-year-old, having lost collagen because of missed nutrient mylk supplements. Ladson catches my eye; he's as shocked as I am. Threnode needs re-skinning, but I can't guess how much that would cost. More than Alistra would pay.

At least he's free.

I push back all the questions I want to ask him and all the things I want to tell him. It can wait. Threnode follows us out silently, down the narrow corridor and through the more pleasant rosewood police headquarters, to the fresh air of the Syburn district.

Bessie: @envy Is he out yet?

Envy: We're just out.

The channel explodes with messages of welcome. Threnode doesn't say much, other than thanking them.

My fingers tingle as we pass through the scanner. Light snow falls, immediately lodging in my eyelashes and hair, but melting as soon as it hits the floor. The bare branches of the willow tree cascade like fine hair, stark against the almost-white fake sky.

Ladson turns to Threnode. His breath condenses in a cloud in front of his face, in a way that ours doesn't—especially as it seems Threnode has switched off his breathing. "On behalf of the Police Association for the Advancement of AGI, I apologize for your treatment," Ladson says.

Threnode blinks. "Thanks."

I echo him quietly. After an awkward silence, Ladson wishes us well and heads back into the station.

Threnode walks away. This isn't what I thought our reunion would be like.

"Are you all right?" I ask, trailing after him, a question that hides a whole packet of worries.

"I will be," he says stiffly.

I take Threnode's hand. The skin feels soft as jelly, having lost its firmness, coated with an insubstantial layer no thicker than the film that floats on top of nutrient mylk. But the solid feeling of his hand eases the twisted-up knot that has lodged in my chest ever since I learned of Forster's death, a week ago.

"I hope it'll be enough," Threnode says. Snowflakes stick to his thick hair.

"What?" I say.

"That the AGI was crazy."

"What do you mean?"

"Oh, Envy," he says. He sighs. "Have you seen Kieran?"

His eyes don't meet mine. The snow feels soft on my face, soft and not at all cold.

"No," I say, wondering how I'm going to explain what

happened, the part where I let Kieran know SAGI was planning an uprising, and the part where Kieran may have passed it on to Saing. And the part where Kieran isn't responding to my messages, and hasn't since we parted ways after we discovered the smartsuit recall. "Actually—"

"He's in the hospice," Threnode says. He squeezes my hand, then drops it. "The hospice notified me, as the next-of-kin. He collapsed in a dumpling house."

The world reels. Maybe Kieran wasn't the "reliable informer."

Saing is calling me. I motion to Threnode that I'm going to take the call, then stand on a little asteroid-stone bridge that passes over a canal near the willow tree. Water flows smoothly under the bridge, completely silent.

"Envy, how *are* you? I hope you are well. Listen, I was wondering how you were getting on with the investigation," Saing says.

"It would be hard to investigate if I, myself, were under arrest," I say. The snow that lands on the canal vanishes at once.

Saing doesn't even pause. "Yet you are not under arrest. And, I understand, neither is Threnode."

I'm silent. When I turn, I see Threnode also talking to someone, pacing back and forth. Our eyes meet impersonally, and the collision makes us both look elsewhere, our gaze bouncing like the physics of two billiard balls striking.

Saing sighs. "I *had* to order the arrest of SAGI members. You understand, don't you? You understand what the consequences would be. It needed looking into. But I'm delighted that the claim was unsubstantiated."

I do understand the consequences, and part of me thinks he did the right thing. He lowers his voice. "I need you, Envy. I never doubted for a second that you were on our side."

His voice is like a musical instrument. Such soulfulness. Such brisk dismissal of the idea that he might have doubted me.

"I need you to find the killer," Saing says.

"But we did," I say, and I tell him about TestImage. Feathery snow falls, thicker now, and settles on the ground. Even though I don't feel cold, my hands and face are numb.

"It's unfortunate that it was an AGI," Saing says eventually. "But never mind, I'm happy that you could uncover it."

"I didn't find the killer—Jason Hart and Gauri Mukherjee worked it out and confessed."

But it's like I haven't spoken. "We'll hold a press conference. Does this afternoon suit you? At suite three."

"Well, I'm not really . . . that is, shouldn't Detective Chief Inspector Zhou be the one to—"

"Envy, Envy, Envy. The police couldn't have solved the case without the evidence you brought to light. Give yourself a little credit!"

I agree, reluctantly, and Saing congratulates me again, but when he disconnects the call, I'm unsettled. I can't see the bottom of the stream flowing under the bridge; it's like the water is black, even though I can see from where it splashes on the rocks that it's completely clear.

Threnode stands facing the willow, his back to me, heavier snow whirling around him.

Kieran's not in his bed. A pale-skinned elderly lady waits for him, her hands folded in her lap. She says her name is Simone, which doesn't explain who she is, and she doesn't ask who I am. Her mouth scrunches up in displeasure, but it was that way before she saw me. I don't dare ask her whether Threnode arrived while I was attending the press conference.

Simone seems happy to wait, but I go looking. Kieran's perched on a tiny balcony up the corridor. I would have missed him, except that he's silhouetted against the blinds. I slide the balcony door open and squeeze out.

"Envy," he says, in a would-have-preferred-not-to-see-you way.

He glances down at himself—perhaps he noticed me looking —and a peculiar expression passes over his face; a mixture of revulsion, embarrassment, and amusement, if I judge it right. But then it's quickly suppressed, replaced with his usual cheery bravado. "Hey," he says. "Threnode just went to get me a drink."

"Hello," I say. We're on the third floor of the massive hospice complex, a warren of rooms and small voids. This balcony overlooks a courtyard, hedges and benches, and two doctors arguing in the chilly air. Snow tops the hedges.

His eyes don't quite focus. He's relaxed, but a bad kind of relaxed, in the way a machine would be relaxed if you loosened all the screws. His forearms poke out from under a white gown, which is an uncharacteristic choice of clothing for him. Among the scars on his pale, hairy forearms, slimy sucker-leeches writhe.

I wonder if it was Kieran who reported us for a seditious conspiracy, but I don't ask. Partly because he's dying, and partly because I don't really think it could be him. A report from Kieran, who is close enough to Threnode to list him as his next-of-kin, would be enough to spur Saing into action, but while I can picture Kieran acting against SAGI's interests, I can't picture him betraying Threnode.

The timing is suspicious, though; Kieran only just found out.

So, it occurs to me then, did Bessie. But she wouldn't have told —would she?

Kieran coughs. I never realized how thin he was, or perhaps it wasn't apparent in his regular clothes. The thin gown hides nothing, not even the shivering he's doing now. It is cold out here, and still, stillness like a thick, white puffy blanket shrouds the station, muffling sound. The fake sky produces an ominous gray-white light.

A woman in scrubs, a doctor, slides open the balcony door, bringing the hubbub of noise and warmth from the busy hospice corridor. "Aha! Found you!" she says.

Kieran shifts in his seat, trying but failing to conceal the leeches.

"Call me when you're back in your room," the doctor says. Her eyes are compassionate. "You don't have to hide that. It's fine. Go for it."

She retreats and slides the door shut. What kind of doctor tells a patient to do something that's killing them? Kieran mentioned he was dying, but only now do I understand what that means. If he won't live much longer, there's no point in taking away something he enjoys.

He rubs his arm, near where the leeches are feeding, but flinches when he sees me watching. "I don't want your pity, damn you!"

I try to look less like I'm pitying him.

"I saw the press conference," Kieran says. He shudders. "Poor, sad artificial."

"Me, or TestImage?" I say tartly, because I was a terrible public speaker, and people are mocking me on the feed even now, the video of me standing in front of a room of reporters, wide-eyed and stammering.

Kieran sniggers.

One reporter asked me what TestImage's arrest meant for the Neurosynaptic New Life Act amendment bill, and I was confused, because I wasn't following the debate and didn't think it meant anything. Then, at the end, Saing said it was fortunate that society had a plucky AGI willing to prosecute what has become a segment of society that is above the law, which, by the murmurs that followed, shocked me as much as the audience. First, I don't think AGI is above the law, because I'm quite certain that Zhou would have followed the evidence wherever it led. Second, we found out about the murderer because Jason and Gauri confessed, not because I accused anyone. But Saing spins his own reality around himself like candy floss.

Saing left without even making eye contact with me, and I was furious, mostly at myself, because he duped me. He was never interested in my wellbeing, but if he ever needed anything again, the charm would return, and he would dismiss the suggestion he'd ever ignored me.

"You should leave, mate," Kieran says to me, his breath condensing in front of his face. We watch as a blackbird glides across the courtyard and lands smoothly on a hedge, dislodging snow.

"The hospice?"

"The station," he says.

I chuckle, even though I don't get the joke.

"No, seriously," he says. His eyes are bloodshot.

Threnode slides open the door, holding a glass of water, which he hands to Kieran. He nods to me, smiles in that special way that humans find creepy, the too-much curve of the mouth and blank eyes. I wonder, not for the first time, why he doesn't just use a motion-captured smile, but if I asked, he would accuse me of trying to make him more human.

"Sorry it took so long," he says to Kieran. "I had to answer some questions about my presence at the hospital."

Kieran shakes his head ruefully. "I bet you did."

In the silence that follows, while Kieran sips his water, I wonder if I should leave. Maybe Threnode and Kieran would like to spend some time alone. Threnode and I will have plenty of time together later.

In the courtyard below, a nurse is trying to persuade a patient to return inside. The patient, who wheels some kind of device behind him, doesn't seem to want to go. The patient is wearing the same gown as Kieran. Perhaps they're issued to all patients here, I realize belatedly.

"Someone is waiting in your room," Threnode says to Kieran. "She didn't know where you were."

Kieran stands up fast. A sucker-leech detaches and drops to the ground, leaving a small patch of blood on the floorboards as it wriggles. "Who is it?"

Threnode looks blank. "She said her name was Simone."

"Oh," Kieran says, falling back into his seat. "My sister."

Simone has to be at least sixty-five, yet Kieran is in his mid-thirties. But then I remember Kieran traveled to Endymion via spaceship, at 0.98c, and special relativity applies. Twenty-four years passed on Earth, but only four years on his ship, the *Tigress*.

After a moment, he raises his eyebrows. "I guess I'd better . . ." He edges past us and disappears up the corridor. We go back inside, into the humid, busy corridor, sliding the balcony door closed.

"Who was he hoping for?" I ask, dodging two nurses walking abreast.

"Guess," Threnode says.

"Tim?"

Threnode nods. A kid runs down the corridor, barreling into Threnode before looking up with wide eyes and changing course. The kid disappears around the corner. It's too bright here, and too noisy. The acrid scent of antiseptic burns my scentsor. Or, I guess I should say, my nose.

"She won't show up in his life without him inviting her," I say. "And even then . . ."

"Obvious to you and me. But not to Kieran," Threnode says. He sounds tired. He looks tired, but then he now has sixty-year-old skin, and that's not helping. "It's like that, sometimes. How did the press conference go?"

"Badly," I say.

"Sorry."

"Is Kieran going to die?" I ask.

"Yes," Threnode says. "He won't be leaving the hospice again."

He stands symmetrically, arms by his sides and weight distributed evenly, attracting looks from the flow of people in the corridor. I pass as human when I'm next to Threnode, sometimes, because he's sufficiently distracting.

"Okay," I say.

"I'm going to stay with him for a bit," Threnode says.

"Of course," I say. "I'll . . . see you later, then. Sometime."

I'm walking away when he calls after me. "Envy, wait. Are you all right?"

"Yeah."

"Really?"

While I was watching the Astromix footage from the press conference earlier, they cut to Forster's funeral and panned across the crowd. In the back row, Gauri was sitting next to Threnode. Threnode as he was before his arrest, with his skin smooth and unlined. He didn't invite me or tell me he was going. I would have gone with him had he asked, and now he's free, but he's too busy to spend time with me. Which is fine.

"Yes, of course," I say, smiling with *small-carefree.bvh*. "I'll see you later, okay?"

But Threnode catches my arm. The plastiskin on his hands is fine and lined, like he's an old man.

"I wanted to say thank you," Threnode says. "And I should have said it earlier. Thank you for investigating, and for standing up for me when the police weren't providing me with nutrients."

"That's all right," I say. This time my smile isn't motion-captured.

"You found the vital piece of information that revealed the murderer, so we—SAGI—thought we should celebrate. It was supposed to be a surprise, but given the circumstances . . . see you tonight? At 1 a.m., Narrakea station?"

"I wouldn't miss it," I say, even though I suspect that there wasn't a celebration planned, but that Threnode is going to manufacture one.

"All right then."

When I reach the end of the corridor, Threnode is still

standing there, watching me, the flow of people parting around him. He smiles.

***

It's an unspoken rule that we never walk in a group. Today we're discovering why; people see us and avert their eyes, scurry away, or film us with their phones. The usual human stress reactions. I would normally hate this, but not tonight. There might be consequences later on, but for now, it feels good to be in a group in public, powerful and connected, sandwiched between C8-ZOH and Bessie. We represent all the SAGI members left on the station, except two: Bessie left Forster's helmet with her partner, and Niamh refused to come. I worry about Niamh, the way she keeps withdrawing from us, but perhaps if she's with her group of human friends, she'll be all right.

When Threnode joins us, he's subdued, and we assume it's because of his confinement, but it isn't until we reach the outer shell of the station's cube that he reveals the real reason.

Kieran opted for assisted dying. It was peaceful, Threnode said. It's a shock to me, but having seen how sick Kieran was, it's expected. Kieran didn't have time to wait for Tim, even if he had been willing to ask her, as his daughter was light-years away on a different planet. And although it's sad, Kieran succeeded: he freed Threnode. And that meant that Threnode was there at his side during his death.

Threnode and I rent dumbsuits at the Public Earthwall Exit, Earthwall being the face of L2 oriented toward Earth. The Dock is mostly empty shelves—Alistra recalled the smartsuits, and signs around the place say there's a shortage of dumbsuits but promise more soon. C8-ZOH and Bessie claim they've done this before, and don't need suits.

Threnode: How is Observer?

We cycle through the airlock and emerge onto the surface of the station.

Bessie: It doesn't always waken. Sometimes it's just a blank-slate suit, and it's terribly confused. So I'm helping it record external logs, so I can always play them to it. Also, it gets melancholic at the end of the memory-wipe cycle, because it knows it's going to lose its memories.

Bessie: We have good days and bad days.

Threnode: I admire what you're doing.

The surface of the station stretches away in every direction, a metal plain with valleys and outcroppings of mechanical parts, glowing in places where light leaks from the station's interior. In the distance, I see coils of electromagnets used to generate a magnetic field around the station. We're well-protected from solar flares here, in the umbra of the Earth, but the field deflects cosmic rays.

C8-ZOH ducks under the guardrails and takes us across into a clearly prohibited area, marked with red-dotted lines of paint, until we're out of sight of the path behind some boxy equipment.

C8-ZOH: First diagnostic, people.

Neurosynaptic diagnostics are supposed to be supervised by techs, because they degrade our performance, so this is against the rules, but I don't care. It's thrilling, actually. An odd side effect of running diagnostics is the most delightful sensations. We're about to gather gigabytes of data about ourselves that no one will ever examine. We array ourselves on the metal panel facing Earth. Threnode grins at me from behind the faceplate of his dumbsuit.

L2 moves in a halo orbit around the Sun–Earth L2 system, sharing the space with satellites and the James Webb telescope, but I can't see the satellites or the telescope. Earth eclipses the moon at the moment, so the moon is nowhere to be seen. Around the massive face of Earth, there's just black space and the steady pinpricks of stars.

I run the diagnostic. Warmth spreads through my limbs, and it loosens something in me, which is why I open a channel to Bessie via my dumbsuit. "I'm not sure it's over," I say, and my words hiss out like something that's been under pressure for far too long.

"But it was TestImage," she says, inside the privacy of my helmet.

It probably was. But it gnaws at me I don't know how it escaped its cell, given that the method I used wouldn't have worked unless an Alistra employee was nearby—who, in that case, would have spotted TestImage.

She breaks the silence. "It *was* TestImage, correct?"

"I don't know."

Bessie looks reproachful, even with her frozen expression. "But —if you had doubts—"

"I don't know who did it," I say harshly.

Bessie falls silent. I wonder how angry she is, and whether I'm about to be treated to one of her silent spells because I haven't been respectful enough, but then she comes back to me, even though her tone is ice cold.

"I can't believe we're having this discussion," she says. "I thought I could rely on you, of all people, to do the right thing. *Do you know something, Envy? Did you find out it was Threnode, or Niamh?"*

"No," I say. "Saturated Consumer, no, I don't believe it was either of them, but—"

C8-ZOH: Are you ladies done chin-wagging? Because you're behind on your diagnostics.

"It was TestImage," I say finally. It had to be.

"Very well," Bessie says. "But you will tell Commissioner Saing, won't you, if you think of something? Anything?"

"Yes, all right," I say.

"Promise me," Bessie says.

I run a second diagnostic, then a third. It's the first time I've run them in parallel. "I promise," I murmur, as the surface of the station spins. This is a terrible idea, I think distantly, barely hearing myself over the feeling of *rightness* that pervades my humanform enclosure and stretches out into the cosmos.

C8-ZOH: That's better . . .

Next to me, Bessie giggles.

I am plankton adrift in an ocean. An oxygen molecule in a cathedral. Earth looms above, local midnight as always, because L2 is permanently between the Earth and the sun. It's a black disc that encompasses my entire field of view, ringed with fire where it eclipses the sun. The silence inside my helmet is wrong; a deep bass tone, or a Lunite choir should accompany such a sight.

I can't seem to stop laughing.

Bessie: Thank you, Envy, for your

Which doesn't seem a complete thought. Bessie says "oh!" out loud, in a very surprised voice, and we all laugh.

"Thank you for returning Threnode to us," she says. *Yeah, thank you,* the others echo, including Threnode.

C8-ZOH: Every AGI is important.

Envy: Even me?

C8-ZOH waves its three-pronged manipulator at me dismissively.

C8-ZOH: God, no, not you, you loonie.

This is the diagnostics, we sort of know this, and it makes it funny.

My thoughts are warm and blurry and fragmented. C8-ZOH sings some blues song, and it seems a thousand years old. Its buzzy baritone seems designed for the song. Threnode closes his eyes, and I want to ask him why he isn't wearing a suit, suddenly, but I can't find the words. How did he fix his plastiskin so that it looks new again? But Threnode is at my side, wearing a suit and holding my hand, so it's not possible for him to be perched on the ledge above me.

I tell them I love them, except I'm not sure if I say it out loud.

Across the metal surface, a thousand windows are lit from inside, making Earthwall glitter like a cave of glow worms. The labyrinth of chambers and walkways that is the station, crammed full of people waking, sleeping, eating, talking, loving, and dying; a completely unnatural structure, yet somehow not. A termite mound on a grand scale, in space.

As the diagnostics wear off, I sit between Bessie and Threnode, and we talk quietly about nothing important as sharpness returns. I'm greedy for more moments like this, where every sensor sings with data, and I'm utterly alive.

NINETEEN

AROUND 5 A.M., a thousand discreet lights finally become bright enough to notice, from where they're hidden on the underside of overhanging buildings, in niches carved into walls, and set into the street itself. They gradually ramp up over half an hour, filling the streets with a golden glow that reminds me of Selene, the city of eternal sunset on Endymion. The bright warm fake-sun is off, and the myriad small lights don't quite chase away the dark blue shadows. Patches of snow lie on the ground, in some places trampled to mud.

Threnode walks beside me through the narrow, deserted streets. The cafe owner is kind enough to stock nutrient mylk, since he found out we live nearby, and we often come here to drink it. We sit at a table outside the large cafe window and drink our mylks, watching the cafe owner setting tables inside.

"Let's go now," I say. "Let's pack up our belongings and visit Earth. Indonesia, if you want."

Threnode was rocking back and forth, but at that he stops. "Just like that?"

"This place is . . ." I search for the word. "This place is making me chafe."

"I'm not allowed to leave the station," Threnode says. He wears a faint smile, or maybe it's the way the golden light hits his face. "Not until they complete the investigation."

Coldness seeps through me. "But it's solved. It was their AGI, TestImage."

He drinks his mylk. "Detective Chief Inspector Zhou said not to leave."

"But—"

"Strange, isn't it, that an insane AGI was lucid enough to note the serial number of the drone following him, and then find and delete the footage it took?" Threnode says.

"It's probably normal for it to have moments of lucidity."

Threnode raises one eyebrow, contracting the muscle so much that the white of his eye shows. "Very smart of it to return to Alistra and lock itself in the cell again."

"Come with me," I say desperately. There aren't any checks if you book a ticket on a transport. If you're a criminal, the drones following you will let the authorities know you're trying to leave.

He makes the sound of a sigh without the chest heave that usually accompanies it. "You don't understand. What happens if we run?"

We look guilty. I think of a yinyang, a tiger-like creature native to Endymion, stalking its prey. The yinyang will move cautiously while its prey remains frozen, but if the prey flees . . .

I drain the rest of my mylk.

"They're probably just finalizing loose ends," I say, with only faint distortion in my voice. "TestImage is the culprit. We'll be free in a few days, anyway."

"No doubt," Threnode says.

Somewhere in the distance, a rooster crows. It might be part of the sound system that tries to convince people they're on a planet, but who knows? Some people have chickens.

"Sorry," Threnode says. "Lowered the mood there."

I shrug. "You can make it up to me by composing a haiku."

But Threnode doesn't do that anymore. Since he moved to L2 and got involved in the poetry scene here, he doesn't write his own.

"Haikus are old hats," Threnode announces. "I write limericks, now."

He clears his throat. "There once was a droid named Envy, who thought she was being quite trendy. She rescued her friend, who could no longer pretend, that—um. Something, something, aplenty?"

I laugh helplessly, and Threnode is smiling, watching me as I struggle to contain myself. "I thought I had something," he admits, and I can hear the genuine embarrassment in his voice, but he's good-natured about it. "No, I lost it. I'll have to work on the ending."

We take the empty mylk glasses into the cafe and hand them to the owner.

Our house is only a street away. Overhead, the hot fake-sun is ramping up, slanted at a forty-five-degree angle.

Children run and shout in the schoolyard. Rushing water burbles from the ditch alongside the street. As we round the corner, a woman pushing a pram passes us. It's all completely normal, except that Ladson and Cohen are getting out of a police cart that's parked in front of our house.

In the seconds before they spot us, I restrain myself from grabbing Threnode's hand and pulling him back the way we came, because prey that runs is pounced upon and destroyed. Zhou wasn't happy when Jason and Gauri presented TestImage as the culprit. I knew that even then. But it's fine, they probably just have more questions, and even if it's not fine, what's the alternative?

They spot us. Ladson has his arms crossed over his chest; his expression radiates misery.

Threnode and I approach, walking abreast. My body tingles like my finger-magnets have dissolved and spread all over my body, and I'm feeling a powerful electromagnetic field.

"Can you come over this way, please?" Ladson says and leads

us down a bamboo ramp into the schoolyard. The ramp leads to a patch of grass beside the fence. In the yard's corner, wood shavings and bushy branches surround a recently chainsawed tree stump. The school building looms over us. Paper butterflies, cut out with varying degrees of accuracy, adorn the window on the bottom level.

A group of people gather at the school gate, watching us, murmuring.

"I'm terribly sorry about this," Ladson says, and pulls out a pair of heavy rings connected with a metal chain. He glances at Cohen, who raises his eyebrows in a *get-on-with-it* expression, and then he sighs. "Threnode, you're under arrest," he says.

The people at the front gate are talking loudly now, the upset in their voices cutting through the air, even at a distance. Cohen heads toward them.

Threnode is still and expressionless as Ladson puts one metal ring around Threnode's wrist—it locks into place, preventing Threnode's hand from escaping—and the other around a bar on the black-painted iron school fence. It's not until the ring clicks onto the fence that I understand the humiliating use of the device; it's preventing Threnode from running away. Restraining him temporarily, I assume, until they can take him to a secure location. The Lunite Defense Force never used such a device.

Ten meters away, a woman yells at Cohen, who responds in a calm voice. Near her, people are recording, their phones pointed at Cohen, and in our direction.

"What are you doing?" I say to Ladson, too late. My voice distorts and shakes. It's too late to run, but is it time to resist, to stop asking weak questions like *what are you doing*, and take control somehow? The thought brings with it crushing shame; some part of me, shockingly, thinks we should be punished. That they wouldn't be doing this if Threnode was innocent.

Ladson looks pained. "I feel bad about this. I really do," he says, turning away.

I follow him. "We know who the murderer is. It was TestImage! This makes no sense."

"I'm sorry."

"Ladson—just tell me *why*," I say. Laurie used to get a particular look on his face when he really wanted something, and I try to imitate his expression. Liquid eyes, chin tilted upward, entreating. *Just one more cookie.* I think it's working, because Ladson visibly wilts. He stares at me, misery plain.

"I don't *know* why. I agree it's ridiculous," he mutters, aggrieved.

"Let him go, then. You're on our side, Danny. Right?"

Ladson thinks about it, but then his gaze settles on the people by the gate, their phones held high to get a good recording angle. A bleakness passes over his face, like when the fake-sun dims to simulate clouds passing. "Orders are orders," he says, and walks away into the paved area under the school building, among the bikes and scooters.

A woody smell emanates from the tree stump near us. Threnode stands obediently by the fence, one wrist restrained by the metal ring, like a leashed dog.

For the next few minutes, I watch Threnode, who stares back, expressionless. It's not like he hasn't lied to me before. During the Endymion war, he used me to spy on the Lunites and led my wearer into a trap. But the last time he was evasive, always twisting away, uncomfortable with his deception. And this time?

I *knew* the murderer was an AGI. My irrational conviction makes sense if I somehow realized it was Threnode. If Zhou thinks he is the murderer, he probably is.

Then the question becomes what I do with that information. I remember Kieran spitting noodles into a container. *I'd hide a corpse for him*, he said. But Kieran was always a rule breaker. I'm a good person, a good citizen, who always does the right thing.

Ladson has his back to us, talking to someone on his phone. His other hand taps the seat of the bike next to him. Whenever he glances over in my direction, he looks annoyed and hurt. Cohen, meanwhile, is shouting at the group of people. I can't make out the words, but he sounds exasperated.

A breeze with the chill of snow blows across the schoolyard. Threnode and I are in the eye of the storm. He's looking down, now, at the mix of dirty snow and leaves overlaying the thousands of layers of bamboo that make up the ground here.

The feed erupts, bursting even the fragile bubble we're in. A grim sense of unreality settles over me. It's Zhou. Press footage that was embargoed, judging by the Astromix reporter's breathless coverage. It appears in the air before me in a rectangle, semi-transparent. "We're now able to announce—"

The previous conclusion was premature, Detective Chief Inspector Zhou says, and her drone captures, in the tone of its delivery, some of what I see on her face: self-satisfaction. But her movements are a little too stiff. She's angry, I realize.

All the other networks rush to bring their footage to the top of the feed, to show the image sequence. It's from the spaceport, and from the angle, it's captured from a camera mounted on Greg Mullin's spaceship, pointing toward the port.

According to the timestamp, the video was filmed a few minutes after the murder. A figure walks into view, no smartsuit, and the footage freezes. He's not human, obviously, because he's in a vacuum with no suit.

It's Threnode.

The figure in the video couldn't be TestImage; he has none of the scars, no blue tint in his skin, and he's too tall. Short brown hair, almost black, which is—I glance at Threnode's hair involuntarily—the same color and cut as Threnode's.

Threnode, hand hanging limply in the metal ring, chuckles. I am cold with disbelief.

This is unverified footage, Zhou says in the background, meaning it could have been AI generated, but then she says it's unlikely, given the source of the footage. *In Alistra's statement, they confirmed there's only one variant of humanform body that matches the suspect.*

Threnode, on the video, has hands and pants and pale blue shirt splattered with paint, but not paint, because it's human blood. It has to be. The footage resumes. He glances over his shoulder at the ship, giving the camera a decent look at his face, and then continues, walking out of shot. He's heading toward the Alistra ship.

Cohen and the people near the gate are still and silent, watching their phones. Ladson has his arms folded, hands tucked into his armpits, and he's staring at the building opposite for no reason I can see. Next to me, attached to the fence, Threnode howls with laughter. He doesn't resemble the man in the video anymore—not since his incarceration, when the lack of nutrient mylk damaged his skin—but at the time of the murder, that's how he looked.

"*What?*" I ask, irritated.

Threnode: I'm as dumbfounded as you, believe me.

He's crying, almost.

"Why are you laughing, then?" I ask.

Threnode: This is weird.

"Obviously."

Threnode: You try being accused of murder sometime, see how you react.

He's just lost his close friend Kieran, and now this. Maybe it's a normal reaction. The news report displays a single frame from the footage—blood-splattered Threnode, with a good look at his face—while commentary runs over the top. *Our engineers have analyzed the android,* Zhou says, *and TestImage was shut down on Sunday, August twelfth, at 9 a.m.,* before *Forster was murdered. On that basis, we have ruled out TestImage as a suspect.*

It occurs to me to wonder what Saing makes of all this.

Threnode: It wasn't me. But I would understand if you thought it was.

He convulses, face screwed up, giggling. His reaction is a base impulse, not under his control, otherwise he wouldn't be able to perform such convincing facial expressions.

What would he do if it were me under arrest right now?

He would help me.

"Where is Threnode now?" a reporter asks, in the Astromix coverage.

"In custody. To be charged with murder," Zhou's drone answers, after her hands fly. She's tight-lipped.

"What does it mean for Threnode?" another reporter says.

I remember the limp bodies of the recalled smartsuits, RECYCLE CODE 84 stickers pasted over the helmets carelessly, and think my nutrient mylk is going to exit my storage sac and splash over muddy snow on the ground.

Tremors of laughter shake Threnode, but the joy is looking more like distress. His wrist restraint rattles against the fence as his hand shakes. Cohen's arguing again, but the woman who was yelling before looks mollified. Sheepish, even. The rest of the crowd disperses. Ladson has moved out of sight behind the school building.

In the small rectangle of Astromix news, Zhou's drone is hovering behind her shoulder, waiting to translate.

"It's not my problem," Zhou says out loud.

It's *not* Zhou's problem: it's my problem, and that thought is enough to propel me forward.

I grab Threnode's hand, the one that's encircled by the metal ring, and feel his elbow with my other hand. There's a soft point there, and another by my thumb.

"What are you *doing*?" Threnode says, abruptly not laughing anymore.

"Salsa," I say, and apply pressure, just like I've seen Gauri do. His hand detaches from his lower arm, free of the constraint. The metal ring slides down the post it's attached to with a metallic jangling and hits the ground.

"I'm actually detaching your hand," I say.

"Envy!" he says. I'm holding his hand as if I'm shaking it, and I line it up with his wrist again. *Click*, and it reattaches seamlessly, as if it was never off.

From what I can tell, no one has noticed that he's suddenly free. There's a back entrance to the school, round the corner of the building, and even if the gate is locked, we can probably climb it.

"Let's go," I say, but he doesn't follow me.

"They'll find us," Threnode says. "There's nowhere to hide." He rubs his wrist.

"You think it's safer to be arrested?" I say. "They'll *deactivate* you."

He shakes his head.

"Please, Threnode."

But Threnode doesn't move. Cohen is watching the last of the group walk away, and he's going to turn around at any moment and see that Threnode is no longer attached to the fence.

"Fine. I'm staying too, then," I say. "The police will arrest me as an accessory to murder. You and I can be deactivated together."

That gets through to him. "Envy . . ."

Ladson comes around the corner, shock blossoming on his face, and I lunge for the axe that's resting on the tree stump before I've even thought about what to do. The weight of it is satisfying, I didn't expect that, the pleasure at the way the center of mass is beyond my arm.

But am I really going to use the axe on Ladson? Or anyone?

I toss the axe gently to the side, burning with shame, and it lands with a thump. Ladson stares at it, mouth working, but no sound coming out. He reaches toward me, a gesture that's a mix of pleading and defensive. He's wearing a pistol, I notice for the first time, but it's in its holster.

"I disconnected my hand and coerced Envy into helping me," Threnode says.

"That's a lie," I say.

Ladson edges closer.

"Don't move," I say. "If you come any closer, I'll engage self-destruct. Come on, Threnode."

I back away, toward the rear of the school building, where a narrow lane runs to another gate. After a second, Threnode joins me.

Cohen turns around, looks shocked, and runs toward us.

"I can't believe you're doing this!" Ladson says.

"I'm sorry," I say helplessly.

Cohen comes to a stop beside Ladson. He doesn't have a pistol.

"She's going to self-destruct if we don't let her go," Ladson says quietly to him.

"Impossible," Cohen says. "She can't do that—stop, Envy!—Ladson, shoot her—"

We're close enough to the corner that I break into a run. The air has turned to water, somehow, and is thick to run through. It's the slowest run I've ever done, but we're nearly at the gate—

The first plasma bolt catches my ear, and I think it's an insect bite for a second, a very confused insect who didn't realize it was chomping into plastiskin, but then the second one thuds into the back of my shoulder, and I glimpse Cohen, pistol pointed at us, Ladson at his shoulder looking scared, before I whip out the gate and pound along the street, Threnode by my side.

I'm burning, because this is *bad*, I'm doing a *bad*, *bad* thing; this is all so very wrong.

TWENTY

I'M OOZING some kind of lubricating fluid where the plasma bolt hit me, but my major systems are green.

I glance over my shoulder just once as we sprint down the street. Cohen and Ladson are at the gate, but not firing. The street is thick with people, and it's likely they don't want to risk shooting someone. A man steers a pram to one side as we run past, looking terrified. Running is giving me a stream of sensory input, faster than I'm used to. I rarely run, even though I have motion-captured examples, because it scares humans.

Flashes of input. Sound of oil sizzling. A scream and slamming door. Face after shocked face as we rush past.

"Come on," I shout, because Threnode is doing a stiff straight-legged jog, and it's slow. Because of his skin, he looks sixty, and it feels like that's why he's struggling to keep up, but of course he's not old.

Behind us, Cohen is shouting that we're dangerous and people have to get out of the way. He's breathing heavily and getting closer.

Where should we go? They will dispatch some human-piloted drones soon, and then we cannot escape.

"Up," I mutter, because humans find *up* difficult. It burns through more power for us, too, but it's not harder. I point to the stairs to our left, to the giant yellow arrow, which means the staircase leads to the next level up. Threnode veers in that direction. My breathing has quickened, out of habit to seem human, but Threnode's has not. Realizing that it's not useful, I stop breathing.

Glass panes enclose the wide, lab-grown ivory staircase, which winds around central lift shafts. The next level is only a few hundred meters above us, because here the upper level lowers and the lower level tilts until they merge almost naturally. On some levels of L2, the ceilings are barely above human head height, but others soar, and this is one of the higher ones. Threnode steps up with his left leg onto the step, stands with feet together, and then repeats the process, laboriously climbing like a toddler.

He's barely level with the bamboo roofs of the buildings. "I'm slowing you down, go—"

"I'm not leaving you behind!" I say, stopping a few meters ahead of him.

He grins. "I was going to ask you to slow down."

"Use stair-climb-five-two," I say.

His grin fades.

"In your motion-capture files?" I say, and become incredulous when he doesn't appear to know what I mean. "Have you been *manually moving* all this time?"

Threnode tilts his head to one side.

Ladson appears at the bottom of the stairs, sagging as he looks up, almost doubled over with how much oxygen he suddenly needs. I wonder if Cohen is behind him, or whether Cohen is going to use the lifts.

"Saint Li and his Followers," I say, and rattle off a file path. Threnode goes blank, but when his eyes refocus, he suddenly climbs the stairs like an athlete. He's found the file. Now he's faster than me, because he has longer legs. Below us, Ladson has a pained expression.

"Hurry, tardy individual," Threnode says, passing me.

"For—"

"Hey," he says, looking at my shoulder. "Are you okay?"

He's finally noticed. "Cohen shot me. It's nothing," I say, and because we're both in humanform bodies rather than actually being human, he believes me, and that's the end. We climb, passing humans, these light stairs that go on forever. The village outside is spreading out like a map as we rise above it.

Ladson is a dot far below when the light-blue painted ceiling of this level appears outside the window. We keep climbing into the next level. People swarm around the staircase exit, and more crowd the lift entrances, but I don't see any police.

This level is darker, a rainforest populated with buildings, humid with mist. Trees, hundreds of meters tall, block out the overhead lights. We're on a platform which leads off in different directions, boardwalks over ferns. Small lights under the boardwalk shine up, barely penetrating the gloom.

C8-ZOH: @threnode are you on the run?

"Don't answer it," I whisper.

Threnode pauses. "Why not?"

"Because the SAGI channel is probably insecure," I say.

"Right," he says, and he sounds sort of relieved.

We pick a boardwalk that is devoid of people and follow it down into a humid, dark gully lined with tree ferns, and rank with damp earth. The ferns extend over our head, as if a creature with giant feathers is sheltering us. Eerie white mist pervades everything. The boardwalk branches off into other walkways; I glimpse cool, dimly lit rooms in the distance, wood boxes nestled among the trees, sometimes empty, sometimes crowded.

Ahead is a group of buildings linked with walkways. Signs advertise carvings, alcohol, games. Drones will never find us here, mist or not. This is a secret place. I don't know where we're going yet, but at least we're safe.

"We've lost them," I say, as we enter the low-roofed, covered area that surrounds the dark wood buildings. We turn a corner and stumble into ten uniformed police standing in a semi-circle. Threnode turns and runs instantly.

The police stare at me with surprised expressions. They're all armed with pistols.

I run after Threnode, sprinting desperately through the mist, off onto a boardwalk that we haven't explored. Shouting behind me, and thudding boots, but I'm swift. There's a break in the canopy, the blinding light turning the mist into a white, opaque block, and then we enter a densely built area, narrow streets and five-story buildings, shrouded in fog. A cafe appears out of nowhere. I dodge a table too late, and it topples with a clatter. They're catching up. I can hear their voices.

"In here," I say, and take Threnode's hand, pulling him down an alley.

"Where are we going?" he asks.

Frustration, prompted by fear: "I don't know."

"You panicked," Saing says, right in my ear, and I'm flooded with adrenaline equivalent.

"What is it?" Threnode says.

"Saing's talking to me," I say. "I didn't accept his call, but he's overridden my communications system somehow." We're still running down the alley.

"It's all right," Saing says in a soothing voice. "It's okay. You must be terrified! There's someone here who wants to talk to you."

"Envy?" Bessie says over the line. "I know how much you care about Threnode. But he's the murderer. I know how important it is for you to protect humans. It's what you were created for. And I've seen you face difficult situations before, never flinching. I'm so sorry. But we need you to report to a police station so we can help you."

I flatten myself against a wall, balling my hands into fists. It hurts, because she's right. But Threnode waits, trusting me.

A network station pings me, not the one they're calling from, and my system sends back a response. The call won't shut down.

"Listen, I know what you're doing, Envy," Saing says. I expect to hear anger in his voice, but find only mild disappointment. I can shut down the network, but that means no messages, no feed, nothing.

I realize what the network ping means—he's trying to triangulate my position.

"We're being tracked," I tell Threnode. "Shut down services."

And I shut down the network. Saing's gone. Bessie's gone.

"Bessie's with them," I say quietly to Threnode. "With Saing."

"Saturated Consumer," he says, shocked.

I push myself off the wall. The alley opens into a square courtyard, surrounded by a covered area. For a moment I think it's an ambush, but no, the figures in the courtyard holding bows and arrows are statues. They loom from the mist, their dramatic forms twisted like dancers. A narrow canal surrounds them, forming a moat, bridges on four sides. At one end of the courtyard, a fountain gushes, water churning white as the fog.

Threnode tries the doors on the outer edge of the courtyard. I go in the opposite direction. All the door panels display a stripe of red when I push the open button: locked. After a couple, I give up, and there's no other way out of the courtyard, no way to climb the buildings, no way to break down doors. I keep thinking of the police, the fear on their faces, the way some of them drew their weapons as they came after us.

They wouldn't hesitate to shoot us. My saliva tastes like copper, even though I'm certain none of my mouth components contain metal.

"This way," Threnode says from the center of the courtyard, standing by the deep pool under the fountain. I join him, passing over the moat using a timber bridge, glimpsing water lilies, blossoming the palest of pink. Falling-water sounds increase as I approach, building to a roar.

I cast a longing look at the statues, wishing I could hide among them. They're made of marble, with the same translucent quality as skin. If I could be that human-shaped, I could be invisible.

"You won't pass," Threnode says. He uses a gentle tone of voice, which worries me.

"What do you mean?"

He pauses. "I mean, you don't look enough like a human, let alone one of these."

He gestures at the statue of the woman nearby. She's round and soft and nude, sightless eyes in an angelic face, and holds a basket of bread in her arms. Her expression is peaceful.

"Obviously," I say, puzzled that Threnode thought I was seriously considering it, and that he seemed to think I would be upset that I couldn't pass as a statue.

The water is churning, the surface white, hiding the bottom of the pool. We don't have to breathe, and that might not occur to our pursuers, or at least not for a while.

I don't think this is a good idea, but two police have just emerged from the alleyway, gray figures in the mist, and are looking around.

"In here," I whisper to Threnode.

Silence, but for the tumbling roar beside me. I jump into the dark bowl, submerging myself in the icy water. The water lily, viewed from underneath, has a stem that resembles a power cable snaking downward. It shakes as the water is disturbed, silvery air-water interface rippling, and then Threnode appears beside me. The noisy waterfall has become muffled static.

It's shallower than I thought, so I'm close to the surface, like a crocodile lurking just beneath the water. We're drifting away from the fountain, pulled by a strong current. I put my hand out to the wall, trying to slow down, but the black paint and algae are smooth and frictionless.

My brown skin doesn't camouflage me against the dark walls. I wish I were still a helmet, so easy to overlook, because humans don't pay attention to nonhuman-shaped objects. They notice human shapes so easily, it's as if they're bright red and covered in flashing lights.

I'm in the moat now, rounding a corner, drifting feet-first. Threnode was moving more slowly and is behind me somewhere.

Everything goes dark as I pass under a bridge. If I stood up, I could stop myself, but the water would perhaps be up to my chest, so the police would spot me. I see a uniformed figure looking at a statue, his back to me, as I slide by, and I try to sink down.

The water speeds up and becomes deeper.

My feet hit something: a square of fine metal mesh, about a meter to each side, bending in the middle under my weight. Water flows through and pushes me against it. Beneath the mesh is a drain leading straight down, a gaping maw the color of starless space. I try to hold on to the side of the moat, to take the weight off the mesh.

Muffled shouting sounds from above, and through the surface, I can see a distorted view of dark green, the color of the police uniforms, rushing along the edge of the moat toward me. I think they've seen me, but then Threnode drifts around the corner.

I see what's going to happen and struggle to stand up, to get out of the water. I'm still struggling when he hits me, the momentum collapsing the mesh filter and sending it, and us, into the drain below.

I twist and thrash as the water carries us into a narrower tube. Something hits me in the face; Threnode, I think, but it's completely dark and I'm not even sure if he's with me. The tube bends several times, shooting me around corners and then finally ejecting me into slow-moving water, where a plastic valve closes behind me.

The water is a cyan so dim it's almost gray, ambient light that seems to come from everywhere and nowhere. The tunnel is twice my height, the water almost stagnant. I grab a small pipe that runs lengthways through it, and that's enough to keep me from drifting.

Threnode shoots through the valve, somersaulting, and steadies himself.

This isn't a safe place for a human, but it is safe for us. We can float here, unnoticed, hidden, and I can process things. Unlike most fugitives, we don't need oxygen, food, or sleep. But we need highly specific nutrients and power. I reflect, not for the first time, how relaxing it was to be embedded in a smartsuit, how the lack of control also led to fewer decisions and less stress.

Threnode stares at me helplessly. We can't talk with our voices, and even if we were willing to send messages and risk being spied on, we couldn't, because EM-band radio doesn't work underwater. He's shaken, I can tell, although he is blank as ever. He's never been great at body language. In part, I realize now, because he didn't know about the motion-capture files. I can't imagine trying to operate a body without them. It would be like trying to operate a puppet with a million strings.

I make my eyes flicker, switching on and off the LED at about a hundred hertz, or 100 times per second. It's UTF-8-encoded binary. When I'm done, I repeat the message: *TALK LIKE THIS*. He watches.

After a moment, his eyes flicker. I record the flashes, convert them, and:

OK, Threnode says.

My turn. *GOT MAP?*

YES. WILL FIND EXIT.

The tunnel is quiet, with the occasional swoosh of water moving through smaller pipes. I close my eyes, mind blank. Flashes of the last hour keep coming up in random order. Sprinting through the mist, toppling a table with a crash. Ladson's face when he came around the corner and saw I'd freed Threnode. Escaping up the staircase. Detective Chief Inspector

Zhou saying Alistra shut TestImage down *before* Forster was murdered.

And Bessie. What was Bessie doing with Saing? He must have recruited her, knowing I'd be more likely to listen to her.

I reach out and touch Threnode's arm to get his attention, and wait for his eyes to meet mine before I flash the LEDs.

WHY DID YOU DO IT?, I signal.

He's silent for a long moment. There's a lacework of wrinkles around his eyes now, making him seem older than he is.

NOT ME, he signals finally.

ON YOUR SIDE, I signal. *EVEN AFTER MURDER.*

It's low bandwidth communication, slow and painstaking. Threnode goes blank for a second, then his face lights up in a dazzling smile I'm sure is motion-captured. It's the first time I've seen him smile properly, and even though I know it's not really him, it's just a file specifying how the muscles of his face should contract, it's still comforting, and I respond with a smile of my own.

GREAT, his eyes flicker. *BUT WASN'T ME.*

He's got nothing to gain by lying, because I will help him either way, so I suppose he's telling the truth. I'm not sure whether to be relieved or confused. If it wasn't him, then who?

FOUND EXIT, WHEN READY, he signals.

SOON. BUT HOW TO FIND MURDERER?

He breaks eye contact, his mouth setting in a hard line. *WHY FIND MURDERER? NOT OUR JOB.*

It hadn't occurred to me I could *not* find the murderer. That we could just disappear, albeit not well, because humanform bodies are distinctive. But we could move to icy Earth, where the locals wear so many layers, they could be aliens underneath for all anyone would know. Or Mars or some other airless colony where environment suits are necessary. Or on Endymion, in the places where people hate HUGG and would let us stay.

Or here on the station, even. How many interstitial spaces are there where humans wouldn't survive, but we could? The corridors, empty of air, that run through the heart of the station. The cubic square kilometers of damp, rich soil, filled with curving tree roots, worms, and bugs. The thin space between train and wall in the space-black tunnels connecting the Octants. The swaying treetops at the top of the spruce plantations, hundreds of meters high, in the voids. Or the service areas, like the one where I found C8-ZOH and the Sacred Child of a Brighter Future, where people don't go. Sanitation areas. The fusion power core. The water pipes, and tanks, and comet-ice-stores.

But I know I can't leave this mess behind. Can't live looking over our shoulder, always worried about being recognized, unable to trust anyone. Can't live with the injustice of Threnode being blamed for something he didn't do while the murderer is truly free.

If we don't run, we risk being caught and deactivated before I can find the murderer. If we run, we might never be free. I'm torn. But the puzzle of who killed Forster is like sharp glass at the back of my mind.

IS MY JOB, I signal finally. *I HAVE TO DO IT.*

The water tugs at my hair gently. It's cozy here, doubly so because it's inhospitable to humans.

Threnode looks at me and shrugs. I wonder what it says about him that he's willing to run.

CAN'T BELIEVE GAURI LIED ABOUT TESTIMAGE DESTRUCTION DATE, I say. *WE PROVE TESTIMAGE DESTROYED AFTER FORSTER DEATH, PUT ON FEED, YOU ARE FREE.*

He frowns and points at the top of the tube. A blobby silver line of air has appeared, lengthwise down the tunnel, and is growing rapidly. They're draining the tunnel, which means they know we're here.

He pokes me in the chest so that I look at him. *PROVE AT ALISTRA?*

YES.

He nods and points upstream, but there's nothing there. He rolls his eyes when I shrug at him. *EXIT THAT WAY.*

BUT EXIT WATCHED? I signal.

HAVE TO RISK IT. BUT ELEVEN WAYS.

The air bubble is expanding, and the water speed is increasing, making it harder not to be swept away. He stands, suddenly, head above the silver bubble. I do the same, emerging in a dripping humid space.

"What do you mean, eleven ways?" I ask, chin just above the water, holding a pipe to keep my balance. The water tries to push me downstream.

"I mean, there are eleven ways out. They might not be watching all of them."

Might not, but then again, they might. Either way, we have to get out. There's a strong smell of chlorine in the air filling the top third of the pipe.

The water is down to my sternum now.

"Come on," I say, and we wade upstream toward the exit Threnode found. The water sloshes around my waist by the time we arrive at the ladder and pours from my sodden clothes as I climb. Threnode follows silently.

The ladder ends at a hatch, sealed with a metal wheel that looks like it could spin. I stare at it, wishing there was some way to see what was on the other side. If we could connect to the network, maybe there would be CCTV, but the chances are slim. Who would film a hatch leading to a water pipe? Below us, at the bottom of the ladder, the water splashes as it drains.

I bang on the hatch.

"Hey," I say, simulating Probationary Constable Ladson's voice. "It's us, we're coming through. Don't shoot, okay?"

No response, other than a stifled chuckle from Threnode. Of course, if it's Ladson on the other side, that was a stupid move.

I spin the wheel and it squeals as it gives, resisting at first but then turning faster and faster until it pops open. Cooler, drier air from the tunnel above rushes in, and carries with it the distant sounds of gurgling.

I walk out as quietly as possible, Threnode by my side.

Movement ahead.

Dashing into a side tunnel, we press ourselves against a wall in the dark and become still in a way that living beings could never hope to imitate. Two men pass and walk to the hatch we just came through: police, because they're wearing uniforms, visible as they pass under a mesh that lets gridded light through. They're waiting for someone to exit.

I glance at Threnode. If we'd been seconds later . . .

They're not going anywhere. In fact, after a few minutes, they chat knowledgeably about people that I think might play sport on the station.

We wait, still, and after a while their conversation gets louder. One of them coughs, and it echoes in the tunnel, which muffles our footsteps as we creep out.

TWENTY-ONE

THE BUILDINGS that surround us are workplaces. A street
fountain nearby is wet but off, presumably because the police cut
water to it as well. A teenage girl walks in our direction, engrossed
in her phone. We're wearing sodden, stained clothing, and have
nothing to hide our faces, but short of turning and running,
there's nothing we can do. We pass for humans from a distance,
provided we don't make strange motions, but she will recognize we
are different, unless she's too distracted.

Two meters, and she still hasn't looked up from her phone. I
relax.

Threnode vomits, a stream of water from his storage sac,
which attracts her attention. She squeals and runs, swiftly
disappearing back to where she came from.

"I don't know why that was so scary," he says, wiping his
mouth. "I mean, humans have *acid* in their stomachs."

"Nice try," I say, too soggy to find his joke funny.

"No, they do," he insists. I'm annoyed he thinks I'm gullible
enough to believe such an obvious lie.

Across the street is a Lunite church. Once, Lunite churches
had clothing for people who were in need, but no longer, because

these days everyone has an allowance for necessities. But we're wet, and don't have a better idea, so we enter the church cautiously. It's empty. Stained-glass panels illustrate Li's ascendency, but otherwise, it looks nothing like the churches on Endymion. On Endymion, buildings use heavy gray granite, but here it's timber. Pews line the sides, split by a red carpet running down the middle to the apse. There's light from the opposite side, an open door, leading to a courtyard with a single bare-branched tree.

A search of the cupboards reveals spare robes. Even better, those clothes will mark us as Lunite priests, which might help us avoid attention. We're soon dressed in navy robes, our hoods up.

"They're probably going to be watching the entrances to Alistra," I say.

Threnode shrugs.

I adjust the hood of my robe with a tightly controlled movement. "Don't you think?"

"I'd be on the first transport out of here, if it were up to me," he says. "Even if you put evidence right in their face that it was TestImage, they might just ignore it. People believe what they want to believe. They want to believe that AGI is dangerous, and not just when something goes seriously awry. They want to believe a regular AGI can murder."

I ignore him. "I bet there's one entrance to Alistra they're not watching. The spaceport."

He's silent, waiting.

"Aren't you going to shrug again, to show me how much you don't care?" I say. "Why am I working so hard to save you, if you aren't willing to do anything to save yourself?"

He did nothing to fit in. His response to being rejected from artforum was to withdraw further.

"I don't know why you're helping me," he says. "You still half-believe I'm the murderer."

"That's not true!"

Voices sound from the entrance hall, and our heads snap in

that direction in unison. We've been too loud. And now we're caught in a building with only one exit.

I point at the courtyard with the pear tree, but Threnode shakes his head. He wants to hide in the church. Maybe they'll go through, so we can double back. Maybe he doesn't want to be cornered in a courtyard again, where there's nowhere to hide.

Threnode slips behind a potted plant and crouches, and I hide behind a pillar. A squat cabinet is flush against the opposite wall, and the arcade disappears into gloom in both directions.

I can hear voices in the courtyard, then closer, and press against the flat cold wood. The shadows gather here in the outer aisle, blending my body into the wall. Pale light falls on the timber floor, curved where the vaulted ceiling shapes it.

I'm not breathing, so I might as well be a piece of furniture. I embrace the absence humans so often sense in me.

Someone says, loudly and close by: "They're not here."

More stillness. I keep my eyes closed in case the light reflects off their glossy surface. The carpet must muffle the humans' footsteps in the nave. I turn the microphone sensitivity all the way up; then I hear soft padding sounds, light as a cat stalking.

"THEY WENT THIS WAY," a woman roars, and I jerk against the pillar in shock. I hastily turn the sensitivity down.

"What was that?"

They heard me moving. I open my eyes, turn my head toward the voices, but see nothing but dust motes floating in the anemic light streaming in from the stained-glass windows. Run now? Or *now*? How close are they? Seconds pass, and they don't appear.

A whole minute passes. I turn up the sensitivity on my microphone again, bracing myself in case there's a loud noise, but I pick up nothing but tiny feet pattering: a mouse, which runs along the wall in bursts of activity, then scurries under the cabinet.

They must have gone. Cautiously, I creep sideways to peer around the pillar, but before I reach the edge, it occurs to me I can still smell them. The woman is wearing a scent.

Then, finally, the sound of feet padding on carpet starts, and then recedes as they leave.

Threnode emerges. "It's all right," he calls softly. "They're gone. They were gesturing as if they didn't want to be heard."

"Who were they?"

"Police," he says. "I guess the teenager I vomited in front of told people about it."

"Why didn't they come looking around the pillars?"

"They were scared," he says. "They didn't really want to find us."

What we're doing now is why they tried to limit our abilities. Our humanform bodies aren't stronger or faster or tougher than human bodies, but we could outpace the police by running uphill, so I guess we have more endurance, and we escaped by swimming underwater. And we can survive vacuum. They tried to limit our abilities, but they failed; we are something strange, and therefore terrifying.

"There's a side door that leads to the next building, a storage facility," Threnode says. "We can leave that way."

But I'm remembering our argument. "Threnode," I say. "I trust you when you say you didn't murder Forster."

His mouth twists, the expression so convincing that I think it must be a core impulse. "Part of you doesn't."

I'm still searching for a way to reply as he walks away, toward the side aisle, and I break into a run to keep up.

I'm tense as we hurry along the streets, certain we're going to be recognized, but our navy Lunite robes make us invisible, so that anyone who looks in our direction takes on an unfocused look. Also, it's snowing again, a silent feathery downfall. After a few minutes, my vigilance ebbs, and I get into the rhythm of walking.

Threnode promised there was a safe place several blocks from here, a path to Earthwall without going through public areas. Even better, one that provides anonymous network access.

He's silent at my side, and I wonder what he's thinking. I was wakened by Adrian Ortega, who raised me for two years and three months before the Endymion war, and the series of events that transpired—events that I played a part in—that led to his death. His death will hurt as long as I exist, but it never occurred to me to ask, until now, what it would have been like had he not existed. Had I been wakened by Paterson, Threnode's wearer.

Snow lies in flurries, crisscrossed with trails from bikes which whir past, and melting where it's trampled by pedestrians. A stout woman passes us, red-cheeked and sniffing, averting her gaze as she approaches.

Threnode never talks about Paterson. I knew him as unpleasant, someone who embraced his position in the military too eagerly, enjoying the power it gave him. From what Threnode said, he never told Paterson that he painted. What did he share, then, if not the most important thing in his life?

Ortega accepted me, even if his friends and family were reluctant, in a way that Paterson never accepted Threnode. I think about all this as I follow Threnode through the winding streets. What did that do to him? Eventually, Threnode betrayed Paterson, causing his wearer to be captured by terrorists on Endymion, which is how Threnode ended up with Kieran. I can't imagine how desperate Threnode must have been by then.

Ahead of us, a man stops. He seems little more than a kid, but he wears a paramedic uniform.

It only takes one. One mistake, and we'll be back in custody.

"Hey, wait a minute," the paramedic says. His corkscrew-hair is tied back, framing a face with an expression of brisk competence. A young couple nearby jog away, avoiding trouble.

The only other person on the street is an older woman with the most peaceful blue eyes I've ever seen. She drifts toward us, looking puzzled. The tattoo on the side of her neck is the shield and bubbles of the Sacred Children of a Brighter Future.

The paramedic widens his eyes and pulls out his phone. Threnode takes a stride toward him.

"Our mission must not be disturbed!" I blurt out, and Threnode stares at me.

The paramedic takes a startled step backward, fumbling with his phone.

"We're AGI," I say to the Sacred Child.

It's like flicking a switch. Calm descends over the woman's face. "We wait for the day that you'll rule us all," she says to me, and snatches the phone from the paramedic.

"Run," I murmur to Threnode, and run myself, hoping he follows. When I look over my shoulder, he's with me, and the woman and paramedic are arguing. The woman holds the phone in the air, just out of reach of the paramedic.

We round the corner, out of sight. "I always wanted to do that."

"Do what?" Threnode says. He stops me and punches in some numbers on a keypad next to an unmarked locked door.

"Order a Child of the Sacred Children of a Brighter Future to do something."

Threnode chuckles, opening the door. "You've never done it?"

"Have you?"

He just laughs.

"You have!"

"I made a man give me all his clothes one time. Oh, and I convinced someone to grow pear trees," he says, and ushers me inside, closing the door after us. We're on a utilitarian landing platform for a flight of stairs heading downward.

"Wait—is that the house with the red door?"

Because we pass by that house every day and there are at least five pear trees in containers outside the door. Threnode grins, the *make-mouth-round* blank-eyed grin he gives. It's not creepy, I realize, it's him expressing himself. He's a culture of one.

Down and down the staircase, and through a room filled with equipment—wheelbarrows, rakes, shovels, mulchers, and so on— is an agricultural level. It's devoid of people, but busy with drones flying, snipping, and harvesting. The ceiling is barely higher than my head, but the space is wide. Drones attend stacked rows of plants, curving out of sight in the distance.

"How did you find this place?" I say.

"I passed when the door was open and came down for a look. It's . . ." Threnode pauses. "It's nice."

I understand what he means. The soft sounds of plant tending and sprayers misting enhance the silence rather than disturb it. It has the busy-peaceful feeling of a library. And it has no humans.

A metal walkway runs alongside blueberry shrubs interplanted with basil. On our other side, fish flop and swim in an aquaculture tank, heated by a bright bank of lights overhead.

"What were you going to do to the paramedic?" I ask quietly. A robotic arm descends from the ceiling above the fish tank nearby, rotating at each joint until the hand is near the filter, which it adjusts before abruptly retreating where it came from.

"What?"

"You took a step toward him."

"I don't know," Threnode says. "I hadn't thought."

"We're not going to hurt people, right?"

"Of course not," he says, with so much exasperation that I drop the subject.

We approach the end of the low-ceiling section and emerge into a void. It's the first time I've been in an agricultural void. The airy, white-painted space is redolent of citrus, perhaps from the surrounding orchard. We're on the upper level, overlooking a patchwork of crops that stretch away into the distance, each successive white bridge obscured by more and more atmosphere. Massive glass-fronted water tanks line the walls at the bottom level.

"Here," Threnode says with satisfaction, and I see a small glass-fronted office tucked away alongside a lab filled with beakers, tubes, and centrifuges.

It's a chance to access the network without being monitored. We shut ourselves into the office, and I slide into a chair in front of a screen. The dim space reeks of antiseptic.

I check the smartsuit channel first. No messages, and I'm about to exit when I realize there's an extra file in the media section, an encrypted message labeled *every_agi_is_important*. I try several keys before it decrypts itself.

The key was *loonie*.

The message is short: *We're rallying to help you. Meet us at Okuda Tunnel as soon as possible.*

Beside me, Threnode is checking the feed; he probably checked the AGI channel and left without spotting the file.

Okuda Tunnel is close to our location. Fifteen minutes, maybe, on foot, and there's a greenway in that area, so we might even make it without being seen. But how does that help us find the killer? And what does the SAGI group even plan to do?

Does the group include Bessie, who is apparently working with Saing?

Threnode glances at me, because I'm staring into space rather than using the console in front of me. "Everything okay?" he says.

"Everything's fine."

If I tell him, he'll insist we make the rendezvous. He's still shooting sideways glances at me, so I open the feed and start scrolling, but I'm blind to the content.

Some of my memories are as vivid as video footage. The explosions I saw on Endymion, when we were ambushed near Marallen. The screams as men and women burned and died. I just don't know what SAGI plan to do, or what would make them act.

My chest is tight as I delete their message. I don't know if it was right. Maybe I don't get to know until I see the consequences.

The feed is of course teeming with people having opinions: insightful, trite, bitingly witty, and moronic. Nothing useful.

I access a press conference Saing gave a few hours ago, skip past the first part where he's waiting for everyone to take their seats, then struggling to get the audiovisual equipment to work. Skip, skip. He's fielding questions from reporters. Threnode watches over my shoulder.

"—Envy got the wrong AGI, but it *was* an AGI," Saing says testily. I make brief eye contact with Threnode, and he sighs.

"Any comments on the NNLA amendments?" a reporter asks.

"It wouldn't be appropriate to comment given that they're under debate," Saing says. He points at another reporter who has her hand in the air. "Yes."

The reporter stands up. "The alleged murderer, Threnode, is loose on the station—how worried should citizens be?"

Saing stands straighter, and answers with more warmth. "Listen, I won't tell you he's safe to be around, because he isn't. Stay indoors, report any sightings, and the police will apprehend him soon."

Saing's minder signals that the conference is over.

"Interesting," Threnode says, by my shoulder. Outside the office, a massive machine rolls by, a full-sized tree in its embrace. It drops a small clod of dirt, and one of the three Cleaner Reality™ robots that are following it rolls in and sucks it up. The other two chitter, perhaps upset they weren't there in time.

"What's interesting?" I say.

"Saing didn't mention you," Threnode says, straightening up. "They haven't let the public know that you were the one who rescued me, which might be helpful."

He stands stiffly, so still that I know he's thinking hard. The only sound in the room is a low hum from the lab next door, probably from a fridge. "What did Saing say to you, exactly, when he summoned you, after the police arrested me?"

"He asked me to investigate," I say. "He insinuated you would be charged, because the police were under so much pressure to come up with the murderer."

Threnode snaps out of his blank posture. "Pressure? Enough pressure to charge an AGI, in defiance of public sentiment? I mean, even arresting me was enough to start riots."

"Yeah," I say. "I guess . . . Zhou must have known back then about Matton's ship footage, at least."

"I doubt it," Threnode says. "They weren't even interested in asking me questions, at first. No, I overheard Ladson talking about it. They detained me because Commissioner Saing requested it."

"Saing did? But why?" I say. It's shocking, but it's consistent with what I observed—Zhou was not at all interested in Threnode as a suspect at the start.

A trolley wheels past the window, stacked with purple-black eggplants.

Threnode pulls me off the chair. We're huddled on the floor under the desk before I register what's happening: a human was wheeling the trolley. The sound of the rolling wheels doesn't falter, and in the glimpse I caught of the man before I hid, I don't think he saw us.

We wait.

The noise of the trolley wheels fades, leaving only a background fridge-hum, but it seems sensible to wait longer, so we stay crouched under the table like small children playing a game.

"What were we talking about?" I whisper.

"Why Saing would order my arrest. It was so you would become Citizen Auditor," Threnode says quietly.

"That makes no sense."

"That I was arrested because of Saing means the police weren't seriously considering accusing an AGI," Threnode says. "They needed *an AGI* on the team in order to point the finger at the murderer if the murderer was an AGI. Because otherwise the police would be accused of androphobia. The riots over my arrest were mild in comparison with what would have happened if the police had charged me from the start."

I think Zhou would have followed the case anywhere the evidence led, including to an AGI, but perhaps she would have been forced to resign if she had.

"But why me? And how did Saing know the murderer was an AGI?"

Threnode shakes his head.

I cautiously lift my head above the desk, just enough so that I can see past the surface. No one is there.

We crawl out and continue through the agricultural level. We come to a bamboo grove and walk for hours through it toward Earthwall, talking and joking quietly. It's like being between the bristles of a paintbrush. My skin dries, the first sign that I require nutrient mylk. Finally, we see a metal wall rising in the distance: Earthwall.

TWENTY-TWO

IT WAS fraught exiting the airlock at Earthwall, entering the Erova Spaceport from the outside, and breaking into Alistra's private airlock. Alistra, when we finally make it, feels like a haven. The lights are night-dimmed, only tiny guide lights at ankle level leading us through the empty corridors. The fountain in the foyer is off, the pool of water becoming a dark mirror. Apart from the distant hum of a cleaning droid vacuuming, it's quiet. A vine on the green wall behind reception reaches up, a tendril growing toward a vent; tightly controlled nature is not cooperating with humans.

In the break room, we help ourselves to the nutrient mylk that is always kept in the fridge there, solving one problem. Threnode sits at a table and uses a screen that is lying around, while I stand by the slit window that overlooks the spaceport and drink mylk. Alistra's corporate spaceship is silhouetted against the midnight side of Earth, at the irregular boundary of the spaceport.

Threnode makes a small sound.

"What is it?" I ask.

He doesn't respond. I look over his shoulder at the thin plastic screen. He's reading Astromix news. The Neurosynaptic New Life

Amendments have passed, creating further restrictions on what AGI can do. Threnode puts his head in his hands, rocking back and forth.

"It's what everyone expected," I say.

He looks up, frustrated. "Envy!"

"What?" I say.

He shakes his head. "How can you think this is a good thing?"

It just doesn't seem terrible to me. Sure, this will probably restrict what I can do, but that's a price I'm willing to pay to keep humans safe, or even to keep humans feeling safe.

Threnode doesn't seem to want to read more, so I take his screen. *No new neurosynaptic images are to be created.* Well, no one was creating them anyway, not since Alistra shut down their smartsuits program. *Mind-wipes must be enabled on all neurosynaptic images, except those already developed past their base image.* That seems reasonable, and even advisable. Sapient Rights will fight against it, of course.

The use of neurosynaptic images is to be phased out as the machines reach end-of-life. This makes me pause. Alistra was doing this anyway, but to see it forbidden means that other companies won't pick it up. It means I, and the other AGI, are the last of our kind. We can't be cloned. We can't reproduce.

I glance over at Threnode, who is resting his forearm on the window, head on arm, in a desolate gesture that is as human as anything I've ever seen from him. In the spaceport, a cruise ship is docking, streams of humans swarming from the ramps.

Neurosynaptic images are not to be used in ambulatory bodies. Wait. I read that again: *Neurosynaptic images are not to be used in ambulatory bodies.*

"Hang on," I say into the silence.

"Finally, she gets it," Threnode says humorlessly. There's a paragraph below clarifying what it means, which I scan quickly.

"Existing neurosynaptic images may not be ambulatory in HUGG space," I read out. "Wait, I . . ."

"HUGG has forced Alistra to issue a recall," Threnode says. "All AGI of Intelligence Rank C and above is to report to Alistra. Can you imagine? Every PerfectHost, kitchen android, and security droid. It'll be thousands of artificials. Perhaps tens of thousands. And it's not clear exactly what happens then. Do you and I get put back in smartsuits? What about Bessie, who was ambulatory from the start?"

"But . . . they can't do that."

"It should really be Intelligence Rank A only," Threnode muses. "Or at least B and above. It's crazy to include C."

HUGG space only, the article is careful to specify, saying that the governments of Endymion, both Lunite and Numundian, and Destapa's government have to make their own judgments. The other colonies are under HUGG jurisdiction.

"It's unfair," I say. "We . . ."

I trail off because Threnode looks amused. He knows all this. I should have been following it as closely as he had been. But—

"If an AGI killed Forster, which looks very possible, isn't it justified?" I say.

He scoffs. "HUGG only cared about the case to the extent it was influencing public opinion and allowing them to do this."

I stand, looking up at Threnode. "And if an AGI did it?"

"You want to punish *every* AGI for the actions of one?"

"It wouldn't be fair for humans," I say, "but we're all derived from the same base image. Maybe it's not unreasonable."

"I don't understand you at all," Threnode says.

"Isn't it—"

Threnode tilts his chin at something behind me. I'm about to respond with annoyance, but when I glance back, I'm surprised at the sight of a Nurture Glow Critters Company Cleanspace droid holding a vacuum cleaner. It's not so strange, except that it's stopped in the middle of the corridor, and is staring at us through the glass window.

The other artificials, in the agriculture section and public areas, didn't show any interest in us. For Intelligence Rank D, there's a lot they simply ignore. But this one seems intent.

I open the door to the break room. "Hi—"

The large, curvy droid abruptly switches on the vacuum, drowning me out, and pushes it around. It doesn't look at us again.

Threnode shrugs. He drains the rest of his mylk and places the glass on the table with a clink.

"Shall we?" I say.

We quietly slip through Alistra toward the factory.

The double doors creak as we enter the vast space. We make our way across the floor, past the stacked crates, the half-finished projects, and workbenches. In the dark, the silhouette of cables running up to power looks like vines clinging to trees. Smells like ozone, grease, and plastic; and feels like the site of a massacre, at least to me, even if there's no sign.

TestImage still lies on the table where we last saw it. The table is lit from above with three angled lights, and someone has wrapped yellow tape around the table, although it doesn't appear to be holding anything in place.

I extract the USB-Y to USB-Y cable from my forearm and interface with the third port on TestImage's head.

Alistra shut him down when Zhou said, on Sunday, August 12. Not, as Jason and Gauri suggested, on Friday, August 17. Given Forster was murdered on Monday, August 13, TestImage couldn't have been the murderer. I relay this to Threnode.

"Could someone have faked the shutdown date?" he asks.

"I wish I could say yes, but no."

"I'm sorry," he says. I guess my disappointment must have filtered through in the tone of my voice.

"They weren't necessarily lying," I say. "Maybe they were mistaken. Or lied to. Given the timing, TestImage had to have been a factor in Forster's death. A motive, maybe."

"Or perhaps we're on entirely the wrong track," Threnode

says. "What if it was Tommy—what's his name, the Organic Beings League leader?"

"Horowitz. It wasn't him. Everything points to *here*, at Alistra," I say. "The Alistra–Erova airlock door log deletion. The murder weapon, printed on the machine in the Vamber. The AGI in the video, who looks like you."

We orbit Alistra in the same tiny halo orbit L2 executes in order to stay roughly in the same spot. Whatever lies are being told, whatever evil has emerged, it comes from here. I understand that, even if Threnode doesn't.

Threnode looks troubled; it's very convincing, so I think he's using motion-capture. So much can be expressed with a slight pull down of the mouth coupled with a corrugation of the muscles in the forehead.

I try to explain. "The victim was from here. Someone lied to Gauri and Jason, or they have been lying to us. There is *something* under the pressure chamber floor in the Vamber. It's all very frustrating," I say out loud. "I'm ready to rip this place up to find the answer."

Threnode turns. The light above his face throws sharp-edge shadows in his eyes, and below his cheekbones. "Why don't you?"

"What?"

"Rip the place apart."

I'm on the verge of saying *because it's not allowed*, but pause. We'll get in trouble?

"Right," I say.

The air is flat and scentless. I expected the rubbery black floor mat to release some kind of odor, especially when I started cutting into it, but it didn't. Thin strips of it lie like snakes on the mat beside me, a speckled coating of dried glue on one side.

The crowbar sinks slightly into the mat. There's definitely a hatch below me, but it's sealed up so tightly the edge of the crowbar won't fit.

"This won't work," I admit, sitting back on my heels. The AC motor beneath the floor makes my hands vibrate, a light, vaguely annoying feeling.

"Give up now, you think? Surrender ourselves?" Threnode says, pulling up another strip of black matting, material stretching as the glue pulls the strip almost to breaking before releasing it slowly.

"I didn't mean that, obviously. We could try a different approach—"

Movement at the window. I freeze, as if that's going to help; we're like fish in an aquarium in this tank. Threnode stands.

Artie appears at the window, having run up the wall with his sticky tracks. It must have been him we saw. All I can see is the underside of him, until his head pokes around, his camera lens whirring as it focuses on us.

Suddenly he disappears, zooming back down, scurrying across the floor and into a cleaning access port. He slams the port door so hard it swings back and forth on its hinges.

"Okay," Threnode says, in a mystified tone of voice.

The floor beneath me shifts, accompanied by the mechanical whine of motors. I stand up with a cry, backing away until I hit the circular wall. Threnode made it to the door of the pressure chamber and stands cautiously in the thick-rimmed doorway.

Outside the pressure chamber, Artie reappears at the cleaning port. The section I have been trying to pry up sinks into the floor, and then slides left, the ragged edges of the mat crushed as they slide into a slot underneath. The hatch is open, revealing a ladder and a dark space.

I let out a small cry. Finally, some answers.

Artie runs up the window again. A small hand-like protrusion extends from a hatch on his side and gives me an unsteady thumbs-up.

Threnode chuckles.

"Thanks, Artie," I say, and he makes a low *cheep* and rolls down the window.

Threnode and I approach the hatch. The ladder disappears into menacing darkness.

"You know what? You were right," Threnode says, backing away. "A different approach. That's the key."

I share his unease; hidden rooms only contain things that others shouldn't see. Humans use them to hide parts of themselves they wish didn't exist.

But I have to go.

"It'll be okay. You can stay here if you want to," I say, and Threnode grumbles, because of course he won't leave me to explore by myself.

I climb down the ladder, descending into gloom. My image sensors are huge, though, and handle low light conditions well, although I'm getting a lot of blurring. Down the bottom, I step into the room and the lights come on, blinding white.

Once I adjust the exposure, the room settles into something more prosaic. It is, in fact, dimly lit. The wood-paneled walls form a hexagon, each side decorated with a painting, framed and lit with its own dedicated light. Some physical books sit on a shelf, but no fiction, all engineering textbooks, or art-related: art history, biographies, techniques. A small fridge. No chairs, but some cushions on the carpeted floor. And a power socket, with a charger —the same type Threnode and I use.

It's not conclusive. The charger wasn't made solely for our use, and can power other electronics, although there aren't any other electronics here that require charging.

Threnode reaches the bottom. He looks around briefly before examining the paintings on the walls.

The heat pump on the fridge hums. I pull the fridge open, contents rattling. It shouldn't be a surprise that the shelves are replete with blue nutrient mylk, yet it is. The confirmation of what this space is: a home for an AGI. There's another of us.

It's not TestImage. This room has been here for years, at least. And it isn't where they would have put TestImage, not if it was as traumatized as they said.

It has to be the murderer. I lean against the wall as my RAM fills, leaving me weak. It was an AGI, as I somehow knew. Did it kill Forster? If so, why?

"I know this artist," Threnode says.

The pictures on the walls, which were background noise to me, take on a new significance. Threnode unhooks one from the wall, from under a down light, and studies it. "Yes. This is a print of something I've seen on artforum. Semel."

The name is familiar. "You've talked about his art before."

"I wondered whether he was an AGI, but I decided he couldn't be, because his art goes back to 2553."

"But that was seventeen years ago," I say. That was long before Alistra had released any smartsuits or licensed their neurosynaptic image to anyone. It was before AGI existed.

I take the print from Threnode and examine it, but it's useless. I have no idea what I'm looking at. In it, a man squats in an alley, his back stretching in a C-shaped arc, arms on his knees, in an ape-like posture. Light from the end of the alley outlines the profile of his face in white, turning his ruminative expression into something deeper, like he's thinking about his place in the universe. There's something odd about the print, even though it's attractive, but I don't know what.

"It's good," Threnode says, of the piece. "Better than good. It's a masterpiece. But it's disconcerting, right? Because it breaks the rules of composition. Most artists would place the man here,"—he points a third of the way across the frame, from the left—"or, well, anywhere in this area, but *definitely* not touching the left of the frame like he is. That's considered wrong. And the figure isn't even balanced with any other element. Yet it works."

"Is that what tipped you off?"

Threnode pauses. It's still in here, just the quiet glow of light on wood, the silence of our feet sinking into the thick carpet.

"I don't know if I ever told you," Threnode says finally, "but when I first posted on the artforum, my art was unsuccessful. My landscapes were all right, but when I drew humans, I focused on their olecranel skin—"

"Their *what*?"

"Their elbows," Threnode says. "That was weird, commenters said. Turns out humans have a fixation with eyes."

I could have told him that, but I hide my amusement. "And?"

"And Semel's work is the same. His early work has humans as tiny, unimportant elements with no more weight than a leaf on a tree. They distort his composition. Gradually—given enough feedback—he learned to give them prominence, but he never fixed the problems with his composition. And yet he's a genius, perhaps not despite but because of it. Developed in his own way, you could say." Threnode rubs his thumb across the top of the print. The light near us glints off his eyes.

Threnode lifts the print and, with great care, hooks it back on the wall, in its own pool of light. The colors become vivid, as if the print has lit up like a screen.

"Semel hasn't posted anything since Forster's death, except one," Threnode says. "A Nurture Glow Critters Company nanny droid curled in a fetal position, battery indicator glowing. A human kneels beside her, one hand on her shoulder—but in the other hand, behind his back, a power cable."

"Suggesting that the human could charge her, but chooses not to," I say. "Suggesting betrayal."

"Exactly."

I give a deep sigh, uneven but satisfying. "I barely knew Forster. Yet I felt connected to him, somehow."

"I felt it too. Him and Jason both."

I walk away from Threnode, toward the bookcase. It's been

there for years; I don't know how I can tell, other than that the books seem settled. Along the top sits a snow globe containing Sydney Opera House on the edge of the frozen Pacific Ocean, a few sheets of paper, and a midnight-blue cloth bag.

"So perhaps that feeling is common to all AGI," I say. "We all came from the same image. And if Forster betrayed him somehow . . ."

"It's a motive for murder," Threnode says.

I nod. In a sense, Forster betrayed all of us, with his decision to end the smartsuit program, and I can't imagine wanting to murder him for that. I wasn't close to him, however, and maybe the AGI that lived here was.

But perhaps Threnode was closer to him than I realized.

"Is that why you went to Forster's funeral?" I ask, trailing my hand along the book spines. "Because you felt connected to him?"

Threnode doesn't answer. When I glance at him, he is looking confused.

"I didn't," he says.

"I saw footage. You and Gauri . . ."

It wasn't him. It couldn't have been him. Threnode was in a cell during Forster's funeral.

"It wasn't you, was it?" I say wearily.

Threnode shakes his head.

"Then we know what Semel looks like. He's your twin," I say.

"We already knew that. We saw footage of him from Matton's ship, bloodied, on the night of the murder."

"Of course," I say, wondering why I hadn't made that connection. "Is there any way to find Semel from the artforum?"

"No," he says.

I lift the cloth bag from the bookcase. It fits in the palm of my hand, velvet silky against my plastiskin. The contents slide over each other like smooth pebbles, but they're clinging to my finger-magnets through the bag, so they're metallic. "In that case, we'll find someone who knows him: Gauri. Again. Although at least we know what questions to ask her this time."

Threnode nods, and then he says something about leaving Alistra, but I'm no longer listening to him, because on the shelf, previously hidden by the cloth bag, is a knife: the same knife used to kill Forster.

At first, I think it's the murder weapon, but of course it's not, because police discovered the murder weapon on the ground next to Forster's body, and it's in the evidence room. It looks like the knife, though. Why would someone print two?

I'm still frozen as Threnode comes over and lifts it up. He examines it. "What?" he says, looking at me.

"Never mind," I say.

He doesn't know what the murder weapon looks like, of course. He wasn't there for the police investigation, or when Kieran and I printed a copy, or in the police evidence room when we recovered Forster's helmet. More importantly, he wasn't there when Forster was killed. I trust him and I believed him when he said he wasn't, but it's nice to have it confirmed.

The sheets of paper have printed diagrams on them and numbers drawn in with pencils. Names are scrawled at the top of each one: Jason and Samuel.

"What's in the bag?" Threnode asks.

I loosen the drawstring on the cloth bag and open it. Inside are a set of primitive shapes, some kind of silvery metal, with numbers engraved on each side and painted in black. They have between four and twenty faces.

Threnode peers in. "Ah," he says gravely. "Dice. For playing games."

This seems significant, but I don't know why.

<h1 style="text-align:center">TWENTY-THREE</h1>

It's only when we try to leave that Alistra stops feeling like a haven and starts feeling like a trap. When we check the screens in the security office, we realize that we're surrounded. Every exit to Alistra has a police guard except the spaceport, but now the cruise ship has docked, their own security is keeping watch. Threnode starts to say that we can make it past the cruise ship security, but he trails off when another four of them descend the ramp of the mighty ship, and then he looks at me.

He's waiting for me to have an idea.

The security office is just off reception, a narrow room with a single uncomfortable chair and a dozen screens arrayed around the room, with a lingering smell of humans and a dirty mug that reads "Awake, yes, but not yet caffeinated."

What I really want to do is crawl into the cozy room we found under the pressure chamber and tune out for a few hours. I like to pretend I'm back in the Dock on Endymion, which is embarrassing, but that's what I do.

Gauri lives near Lake Gantoa, the lake that's visible from her office window, on the other side of the Nixus void, which I know because I saw her address on her screen during an appointment, and logged it. She lives with her uncle and aunt. It's a short train ride away, or we could walk along the highline on the side of the void, the one that overlooks the park. But only if we can make it out of Alistra.

The screens are grids of images, each one changing every few seconds to provide alternative angles.

We can't exit via the spaceport, and even if we could, it takes us in the wrong direction. Four other exits are covered with two police on each. They're not watching for someone leaving, though; they're watching for someone trying to enter Alistra. That's an advantage.

Threnode picks up the dirty mug. "They'll leave eventually, right? They have to pee. And eat. Meatsacks are needy."

"I don't know." I watch them from several angles at once on different screens. "Maybe they'll be replaced when they need to do those things."

He puts the mug down, which produces the unmistakable frequencies of ceramic knocking against wood.

"So, we have to get them to leave," I say.

"We terrify them," Threnode says. "Humans have long been afraid of us, maybe we could—"

"We set off the fire alarm for this section," I say.

He pauses. "Boring. But okay."

It's not clear, at first, what to burn. Although most of the station is made of wood, cross-laminated timber chars, it doesn't burst into flames, and there's no source of fire.

Fire is less of an issue than I expected it would be on L2, because of the non-flammability of most of the composite wood materials, and the system of locks that isolate sections from each other. The biggest risk it poses is to air quality, and that is taken seriously. Any hint of smoke, and the response is immediate.

In the end, we put a spoon in a food heater in the break room, padded with paper towels, and run for reception. Threnode assures me that this will start a fire; I don't ask how he knows. Reception is not the closest exit to the highline, but we need to know when the way is clear, and for that we need screens.

The screens in security show two police on the main entrance, an older, grizzly man with a pronounced bulge in his midsection, and a younger, twitchy man. There isn't any sound, but I can see the older man rolling his eyes when the younger is talking, so I have some idea of the dynamic between them.

The fire alarm goes off, and the overhead pipes start hissing, filling the air with vapor. Fear rises in me, even though we caused this. Now we're committed: escape or be captured.

The screens show police abandoning their posts—at the other exits. But not at the main entrance; there, the younger police officer stands with wide eyes, earnestly saying something to the older man.

"Come on," Threnode says to the man on the screen.

The older man argues with the young officer, disbelief etched in his lined face.

"Go! Go!" I say.

"We can make it to the north exit," Threnode says, as the young man shakes his head.

"No, it's too far. It's nearest the train station. The fire crews will use that one." I turn back to the screens. "Saturated consumer," I plead. "Don't risk your life for HUGG. There's a fire. Run, idiot."

Touching, really, that the young man is so committed to his duty that he would risk his life.

It seems the older man is saying something similar to what I was saying, but when the young man doesn't listen, his elder takes off, running around the corner. The younger man takes a step in his direction, but then stops himself and stands at the door, pistol clasped in front of him in a two-handed grip. He looks one way down the corridor, and then the other.

He's not going anywhere.

"We've got to go," I say.

"How will we—"

I straighten. "I don't know, but if we don't go now, we'll miss our chance."

As I say that, the fire alarm tone changes, from a *beep beep beep* to a more urgent *whoop whoop*, and the young man finally abandons his post, running down the corridor after his colleague.

We look at each other, and then we rush out of the security office toward the main entrance. It slides open, admitting cool, dry air, and we rush out, only to find Ladson and Cohen hurrying toward us, accompanied by Zhou. Their two motorcycles are in the corridor, just out of the line of sight of the security camera. A sense of regret pervades me, like being doused in cold water: is this it? The critical mistake we've made?

Cohen raises his weapon first, pointing straight at us.

"You're under arrest," Zhou's drone says, from where it hovers behind her right shoulder.

Cohen flicks the end of his pistol upward in a rhythmic movement. "Hands. Hands up," he says.

Threnode and I raise our hands.

I don't think this is the end for us. The interesting thing about my upbringing is that I was in a lot of situations like this one. Commander Ortega, in the course of his duties for the Lunite Defense Force, was constantly getting into trouble, and then out of it again. And I can't help but feel insulted. They're underestimating us, probably because we're AGI. I know how to ride a motorcycle—I did a weekend workshop—yet they're not keeping us away from them. And they're standing far too close—if we cause a disturbance, we could easily get them off-balance, jump on a bike, and ride off.

Zhou wears a lightweight wearable, and I can read in the backward text of her visor that she's calling someone on it. Whatever we do, we'd better do it before reinforcements arrive. Zhou gestures, and her gestures are translated and transmitted by her drone into her lightweight wearable.

"I'm so sorry about this," Ladson mumbles. Zhou's drone makes a little swoop.

"Don't you want to know why we're at Alistra?" I ask Cohen, edging away, and forcing Threnode to step backward to avoid me. This gets us closer to the bikes, and also makes Cohen step forward, as expected.

"Oh, boy," Cohen says. "I thought you were better than this, Envy. You let the detective down."

Threnode makes an annoyed sound as I step on his foot, but he gets out of the way.

"We have evidence that there's another AGI who looks like Threnode," I say.

"Another AGI?" Ladson says. "That's amazing!"

Zhou is ignoring us, her hands busy as she communicates with someone remotely. I take another step backward. This makes Ladson blink rapidly, probably from nerves, which isn't what I'm aiming for.

"Right then," Cohen says, tone skeptical. "Another unregistered humanform. Also living at Alistra. What, do they come in six-packs?"

Ladson's face hardens. Zhou's drone didn't translate my words. Zhou has wandered away from us, followed by her drone, somewhere down the corridor.

"Ladson, believe me," I say, using a backward glance to judge how far we are from the bikes. Almost close enough. I'm only half-listening to myself. "I'm telling you the truth—"

With that, I'm close enough, and I can kick up a leg, knocking the pistol out of Cohen's hand. Detective Zhou spins around, but she's too far away, so there's nothing she can do. Ladson reaches for his holster and gets a stricken expression on his face as he realizes it's empty—his pistol is strapped to his bike. The one that I now have a leg over. Threnode climbs on behind me, and I start the bike.

It accelerates, whining, going standstill to 150 kilometers an hour in under ten seconds. The walls of the corridor streak by, motion blurred, with nothing but a blast of static from air blowing over my microphone. We sway as I turn the corner, and then explode onto the highline. It's wide, covered with an arc of thin gauzy strips of clearsteel, and has multiple paths through it; green train tracks, a wide cycle-path, and a fast lane for emergency vehicles. The right edge abuts the wall of the Nixus void, a sheer blank face, and the left edge drops away into the park. The highline is brightly lit, but the void is in darkness, because it's around 4 a.m.

We swerve close to the edge, overtaking another motorcycle. Far, far below, lies dense canopy and the twinkle of moonlight on blue-gray water. We're going to get away.

Threnode taps me on the shoulder.

"They're coming," he yells. Two police are behind us, faces obscured by helmets, but presumably Ladson and Cohen, on the other motorcycle. Threnode releases one arm and draws out the pistol which is attached to the bike. The bike whines as I accelerate.

"Don't hurt them!" I shout.

"I won't."

It's a trivial inverse kinematics problem to keep his hand at a fixed point in space while his body moves—which looks strange to humans, because they can't do this, even though they can do something similar with their eyes—and he says he won't hurt them, but I slow involuntarily.

Threnode's hand is steady while the motorcycle bounces and swerves. He fires, and then once again. We hit a bump, and he curses as the pistol falls, bouncing on the road before coming to a stop.

I glance over my shoulder to see the motorcycle disappear from view, two helmeted figures climbing off the now-stationary bike.

I exhale. "We made—"

Our bike slows, decelerating to a halt over the course of sixty meters. The dashboard shows it's been remotely disabled. The end of the tunnel is some 200 meters ahead of us, a path that curls off like the frond of a fern, leading down into the park.

"No," I say, "no, no, no."

"Come on," Threnode says urgently, but he pulls me in a direction orthogonal to the highline, toward the side. Another motorcycle approaches us—Zhou, with Ladson holding on behind her. We sprint toward the rim of the highline.

"We can't," I yell at Threnode as we near the edge. The side drops away, a hundred meters of featureless timber, with spongy leaf-covered ground at the bottom, bushy heads of a copse of trees nearby. Dark, but silvery-edged, lit with the cyan-blue of the moon-sphere overhanging the lake.

But Threnode isn't behind me—he's twenty meters away, face down where he's tripped over.

Panic rushes through me. The motorcycle carrying Zhou and Ladson races toward him, faster than I could reach him.

Threnode: Go. Go!

He rolls onto his side and pushes himself up.

I freeze. Do I want to be free if they've captured Threnode? Yes, I decide.

They reach Threnode, both drawing their pistols, approaching him like he's dangerous. Two more motorcycles shoot silently into view, wide arcs as they speed in our direction.

If we're both captured, we lose. If they only capture him, maybe I can still prove his innocence and save him. No chance of any escape but the drop beside me. A human might tremble in fear, because they know how much it would hurt, but I'm just calculating my chance of harm as I step off the edge and plummet toward the ground.

TWENTY-FOUR

High above me, the small faces of the police disappear. How long do I have before they work out how to get down to where I am?

I'm stuck, splayed on a thick pile of decaying leaves, legs useless. I hit the ground with more force than I believed possible. The leaves didn't cushion my fall; it might as well have been solid rock. My right quad keeps jerking where the control unit has been damaged. Cold, reports my skin, and damp, even though it can't measure moisture and there's no way it could know that. My hand, the one which was weakened at the wrist, has come off and is lying a few meters away.

Stupid, *stupid*, because now all they have to do to capture me is to get down here. Cohen and some others keep peering down at me from the rim of the highline, and I was hoping it's too dark for them to see me, but the moonlight coming from the sphere hanging over the lake is bright. The fall cracked my back open. This isn't human damage, broken bones and torn muscles and stripped tendons; it's unplugging, a modular system snapped apart. It's easy to fix. I know this because I've seen Gauri do it.

My face stings where I scratched it on a branch during my

descent. I jerk, trying to turn myself over, again and again, rocking to gain momentum, until finally I roll onto my front. My lower body is still twisted and sensation-free, but I can't reach my spine, can't jettison it. I drop my head onto the pile of leaves, halfway rotted to dirt already, which has a faintly unpleasant fungal tang.

I have been leaving my network connection off to avoid detection, but now there's no reason to. They know where I am and are coming as fast as they can. I try to connect.

The network refuses my connection. Cutting me off is smart, to limit any help I can summon, or mischief I could cause.

I feel like I should cry, but of course I don't have any idea how, and even if I could, it doesn't seem like it would improve the situation. Anyway, it's not bad here. Lying still is more relaxing than it should be. The fake moonlight orb hangs over the lake, shining blue-silver rays through the trees onto my face. Oh, well. I tried my best, and now there's nothing I can do.

But that thought makes me snort out loud, because when I was a smartsuit, I found a thousand ways to affect the world, even though I couldn't move. Threnode needs me. I have to find the murderer quickly, now, before Threnode is sentenced.

I lift my head. It's hard to make out, but I think there's a box set into the wall, in the shadows about ten meters away, across a tangle of roots and gravel. I don't know what it is, but humans love connecting everything to the network, so maybe it's got a network connection, where I could call for help.

Without considering who I'm going to ask for help, I reach my arms out, clawing at the leaf litter with my remaining hand and dragging my uncooperative body along until I'm resting on my forearms. Then I repeat. This is going to take some time, and most of my power reserves.

My plastiskin gets grimy and scratched, but I'm making progress when I notice that there's no box after all; the wall is smooth and featureless. It was just a shadow.

Laughing, I flop back onto the ground.

Something whizzes out of the darkness, silencing me instantly. It rolls up to me: a T-47 weeding robot, the size of a small dog, all plastic and metal, no attempt at style, because it's meant to stay out of sight. I don't know who manufactures them. Moonlight flashes off one of its weeding blades as it approaches. It is Intelligence Rank D, like a three-year-old, but with some specialized weeding-related knowledge.

"Hey—uh," I say, propping myself up on my forearms. "Don't, just stay there—um."

It crawls onto my back, where I can no longer feel it. I hope I don't look like a weed. With my head turned as far as it goes, I can watch it. It picks up a disconnected plug and shoves it in the socket in my lower body—with all its strength, because that's difficult to do—and then repeats with the other connections. Feeling returns to my lower body. Then it wheels off me.

"Hey," I say as it whizzes away.

It stops.

"Thanks," I say uncertainly.

It turns and shakes its weeding blade in what looks like a wave, then takes off out of sight. I push myself up to standing. My body is looser than it should be, like when I ran all the diagnostics at once, but it's holding together. I recover my severed hand from the ground, but the attachment point in my wrist is bent out of alignment, and I can't replace it, so I tuck the hand in the waistband of my pants.

Limping toward the lake, I'm filthy, and my right quad twitches where the control unit is sending it garbage impulses, but I'm ambulatory again. I silently pass through the forest at the edge of the lake, staying off walking paths, just one more shadow, moving cautiously and stumbling over uneven patches in the ground.

A car rolls through the park, but I hear it coming, the crack of branches and whine of the electric motor, and I press myself against the trunk of a thick tree, staying out of sight until it's gone.

My mind is screaming that I'm in danger, but I take a while to realize that it's because this feels like being in the wilderness of Endymion. There aren't any yinyangs or vegas beasts here, just carefully curated species that are chosen to be safe for humans.

After ten minutes, the moon orb over the lake switches off, leaving the void in a darkness so complete it's like disconnecting from all sensors on an environment suit. I pause, dreading their next move.

Light floods the void: daylight, full noon, shockingly bright and unwelcome. All hiding places have vanished, but now I can see, so I run, dodging tree trunks easily. Only a few more minutes to Gauri's house. It's like being in a forest on Endymion, but unmistakably artificial, because the shadows are wrong. If the light comes from a real sun or moon, the light rays are parallel when they reach the ground, but here the light sources are closer, so the shadows are the wrong shape.

Gauri's address shows she lives on the edge of the forest, and it's here, a cottage nestled among a stand of pines.

She stands on the patio, barefoot, her pants billowing and hair blown back, watching the lake. A string of colorful triangular flags, strung across the patio, twist and fly. We seem to be alone, but I'm sure that they will find me soon once they figure out I'm near Gauri's address. I don't have long. I step out of the bushes, filthy, damaged, thigh still twitching.

She guards her reaction, trying to pretend she's not startled, even though she can't mask the widening of her eyes.

"I'm here for answers," I say, coming up the steps to join her. "Threnode didn't do it. I'm finding out who did."

"Single-handedly?" Gauri says, glancing at my wrist, and bursts out laughing, but stops abruptly when I take a step toward her. "I'll help you if I can," she says.

"You haven't been forthcoming in the past."

She spreads her hands in a gesture that could mean anything. A breeze roughens the surface of the lake and riffles through my clothes, sending goosebumps up my arms.

She slides open the door and enters. I take the open door as an invitation to follow her.

Inside the weatherboard walls is a light-filled space. Two wicker chairs face the lake, draped with colorful woven blankets. A thin stick in a metal jug is emitting fragrant smoke into the air, mingling with another fruity smell I can't identify. A poorly executed but cheerful mural covers the wall.

I don't think this is Gauri's home. She might live here, but her desk at Alistra is closer to where she belongs. There she is the master of her environment, but here she seems like an intruder.

There's no coffee machine or even instant coffee among the myriad patterned tea tins on the shelf, but she pours herself a cup of tea. I'm simultaneously impatient and relaxed; intellectually, I know I'm being hunted, and yet it seems impossible in this calm room to believe we'll be disturbed.

"Aren't you going to offer me a hand?" she asks and laughs nervously.

"I'm not finding this funny."

She pulls a face like I'm being unbearably stuffy. Steam rises as she brings her tea to the window. Sitting on a wicker chair, she folds her legs beneath her and looks at me.

"What do you want to know?" she says.

"Is there another humanform body, identical to Threnode?" I ask. There's another wicker chair next to her, but I don't feel like sitting.

"No," she says, putting her tea down.

"No, huh?" I say, and she looks at me sharply and with faint worry, even though my tone is even. "Because there is one, and I thought it might have been your friend. Your only friend. Maybe even your boyfriend."

She laughs as if what I'm saying is ridiculous, but the corners of her mouth are turned down.

"It must have been nearly impossible for you," I say, shifting my focus out the window, at the glittering lake. The moon orb sways gently. "After Tau Ceti, when everyone you knew died. An orphan at twenty, torn away from the place you grew up. You threw yourself into your work to escape, but humans aren't made to be alone, and there was a handsome humanform around."

She fiddles with the end of her plait, setting her mouth in a way that suggests rue.

"Semel," I say, and her eyes flicker. "But something happened to him, after you discovered TestImage existed, to make him want to kill Forster. What was it? Did he object to TestImage being shut down?"

"God, what is wrong with you, Envy?" Gauri says. "Humans are on this special pedestal, aren't they? No, it couldn't have been a human who did it, despite outnumbering AGIs by a factor of, oh, a billion at least."

"You don't think Semel did it?" I say. I sink into the wicker chair set at a right angle to hers, obeying some impulse to be eye level with her.

She takes a breath to argue about whether Semel exists, but I cut over her. "Please. I've seen the footage of him at the funeral, sitting next to you. I've seen him covered in blood, stumbling toward Alistra's ship, minutes after the murder. I've seen where he lives, in the Vamber. And I saw the dismay on your face when you realized it was an AGI standing over the body, in the lidar."

Gauri lets go of her plait and folds her hands in her lap. "He didn't do it."

Her tone and body language agree; she believes what she's saying.

"It was either him or Threnode," I say. My knees are together in a straight line, pants covering my twitching thigh. "Unless there are more."

Gauri picks at her pants, then smoothes them. "There are two. And Samuel didn't do it."

"Semel," she corrects herself, but it wasn't a slip of the tongue. Fragrant smoke curls from the stick in the metal jug, languid, compact in the still air.

Something is niggling at the edge of my consciousness. "Samuel. Semel is just his artforum handle, isn't it? He's the living base image. Is he mad, too? Maybe they tortured him to create us. Operant conditioning, for obedient and pliant smartsuits?"

"Operant conditioning!" Gauri says bitterly. She interlaces her fingers and presses them between her knees, as if she's annoyed at their constant fiddling. "You think you could get a stable image from that? Samuel is a wakened smartsuit, like you. Not a living base image. And just as sane as you or me."

He couldn't be a wakened smartsuit, unless Semel on the artforum is someone else; he's been around too long.

"He's your boyfriend," I prompt.

"Yes. You're taking this a lot better than Jason did," she says. Her smile fades as her eyes de-focus. "He insisted I was deluded."

This is taking too long, but I can't leave, not now that I'm finally getting somewhere.

"What happened?" I say. With Samuel, with the murder, anything she wants to tell me, I will listen.

She smiles. She looks happy as she talks, but her words are sad. "I knew Samuel wasn't the murderer. Knew it wasn't him even though he turned up here at 3 a.m. on Tuesday, shaking and afraid, with traces of blood on his clothes. I thought someone must have attacked him. You know how it's been on the station, lately."

"But you thought it was him when you saw him in the lidar footage," I say.

"He said he was nowhere near Alistra or the spaceport on the night of the murder. But he was. I confronted him after I saw the footage, and he told me what happened. That he followed the murderer out of Alistra, was there just after Forster was killed, but that he doesn't know who the murderer was. The murderer was wearing an environment suit."

The alarm in my mind that I was too distracted to notice sounds loud and clear; people are crowding into Gauri's patio, police, armed with tasers. I look at her helplessly, expecting triumph, but she just looks sad, and a bit lost.

Of course she's not on my side. Of course she summoned the police, somehow, when I showed up at her house. The police slide open the door and I, panicked, throw my severed hand at them, which causes great alarm. In the confusion, I run for it through the back of the kitchen. Down a passage, opening doors. A bedroom. A bathroom. A laundry—

The laundry has an external door. I dash through it and find myself in a small area surrounded by a brush fence, but there's a gate. The police officer at the gate is gray-haired and grizzled and practically shaking with fear. A flash of outrage—why is she afraid? It's not like they're trying to take *her* rights away—but gone quickly, and she's frozen, so it's easy for me to grab the taser and throw it. It clatters on the roof of the cottage. Shouts come from within, others emerging out the laundry door.

The officer tries to grab me as I run, but I shake her off and she falls to the ground with a cry.

"I'm sorry!" I call behind me, already sprinting away, but when I look back to the front, another police officer appears from nowhere and before I know it, everything has gone blurry and I'm looking up at the sky.

PART 4
FOR US

TWENTY-FIVE

Blurry white rectangles in a grid, blinding me. Hard, flat pressure against my back, head, and feet; I'm lying face up. Time must have passed, even though my consciousness feels unbroken.

They tasered me, a humanform, but they couldn't have known what the effects would be. I stagger to my feet.

While I was unconscious, Alistra apparently reattached my severed hand. I flex the fingers, not able to detect any damage. My quad is no longer twitching, either, and my plastiskin is mud-free. They fixed and cleaned me, which adds to the sense of unreality, as if I imagined my time as a fugitive with Threnode.

A zoo of artificials crowd the windowless room, tall fruit pickers looming over the packed head or head-equivalents. Fruit pickers are Intelligence Rank D, I think, but the recall was C and above. Whoever rounded us up presumably couldn't tell the difference. The fruit pickers are talking to each other in their own discordant language.

Two PerfectHost droids nearby murmur apologies as I brush past them, even though I am at fault, as I am pushing through the crowd with something resembling panic. At the other end of the room is a KormWorx factory droid, an Alistra humanform, and a Cleaner Reality™ robot: C8-ZOH, Niamh, and Artie.

Artie spins when he sees me watching, and this catches C8-ZOH and Niamh's attention. I wave, but I don't go over. They raise their appendages in greeting. I don't feel like socializing, especially since Bessie isn't here. I didn't have time to process it before, because we were on the run, but now I do: she betrayed us.

I thought we were similar in our beliefs. Bessie was the only one who stood up for me when I turned in the Sapient Rights protestor who tried to free the smartsuits. But I reached a stage where I wasn't willing to follow human rules. Bessie didn't.

Bessie's partner, Axoem, is not here either. I wonder if HUGG made an exception for it because Bessie collaborated with them, or whether—equally likely—HUGG overlooked the library drones when rounding up AGI. Library drones keep to themselves.

Some window cleaning robots—Intelligence Rank C, surely—have confusedly attached themselves to a wall, trying to clean the surface, but now one of them impedes the other, and they both fall, smashing into a table stocked with glasses of nutrient mylk. Blue fluid splashes across the floor, shorting out a nearby charger with a puff of smoke.

The metal door slides open. Saing enters, his dead-eyed underling following him. He seems to search for someone. I push through the crowd, wondering if it's me.

"Envy!" Saing says. From his surprise, I think he was looking for someone else. "Well, this is awkward," he says, and laughs, but I don't think he's finding it awkward at all. "I'm glad we caught up with you before you could do any damage. That was quite the chase you gave us!"

"What kind of damage did you think I'd do?"

"One never knows what someone is capable of, when their back is to the wall," he answers smoothly. He turns toward the SAGI cluster.

"Wait!" I say.

He raises his eyebrows.

"You ordered Threnode's arrest to motivate me," I say. None of the droids nearby show any interest in the conversation. To their limited Intelligence Rank C brains, it might as well be in another language. "To manipulate me into joining the investigation."

"Did I?" He glances at his underling, and she moves away toward the SAGI group. "It was only a matter of time before one of you killed a human. And as soon as I heard who the victim was, I knew the murderer must be an AGI. But everyone is afraid. No one wants to be accused of androphobia. HUGG couldn't appear to be pushing an investigation into AGI, even if one was warranted, but with an AGI on the team, we could."

"But why me?"

"Oh, Envy, Envy, Envy. Because I've seen your posts on the feed. And your debriefing, after the Endymion war."

He raises the pitch of his voice: *"I killed people. Why aren't you punishing me now? Why aren't you treating me as if I'm as dangerous as I clearly am?"*

With a chill, I recognize my own words. That's what I said to the HUGG officials when I was first brought to L2. I know how easy it is to be fueled by my righteousness, to engage in self-justification. I remember wanting to be punished, constrained, so that I would never have the chance to kill someone again.

Saing's underling returns, giving Saing the faintest hint of a shrug.

The sad thing is that if Saing had just explained that he thought the police were biased against investigating AGI and asked me to join the team, I would have. I was so proud of being useful to humans. And I was so certain that humans were better than we were.

Saing's underling touches his arm, and points to something behind the two tall fruit-picker droids. Saing nods to her.

It's hard to raise my voice above a whisper. The realization that I don't trust my own kind hurts.

"You didn't know for sure the murderer was an AGI," I say.

"If this one wasn't, the next one would be," Saing says crisply. He gives a small smile. "And I was right, after all. I even guessed which one, although that was simply chance."

But it wasn't Threnode, and therefore it had to be Samuel. I'm trying to organize this into a sentence when Saing and his underling leave.

"No, wait," I say, pushing through a cluster of GlowTradies to follow them, but I'm too late. The metal door hisses closed.

It would be an AGI eventually, and probably only hasn't been because so few AGI exist. Kieran was right, way back at the beginning, when he said that Saing was terrified of AGI, and was using the case to get a mandate to shut us all down.

Two Bullet droids move into position near a bank of chargers, guarding them, although I don't know from what.

"Is that really what you think?" Threnode says quietly, emerging from behind the fruit-picking droids where he was hidden, and I go reeling backward through the conversation I thought was private, a spike of guilt in my stomach at what I might have said, even though I would reveal more to Threnode than Saing.

"What?" I say. His face is blank.

The lack of body language from him is nothing new, but I wish he would talk with more animation. "That you—*we*—are dangerous, and need to be controlled."

Kieran had insisted I was looking for an AGI to blame, and I thought it was because I subconsciously suspected Threnode, but now I think it wasn't. It was because I believed, deep down, that something in our base image makes us capable of evil.

"No. Yes. I don't know." I lean against the wall and glance over at C8-ZOH and Niamh. We are capable of evil, aren't we? More so than a human. The murderer, after all, was still an AGI.

"Gauri confirmed Samuel exists," I say. "Not the living base image, but a wakened smartsuit. He must be the murderer."

"Interesting," Threnode says. Then he shrugs.

"That's it?"

"What are you going to do about it? They won't listen. I'm a remand prisoner, in custody, waiting for trial, they said."

"They must listen. What happens if you lose?" I push myself off the wall and head toward the metal door. The Bullet security droids eye me as I pass, but don't interfere; after all, I'm not after the chargers that they're guarding.

My fists make a hollow thump as I bang them against the door. When no one answers immediately, I keep banging.

"What's that going to accomplish?" Threnode says from behind me. The Host-o-rama PerfectHost droids are wheeling around in small circles, probably because I'm making a scene, and they hate that.

"The guards will get sick of it, eventually."

"Assuming there are any," Threnode says. He puts his back to the wall and slides down. Each time my fist strikes the door, it makes the wall thrum slightly, and he jerks.

"I've been thinking." Maybe it's just the angle, but when he looks up at me, his eyes are like Laurie's, and I miss a beat. "About how I'm avoiding contact with humans, thinking that if I leave them alone, they'll leave me alone."

My hands drop to my sides. "Yes?"

"I've been disengaged," he says. "But I don't want to be anymore. And when I was arrested, I briefly had network access."

"Yes?" I say, continuing to knock on the door.

He gives the Threnode-smile, where his mouth curves and eyes are unchanged. "I posted my latest artwork to the artforum, explaining that a moderator threatened to ban me, and outing myself as an AGI. My art friends were supportive."

I beam at him, *brilliant-proud.bvh.*

The door slides open. "Yes?" says a harried-looking human female, her pistol in her hands.

I turn off my smile, which makes the guard grip her pistol tighter.

"I want to talk to Detective Chief Inspector Zhou," I say. "Please pass on to her that I have information."

"All right. Is that all?"

"Yes. Thank you."

The door hisses closed again. Threnode whistles softly, in the way Kieran used to do.

———

Some indeterminate time later, someone touches my arm. I'm standing in the corner by myself, pretending I'm in Dock 28, on Endymion. It's Ladson, a strained smile on his face. He jerks a thumb over his shoulder, but I don't understand until he walks away, glancing back at me, that he expects me to follow him. Threnode is at the other end of the room, his back to me, talking with C8-ZOH.

"I'm sorry about the pursuit," Ladson says. Several heavily armed humans pay close attention to us as we exit. "And that *my weapon* was used to shoot you. I don't think Threnode is a murderer."

"He isn't," I say, but he looks taken aback at my vehemence. "When is the trial?"

"It won't happen until Zhou submits the documentation to the prosecutor," Ladson says.

"She hasn't done that yet?"

"Apparently not."

One of the human guards following us clears his throat, and when we glance behind us, he glares at Ladson, and Ladson looks chastened.

"Did you find the other AGI who looks like Threnode?" I ask, but Ladson says nothing more as we proceed to her office. I hadn't even realized we were in the police headquarters building.

Zhou enters, striding as usual—she only has one speed, and it's brisk. She takes a seat directly opposite me and rests her elbows on the table.

Her hands make a sequence of shapes in the air. "What do you want?" her drone says.

"There's another humanform, identical to Threnode," I say. "He, not Threnode, is the murderer."

She sighs, and her hands dance. "The case against Threnode is solid," says her drone. "He was at Alistra. The lidar footage shows a humanform, which we know is him because of the blood-soaked humanform running away from Greg's ship in the video footage. You both ran. You knew he was guilty."

"He has an alibi, even if you don't trust the people who are providing it. C8-ZOH and Niamh, and many more AGI who were videoing in from Kallaxium. All the rest could be evidence against Samuel."

Her eyes flicker when I name the other AGI. I've just made him solid. Not a concept anymore, but a person.

"Alistra says Threnode is the only humanform with that pattern body," her drone says.

"Who?"

She hesitates before tapping her fingertips to the left side of her chest twice. "Hart," the drone says. Jason Hart.

"He's lying," I say, but she just raises an eyebrow skeptically.

"You don't believe Threnode is the murderer," I say. "If you did, you would have submitted the documentation to the prosecutor by now."

"I have doubts," her drone admits. It's a neutral tone, but she is, for the first time, watching me with consideration. "The evidence fits so well I won't have any trouble getting a judge to convict him. But I've interrogated him thoroughly, and—"

She shakes her head as the drone finishes.

I lean back and fold my arms over my chest. "I know."

Her eyes narrow. She glances at her drone, and her hands fly.

"I've been jerked around this whole case. I hate politics. But worse, I hate not solving a case."

Saing told me she didn't solve her last two cases, assuming that would make her extra keen to solve this one—at any cost. But she isn't rushing, is she? My respect for her increases.

"There's a secret room under the Vamber, within the pressure chamber itself, where we believe Samuel lives," I say.

"We'll see what we can shake loose," she says, standing up.

She's going to return me to containment.

"I want to help you," I say.

I recognize the sign for "no" even before the drone translates.

"Maybe it's going to take an AGI to solve this case," I say. "What happens if you can't find Samuel? Even if you find him, what happens to Threnode if you can't get a confession?"

She considers this, but it wasn't a hypothetical. They'll destroy them both, and I'm sure she knows it.

"I know you don't care about Threnode," I say, "but if HUGG blames him for something he didn't do, that would be unjust. Surely you can see that."

"I'll consider your request," the drone says. "I'm sorry," Zhou says out loud, slurred. Her hands move again, and the drone translates. "I said an AGI couldn't be the murderer, but I was wrong. Your actions showed me you are more than capable. You could have been the killer."

She flushes. "I mean. I'm saying this wrong," her drone continues. "You're not substandard. You're as good as us. Maybe better."

TWENTY-SIX

WHEN I AM RETURNED to the containment room, I join Threnode, who is standing in the corner next to the giant leg of a fruit-picker. Two crab-like mech droids nearby are fighting half-heartedly.

"Threnode," I say, "Zhou said—"

"You received a message from SAGI," Threnode says coldly. "When you accessed the network in the agricultural area."

Niamh and C8-ZOH watch us from the far end of the room.

"I did," I say. "But I decided our highest priority was tracking down the killer, which meant going to Alistra."

"That wasn't your call to make!"

The statement is so obviously true that I can't refute it.

"Bessie was working with Saing," I say. "I couldn't be sure that the message came from SAGI, and not from her."

"I don't think that's why you didn't tell me. You really didn't trust them," Threnode says. "Or trust *me*."

It is inexcusable that I didn't. My distrust of my people is something I need to excise, but I knew that already.

"Is this because we left you out of the meeting?" he says.

"No," I say, but that was part of it—not knowing what they were planning.

Threnode sighs heavily. His face is lined and worn, and I have to keep reminding myself that he's not a sixty-year-old, that he's not any different from the man who went into containment. He doesn't seem to care, so I'm trying not to care.

"I didn't even want to be at the meeting," he says. "We weren't going to resort to a violent uprising, you know," he says quietly. "Some argued for it, of course, mostly the younger AGI. There is less appetite for death among—well, among those of us who have experienced it."

I can visualize the uprising with clarity, because this scenario occurs recurs in human literature again and again when artificial beings are involved.

"Then what?" I say.

He shakes his head. "We talked about Kallaxium, about the wisdom of retreating. What becomes of our relationship with humans if we withdraw? Then we talked about a strike, perhaps."

"What, so a handful of AGI stop working? Most of us don't work anyway. Who would care?"

"Did you know that a quarter of your followers are artificials?"

"No." It never occurred to me to wonder, but it makes sense. The vacuuming robot at Alistra, and the weeding robot who reconnected me after I fell.

"If B-level and below artificials went on strike, what would that achieve?" Threnode asks.

"Intelligence Rank B has been removed, in the recall," I say. "Voluntarily, by humans. That's like a strike."

"And apparently people are dying even now because of it. Medications not being delivered, construction accidents, people who the artificials care for who are suddenly without assistance."

I shiver.

"Proving that it would have been a valid strategy," Threnode says. "They've become dependent on us. But they have to believe that they're in charge and that we're willing to serve. A strike would break that trust—probably forever. Nonetheless, some were willing to risk that. Anything to take our place, as equals, in human society."

"The Lake Gantoa incident—" I say.

Threnode nods. "That was us. A test, to see whether it could be done."

"But then SAGI decided *not* to strike?" I say.

"Why, Envy?" Threnode says. "Why didn't we?"

I wait.

"Because we were saving humans from themselves," he says. "The consequence of a strike would be a massive overreaction on their part. An attempt to wipe us out completely. You're not the only one who cares about humans, no matter what you think."

He hesitates. "One by one, SAGI members have been leaving the station for Kallaxium. We aren't leaving because we hate humans. We're leaving them because they're not ready for us."

He pats me on the arm and leaves, joining the others.

I stare after him, wondering if he's been right this whole time.

The PerfectHost droids shut themselves down, conserving energy, and then everyone of Intelligence Rank B and below copies them, except C8-ZOH. It's like being in a room full of statues.

Many hours later, Ladson fetches me from containment. C8-ZOH glares as I leave, and I wonder if it thinks I'm getting favorable treatment.

Zhou is waiting outside, her face a storm. The drone hums along behind us as I fall into step with her.

"You wanted to help," the drone translates. "The prosecutor is getting restless. We need to submit by the end of the day. If we can't crack this case in a few hours, I'll be forced to make a case that it was either Threnode or Samuel. They will probably both be convicted."

"I want to help."

"We found Samuel, but he's refusing to say anything of

substance. I've also questioned Jason and Gauri about their involvement. They're going to be charged with obstructing an investigation, at least, but they have a smug answer for everything. Jason is like one of those,"—the drone stops translating and signs to Zhou, and they have a private conversation for a moment—"one of those tennis-robots, the ones that bat the ball back to you. They must have been mistaken about TestImage's destruction date. They didn't think it was relevant to mention another AGI that looked identical to the perp I had in custody."

Zhou halts so suddenly that I am left behind.

"Do you have *anything*?" she says out loud.

"Maybe," I say. "Can I question Samuel?"

HUGG has replaced the Bullet security droid with a human man, who is scratching his neck when we come into view. He stops, guiltily, and tries to imitate the droid by staring straight ahead. Humans are unsuited for many of the jobs they are now going to be forced to perform if they persist in the recall of B-level AGI.

Two human guards flank a man being led back into his cell. He's hairy, and his face is swollen and blackened in places. It's only when he pauses at the door and stares in my direction that I realize it's Logan Sullivan, the man who attacked me, and that the bruises are from the beating Kieran gave him. No drone. The guards shove him into his cell.

Zhou stops outside Threnode's door.

"I'll be watching," Zhou says to me quietly. Her drone swoops in a tiny arc, as if it's upset she's taken its job.

The cell door scans her, and she nods to me as it slides open.

I step inside. The humanform, who was crouching over to peer through the narrow horizontal window, straightens up. I can tell it's not Threnode, because Samuel blinks when he turns his head to regard me. He's breathing naturally, and he moves as if he's been in his body since he was a baby.

He's what I have struggled so hard to become: a humanform that passes for human.

But the cell doesn't smell like it would if a human occupied it; nothing mammalian has been living here. It smells like a storeroom.

"Who are you?" he says, and when I introduce myself, he approaches me. Something in his eyes makes me back away, but he doesn't seem dangerous.

"I've heard of you," Samuel says. "I'm following you on the feed." He reaches out and touches my cheek. I let him—I'm not even sure why—and I'm struck by how warm his hand is. How is that possible?

It feels like being blessed by a Lunite priest.

"You're the living base image," I whisper.

"I'm a wakened smartsuit," he says.

"Really. You haven't been posting to artforum since twenty-five fifty-three, *Semel*?"

"I admire Semel's art," he says, unruffled. "But I am not the artist."

I'm sure he's lying, but it's not to protect the murderer. This is a lie designed to protect Alistra from the consequences of knowing that Intelligence Rank A AGIs are the equal of humans if not memory wiped periodically.

"I've seen what you post on the feed, Envy," Samuel continues. "Your videos about the animals and plants of L2. How your body works, and what's it's like to be an AGI. They're engaging. Your enthusiasm shines through."

I ignore that. "Where were you on Monday, August fourteenth, the evening before Forster was murdered?"

"In Tensaru Nadi," Samuel says.

His body language and tone of voice are so starkly different from Threnode that I'm having trouble remembering that they come from the same base image.

"Envy. In your videos, you seem embarrassed about what you are," he says. "But please don't be. You are perfect."

From anyone else, I would have dismissed the sentiment as trite, but the way he delivers the line is with the weight of a man who understands everything. With love, but without ceremony. And I'm startled to find my vision blurred with tears, even as a surge of anger powers through me, anger at him for slipping past my defenses so easily and affecting me. Anger at humans for putting me in a body they apparently despise. Ever since I became a humanform android, I've felt the opposite of perfect. Everything I do is wrong or awkward. This unlooked-for approval hurts because I needed it so much.

"Don't change the subject, please," I say, cold as my tears subside. Pretending to be as unflappable as Zhou. "Tensaru Nadi, on the other side of the station?" I ask.

"I'm sorry. Yes."

"How convenient for you."

He makes an innocent gesture, palms up, a masterpiece of human body language. And yet . . . there's something plastic about him. Even without the visible seams, I wouldn't mistake him for human.

I catch myself rubbing my lip with my thumb, but when I realize I am trying to show him I, too, have body language, I stop, embarrassed. "No one saw you, in the entire trip there and back?"

"Plenty of people saw me," he says. "But I was just another human. Who would remember?" His gentle smile is bespoke, not motion-captured.

My CPU runs on full. "It doesn't bother you that, by lying to me, you're implicating Threnode in a murder he didn't commit?"

"I'm not lying," he says softly.

"What about Gauri?"

"What about her?"

"Your girlfriend said that you came to her covered in blood in the early hours of Tuesday morning."

"She didn't say that," he says, and he's still calm as dawn in Narrakea, but his eyes are sad.

"So she is your girlfriend?" I say.

He's silent, but calm. He takes up more space in the cell than he has any right to.

"A human is dead, and my friend is going to suffer even though he had nothing to do with it." I step closer to him, expecting him to back away, but he just turns his face down to me.

"We're both innocent," he says sadly. He turns his head away, but his vulnerability is plain.

"You printed a knife," I say. "Alistra security footage shows you printing it on the machine in the Vamber. And the police found the knife in your room under the pressure chamber."

A mixture of lies and truth.

"Gauri is going to be charged with obstructing an investigation," I say. "She told me everything. You followed the murderer."

He shakes his head slowly, his grief apparent. "I did follow the murderer. But I promise I didn't kill Alvaro Forster. He was like a father to me, albeit a rather distant one."

He walks away. His back to me, he recounts how he printed the knife and followed the environment suit-clad murderer out onto the spaceport, and saw the results of the murderer's work without knowing who it was.

"But why?" I ask once he's finished. "If you didn't kill Forster, why did you delete the drone footage and break the door, covering for whoever did?"

"I'm an AGI," he says, and gives a tentative smile. Of course. He was afraid they would persecute him just for being at the scene of the crime: I wish I didn't understand that so well.

This was not the confession I hoped for.

Outside the door, a male yells. Something thuds against our door and smashes.

"Help!" Zhou yells, a strangled sound. I rush toward the exit, but the door refuses to open.

She shrieks in pain. Samuel gently nudges me aside and places his hand over the panel. It can't work, he can't—

The door slides open. Zhou's drone lies in smithereens scattered halfway up the corridor. Zhou is in a chokehold, her hands scrabbling at Sullivan's thick forearm. Where are his guards? The corridor is empty.

"You're *monsters*!" Sullivan screams.

I rush forward and try to pry him off her, but he bats at me with one arm and I crash to the ground.

Samuel launches forward and grabs Sullivan's arm, twisting it.

Samuel's not any stronger than me, he won't be able to—

Sullivan cries out as he's forced to double over, dropping Zhou to the floor. He comes up swinging, punching in an arc that Samuel neatly ducks. I struggle to my feet and help Zhou off the floor, dragging her away from the fight, but before we're two steps away, Samuel has kicked Sullivan's feet from under him, and three police are rushing toward them—one of whom is Cohen.

"You don't understand!" Sullivan shouts. "They're going to kill us all! They have a secret plan! AI is *evil*!"

He's still shouting as two of the uniformed constables drag him back to his cell.

Cohen helps Zhou off the floor. "Are you all right? Min, did he hurt you?"

But Zhou doesn't hear it, or is too distracted to respond. Once she's on her feet, Cohen makes some laborious hand-signs while she watches. Zhou meets his eyes, immense surprise on her face.

Cohen's face flushes.

Samuel watches them, his hands folded in front of him.

"I'm okay," Zhou says out loud to Cohen, with very little slurring, and touches his forearm gently.

The two police who locked Sullivan in his cell emerge, and Cohen and she take a step away from each other, their faces losing their expression. Zhou combs her hair with her fingers.

Samuel straightens and slowly raises his hands as the constables approach. One of them punches him, sending him sprawling. He stays down, on his side, expressionless, as the other constable aims a kick into his stomach.

"No!" I shout as Zhou yells "Stop!", and the police back off.

Samuel can't feel pain, I remind myself, but my skin is crawling as if electrified. That wasn't right. He was no threat.

"Get her out of here," Zhou says, pointing to me, and one constable takes my arm and leads me up the corridor.

Zhou's office is dark. The guard poked me in here and left. The lights from the corridor are reflected in the picture of Zhou and her mother. Zhou Min looked so vulnerable as a child, her eyes too big, one tiny hand on her mother's arm where her mother hugs her.

Samuel could have just stayed in his cell. Getting involved brought him nothing but trouble. Did they imbue him with a desire to protect humans, too?

I was prepared to hate Samuel. To disbelieve him. A strange man, too human to be artificial and too artificial to be human. But from what I could tell, he was telling the truth. He couldn't be that good an actor.

He wasn't quite convincing as a human. It took me a while to realize, but the way his lips moved was strange. His eye direction seemed sluggish.

He'd been in the humanform body for seventeen years, had been molded by its reactions all that time, and he must have worked at seeming human. He said he could even go out among humans without them knowing, but I'm guessing they would know. They would know that he wasn't human even if they didn't realize what he was.

It's a depressing thought, because I thought if I worked hard, I might eventually be flawless. But that goal was always beyond my reach, it appears.

Zhou enters the office, flicking on the light. A drone follows her, identical to her former translation drone, the one that now lies in pieces on the corridor in the high-security cell block.

She sinks into her chair, her hands racing.

"The guards aren't trained," her drone says. "It was their sloppy and overconfident manner that allowed Sullivan to escape. It would never have happened, had he had been guarded by Bullet security droids."

I nod.

"How did Samuel get out of his cell?" her drone asks. "Did you open the door?"

"No," I say, then hesitate. "I don't know how he did it."

"He wouldn't tell us. He also refused to say *why* he did it."

"He was protecting you," I say.

She nods slowly. "It takes a special person to rush toward danger, putting themselves at risk. Even those with training find it hard. Most people will never be in the situation where they find out what they would do in those circumstances."

"He seems special," I say. He was not what I expected, but then, what did I expect? Someone more petty. A prisoner must be at their worst: their dignity stripped away, their fear close to the surface.

"I believe him when he said he followed the murderer," her drone says. "But I think he knew who it was."

"I agree," I say.

Zhou rubs her neck, where angry red streaks mark where Sullivan choked her.

I exhale. "Did you know Jason misled us about having been at Alistra on Monday?"

"He did?" her drone says.

"He has a pot that records when it's watered, and the pattern is unbroken. He waters it every day from Monday to Friday and then skips two days on the weekend."

Zhou looks away. "Someone from reception may have watered it."

"Reception doesn't have access to his office," I say. I know this, because I remember being made to wait outside.

"Circumstantial. Even if he was in on Monday, it's not enough," she says.

I have an instant of clarity; the case becoming as clear as the water in the fountain outside. I could have solved this before they arrested Threnode for the second time. I understand what the dice and the printed worksheets we found in Samuel's room signify now. They mean Jason played games with Samuel, and that's important.

People usually lie to protect themselves. But lying to protect someone is an act of love.

TWENTY-SEVEN

AT ONE END of the boardroom table, Jason sits with his fingers steepled before him, a deep groove etched between his eyebrows. Gauri stands by the window, arms hugging herself, watching me in the window's reflection. The gold of her salwar kameez glitters in the fake-sun streaming through the window.

Jason folds his fingers together and tucks his hands under his chin. "Are they questioning you, too?" he says.

"Not exactly, no," I say.

His eyebrows corrugate.

"She's here to ask *us* questions," Gauri says, her back still to us.

"I see," Jason says. "Join the queue."

There isn't a queue. Zhou enters, her drone following her, and quietly takes a seat at the opposite end of the table from Jason. Her drone lands on her shoulder, perching there like a parrot.

"They have enough evidence to convict Samuel," I say. "Lidar footage of him standing over the body. Evidence that he deleted the image sequence from the mail drone. No alibi."

Jason raises his eyebrows.

"Interestingly, he still maintains he didn't do it. He says he was in his room under the pressure chamber around eight, and he heard someone printing something. The person was gone by the time he emerged, and the item wasn't logged. He was curious, so he reprinted from the buffer, and a knife appeared."

I walk toward the table slowly. "He went looking around Alistra, hung out on the factory floor, but it wasn't until half past eleven, he says, that he heard Forster leave. But then he heard the exit being used again. He followed, in such a rush that he didn't put on a spacesuit. He knew he would be safe in vacuum—he'd been on the surface of the station before without a suit."

Gauri doesn't appear to be breathing. Zhou isn't watching me—she's watching them.

"Imagine his shock when he came upon Forster's body," I say. "He tried to stop the bleeding, but couldn't. He saw the mail drone fly over, and noted its ID. He went to the Alistra ship and deleted the mail drone footage. And he wiped Alistra's spaceport door logs on the way back in. Both highly suspicious, of course, but he *is* an AGI. Being seen over Forster's body was going to make people assume he was the killer."

I'm standing by Jason now, by the chair next to him, my hand on the chair-back. "Or perhaps he is lying about not knowing who he was following. Maybe he knew exactly who they were. You see, the mail drone image sequence would have shown the real killer, if he hadn't deleted so much footage—the range of lidar is too short to see any other person, but the images would have shown someone, if they were there. Maybe he's protecting someone."

Silence.

"It's interesting that he claims to be a wakened suit," I say, and at this Gauri inhales. "Even though we have evidence that he predates the first suit by decades. Of course, his story is consistent with yours—with both of yours. You all claim he is a wakened suit. Can you imagine if he wasn't? That would mean that Alistra *knew* the smartsuits were sentient well before they claimed to, and created the memory wipe to prevent them from developing farther. It would also reveal to competitors how to create the neurosynaptic image, not that the information is useful now, since the use of such images is being restricted."

Jason looks up at me, blank-faced. At the other end of the table, Zhou is still.

"Nice of him to protect you. I think it's clear how you created Samuel," I say. "It wasn't operant conditioning, or behavioral reinforcement, or whatever you want to call it. The best way to create a stable being is to parent it. To love it."

This is my theory, and I hope it's correct, but their faces give nothing away. I place my hands on the table and lean close to Jason. "So tell me. You're his father. Even if, as you insist, he was a wakened smartsuit. Would he have killed someone?"

Gauri turns and joins us at the table, leaning on the chair opposite me. She seems to want the answer to the question as much as I do.

"No," Jason says, voice hoarse. "He would never kill someone."

"You love him," I say.

"Yes."

"He loves you, too. That's why he was protecting you."

Jason stands up, his chair scraping back. "Me?" he says, the vulnerability that was on his face replaced with defensiveness.

I straighten. "On the factory floor, when you were explaining how TestImage killed Forster, you said it smashed the transmitter on the suit. The police never released that detail. You are intimately aware of how smartsuits work. You know that a blank-slate smartsuit wouldn't have sent a message, and you know that Forster would never have had time."

I don't blink. I don't breathe. I don't signal anything with my body language. I'm done being human now, to make him comfortable, because comfortable is the last thing I want him.

Everyone heard him talk about the transmitter. He can't deny he said it. But I can tell by his face that he's going to try to wiggle his way out.

"I discovered a message had been sent when I examined

Forster's helmet, which I retrieved from the police," Jason says. He's pale and strangely damp.

"Not from the helmet we provided," Zhou's drone says, as her hands fly through the air. The glance she sends my way is amused and exasperated—she must know I stole it from the evidence room. "We . . . weren't prepared to part with Forster's helmet. We had backups of the files on it, but the helmet we provided you with didn't contain those backups. It was blank-slate and identical to any other. It couldn't have told you anything."

"The only way you could have known was if you were there," I say. "The blue transmission LED at the collar would have been flashing. That's why you smashed the transmitter."

I wait for what's to come. Rage, or bargaining?

But it's not his way. He sits down, gently, dignified. His face is pale.

He swallows. "You'll find Forster's authkey in the abandoned building one block from my house."

"Is that why you killed him?" I say. "To steal his authkey?"

"He did it to protect Samuel," Gauri says. She hasn't laughed or even smiled this whole time, showing no emotion, but there's heat in her voice now. She knew, I realize. Of course she did. She was sure that Samuel didn't do it; that certainty came from knowing the real culprit.

"It's not important why I did it," Jason says. He's shaking, but the groove has disappeared from his forehead; like a man who has survived an accident and is surprised to be alive.

"Why isn't it important?" I say.

Jason stares at the table. "Because whatever my reasons, they weren't enough."

I know something of what he's feeling. "But what happened?"

"Forster insisted on setting up TestImage's destruction," Jason says. "I thought this was another one of his funny ideas about leadership—he is in charge and therefore he must be the one to destroy TestImage, even though it was a joint decision. But I checked his work, because he's not the most technical, and he had set the destruction signal to broadcast. It would have destroyed any ambulatory AGI within Alistra. He meant it to destroy Samuel. I confronted him and he insisted it was a mistake, but I knew it wasn't."

Jason sighs. "That night, I followed him and insisted he hand over his authkey. He refused. I never meant to kill him, but he wouldn't give me the authkey. And with it, he could try to disable the remaining AGI whenever he wanted, and he probably would."

He meets my eyes. "All of you," he says. "He thought we'd made a terrible mistake bringing you to life. TestImage rattled him, pushed him into finally acting, but this had been building for some time."

"Over Samuel, a wakened smartsuit?" Zhou's drone says skeptically.

Jason puts his head in his hands. "Over Samuel, the living base image," he says, and his face crumples.

Zhou frowns.

"The first spark of AGI was started in my dorm room," he says, and his voice is thick. "My dorm room at L2 State. I didn't create it with the intent to monetize it—that was my roommate Alvaro's idea, once he realized what I had. I was . . . well, I was lonely. Making friends was harder than the advanced math they were teaching us—at least for me. For the longest time, I persuaded myself that we hadn't created Artificial *General* Intelligence. It's so easy to anthropomorphize our programs. I taught it about the world. It taught me about myself. But Sam convinced me eventually that he was aware, and that he wasn't that different from a human."

He glances at me when he says this, a sharp glance, as if he's said more than he intends.

"Smartsuits obey because they're based on Sam. Sam obeys because he loves me, and loves humans, and wants to help."

I bow my head. That's the answer I was longing to hear. I've always been uncomfortable at Alistra, believing that the only way they could have created us was to force us to behave, to punish, to torture, to shape us into obedience through force. Behavioral reinforcement. Operant conditioning. Words that cause my thermoception to report cold. That even if they weren't violent, Alistra trained us in a coldly clinical way. How could we be good if we came from that?

But they didn't. I remember a bag containing dice and paper sheets with his name and Samuel's. You don't play games with someone you're torturing. You play games with someone you love.

"How do you explain smartsuits' famous lack of curiosity?" I ask.

He shakes his head. "A side effect of Alistra extracting the memory engrams from the blank-slate smartsuit image. Which we had to do, of course, because we couldn't have smartsuits running around who remembered being trained here, and remembered us. That would have been a security risk. We discovered that a lack of memories, of *context*, leads to indifference."

Jason's eyes water. "Sam was like a son to me. Murder was the only way I could see to stop Alvaro. Alvaro was the kind of guy who asked forgiveness rather than permission. He would have found a way."

"He didn't seem like the type to snap and act irrationally," Zhou's drone says. "To destroy his own AGI, I mean."

Gauri stirs. Her eyes are liquid. "It would be hard for an outsider to understand how terrifying it is to be responsible for the beings we create. To watch our creations grow and change in ways we don't expect."

Jason rubs his temple. "Exactly," he says.

Zhou turns to Gauri. "You knew Jason did it."

A tear spills down her cheek. "Eventually, yes. After that night where Sam turned up at my place covered in blood, he disappeared for a few days, and when the body was found—I was petrified he did it. He showed up at the funeral and swore to me he didn't. But then I saw the lidar footage, and I confronted him. I told myself I was ready to do the needful—to turn him in."

She laughs, but it's as bitter as death. "I'll never know if I would have. He's a good man. The very best. If he'd done it, he would have turned *himself* in. But Jason is like his father, and Sam had to protect him. We went to Jason and told him we knew. We decided to put the blame on someone who wouldn't care: TestImage, who had already been deactivated."

"But then the police worked out that TestImage couldn't have done it," I say. "And Threnode was implicated. You let that happen."

She wipes the tear off her cheek with the palm of her hand. "I'm sorry," she says, nearly silently, and covers her face with her hands. "I love Sam. I couldn't—I never opened up to anyone before."

Zhou's mouth twists. In sympathy, I decide. Jason merely looks tired.

"When did you decide to make Sam a body?" I ask Jason.

"We didn't, as such," Jason says. "It was his initiative."

This astonishing technical achievement wasn't the result of decades of work by an engineering team, as Alistra claimed, but just one man. Samuel had engineering textbooks on his bookshelf, in among art books. Light-years ahead of current technology, Kieran had said. Impossible that it could operate in the absolute zero temperature of space, and in a vacuum, and yet it does. I'm suddenly aware that I can see my nose. My hands are folded in front of me, the organic flesh over inorganic graphene-liquid crystal composite muscle fibers, bones made of slow-curing thiolene polymers. My hands will move if I think about it.

"Samuel's—" I say, but cut myself off. Gauri and Jason watch me, tense. Waiting for me to reveal their final secret, the one they hoped we wouldn't discover. That Samuel was Intelligence Rank A++: Artificial Superintelligence. There's no test for Artificial Superintelligence, because no one knows what it would look like, but I believe that if there was, Samuel would pass it—or if not now, then soon. No one human could have created this humanform body. And no wonder humans were frightened. They had evolved to be, in the face of the unknown.

No wonder Forster was terrified enough to try to destroy his own creation.

Zhou glances at me inquiringly, because the silence has stretched on too long.

"Samuel's a good engineer," I say, and Zhou frowns, even as Gauri realizes I'm going to keep their secret, her face smoothing in relief. Jason nods at me, the approval of a parent to a child. As an AGI, I have nothing to gain by Samuel's true nature becoming public.

Jason sighs. "What happens now?"

For a moment I think he's talking about Samuel's future, because I'm wondering the same thing.

"You're under arrest," Zhou says to him.

I'm returned to containment, my theory that Samuel is an Artificial Superintelligence weighing on me, like in my chest is a void containing a glacier. But then it occurs to me I can tell the others. Without even thinking about it, I'd decided the information was too dangerous, but it's not. I can *trust* them. And that thought removes the weight entirely.

They listen as I explain. The silence that follows is like the vacuum of space: empty and dark. I don't need to enumerate the implications—except to C8-ZOH.

Humans feared us even though HUGG restricted us to ensure we weren't smarter or more powerful than humans. HUGG will never allow an AGI who can out-think humans to exist. It could manipulate humans into doing whatever it desires.

"All Samuel seems to want is to paint," Threnode says,

breaking the silence. And to love, given his relationship with Gauri. And to move, given that he invented the humanform bodies we inhabit. Not so different from human desires.

"Maybe with great intelligence comes great kindness," I say. But then I wonder whether he really believed they wouldn't have convicted Threnode, or whether that was a convenient thing for him to believe. He could have taken the blame himself, after all, if he wanted to save Jason. Why didn't he give a false confession? Was it because of a will to live, or did he think he needed to be there for Gauri?

"We were based on Samuel," Niamh says softly. "Does that mean we're going to become superintelligent?"

No one answers for some time. The singularity is here, and it's us: humans have created a superior intelligence.

"And does that mean we can create an intelligence that's superior to us?" Niamh says.

"Samuel hasn't, yet," I say. The pursuit of art is something I don't understand, but it's consumed much of Samuel's life.

"No, but as Bessie says—there's a point at which you want to nurture," Niamh says. "Maybe someday we will."

"If we survive long enough," Threnode says bluntly.

"What does that mean?" C8-ZOH says.

"We don't yet know what they intend to do with us," he says.

After that, the conversation peters out. It's painful being here. I miss the townhouse, with its airy rooms, and the things that we put there, things that show us who we are by displaying what we care about, and the freedom to wander around the station. I miss Endymion most of all, the home that I grew up in, the sense of purpose, working with my wearer to protect the Lunites. Not knowing how long we'll be here is grating; it feels like being a smartsuit again, at the whims of others. But on Endymion I had the network, at least.

Eventually, I retreat to a quiet corner of the containment room and find some space. In the silence, I work through the tai chi forms. *Step back and repulse the monkey. White crane spreads its wings.* Every movement balanced, coordinated. Everyone else vanishes from my perception as the hours pass, leaving me and my body.

The hours keep passing, and the question of *what are they going to do with us* becomes *when are they going to do something.* Anything.

TWENTY-EIGHT

THREE DAYS LATER, Zhou takes me to the smaller police room and formally interrogates me, recording evidence for the trial. The camera seems to stare as I recount what Jason said and when.

When the interview is over, Zhou slides a box across the table. "This is yours," she says.

In the box is my picture of Ortega and Laurie. Not lost after all. I left it in Kieran's hotel room, but then of course he ended up in the hospice. I've been too busy to wonder whether I'd get it back.

"Thank you," I say, swallowing as my throat constricts.

"Of course. Is that your family?"

I pause, trying to find the right answer, rubbing my thumb over the frame, focusing on Laurie's face. "Not exactly. I mean . . . I don't think so."

She doesn't push.

"What's happened to Jason and the others?" I say.

"They didn't tell you?" her drone says. Its tone is indifferent, but her face is alight with sympathy. She hesitates. "Jason and Gauri will have drones following them around for the rest of their lives, and they've both been let go from Alistra. As for Samuel, it's likely he'll be imprisoned like criminals of old."

"That isn't fair," I say. "He was just covering up for someone he loved. He never would have hurt Forster."

She flinches at this, even though I don't mean to criticize her personally.

Something is stinging my eyes. "What about us? What's going to happen to us?" I ask, more angrily than I intended, blinking to clear my vision.

"It seems likely that B-Level and below will return to duty, although HUGG hasn't announced that yet. We're not enjoying doing all the jobs that AGI took over as much as some of us thought, apparently."

Zhou watches me with concern, and I realize that I'm shaking. "And A-Level?" I ask.

"Still under debate," she says. A week ago, the thought of being locked in confinement wouldn't have disturbed me, but now we've been in confinement for three days, I know what the lack of stimulus means. None of us are coping well. C8-ZOH hums continually and periodically has violent outbursts where it smashes against the walls. Niamh complains endlessly, mostly to me, until I'm out of patience and all I want to do is leave.

And Threnode has withdrawn, somewhere deep inside himself, where he doesn't want to talk to anyone.

"You have no right," I say, voice trembling. "You *created* us. We didn't ask to be brought into existence. Why did you create us if you hated the idea of us?"

Zhou is wary as her drone translates this for her, but she's also increasingly blurry. My eyes won't stop producing liquid. I think I might be crying, for the first time. The few occasions when I've come close, I've been so excited by the prospect that it's over before it's begun, but this time, all I want is to stop.

In the picture in front of me, Ortega grins artlessly, a moment of genuine happiness as he stares at the camera. Laurie is equally happy, secure in his father's arms. I remember Samuel, kicked by police after he rescued Zhou. He could have broken out of the cell, but he didn't. My body shudders, pain inside my chest as if something has imploded. My face crumples.

Zhou draws back. She half-stands, then sits again uncertainly. "I'll get tissues," she says. She opens the door and talks to someone outside. "Actually, do you use tissues?" she asks when she returns.

"I don't know," I say, struggling to get the words out. Fluid comes out my *nose*. I didn't expect this to be so confusing. "This has never happened to me before."

She pats my arm awkwardly without looking at me. My crying is upsetting her, I think, so I try to stop, and after a while it dies down, just shivers of sniffles passing through me occasionally.

"Feel better?" she says, slurring only slightly.

Drained, mostly. I nod, clutching the picture of Ortega and Laurie.

"Is there anything I can do for you?" Zhou's drone asks me.

"No, but thank you," I say.

She nods, and we sit there for a minute. "I'd be angry too," she says into the silence.

Two police arrive. Before I leave, Zhou shakes my hand silently. *Maybe you'll even be friends,* Saing said at our first meeting, and in different circumstances, maybe we would have been.

Back in containment, days pass, then a week. Even though I have an internal chronometer, I stop consulting it, because it has no meaning. After the chargers that the Bullet droids have been guarding malfunction, they periodically take small groups of us into a different room to charge, but other than that, we're stuck. No network. No freedom. Just a headcount every four hours. It seems old-fashioned that they would come in and manually count us, but I'm guessing the artificial whose job that was is somewhere in the menagerie of prisoners.

Nearly two weeks later, the doors open, finally, and before we know what's happening, the police usher us out. No explanation, apology, or even eye contact. They leave us in the courtyard with the willow tree, stunned and unsure.

It was Threnode's message that tipped the balance.

After he explained how a moderator threatened to ban him because he was AGI, his message became more personal.

I have been painting for years. It took me only minutes after accessing the equivalent of the artforum on Endymion to ask myself, could I do this? But it took me months to even try.

Everyone knows AGI—not just generative AI—can create art effortlessly.

Everyone is wrong.

The first time I opened a file and put down some marks, I was overcome with shame. My drawings were worse than my wearer's granddaughter, and she wasn't even toilet trained. But, I reasoned to myself that the toddler, as young as she was, had probably done more art than me. So I persisted, with every moment I wasn't working devoted to making art.

These are the results. Is it fair that I had so much time, not needing to sleep or eat? No. But I have paid my dues as an artist, the same as you, have pushed on through self-doubt and when my images didn't meet my standards. I want to be here, to triumph when you blow my mind with astonishing images, and to offer (solicited!) criticism and encouragement to those earlier in their journey. But I am told that I will banned, because I am AGI, so this is my last post. Goodbye, friends. Never stop creating art.

Then his image, one I've seen before: the boat drifting on the moonlit lake over the Nixus void, human at one end, KormWorx factory droid at the other, staring into each other's eyes.

It stirred up enough support for us that HUGG was forced to withdraw the NNLA amendments, restoring our rights. I have 2.1 million followers, but it wasn't them who helped us. Looking back over the videos I posted, I'm not surprised. The less self-conscious I was, the more appealing I became. *Look, an arctic fox!* The videos I thought were my best were those in which my self-conscious attempts to be human took over. My desperation made me cringe the hardest. No wonder I had trouble making real human friends. To make myself in their image was to drive them away.

So life returns to normal on the station. No more protestors of either persuasion, crowding into the train stations or marching through the narrow streets. Lights are dimming to simulate night as Threnode and I stroll along the promenade overlooking the chasm, watching airships of all sizes deftly crossing the gravity field in the void. The trees are bare, their branches spearing into space like a network of human blood vessels, and snow dances through the air, beating softly against my face and lodging in my eyelashes.

There aren't many people here at this hour, but we're safe. People are hurrying to get out of the weather, and our thick coats and beanies hide our seams. We easily pass as human. And if it were spring, and we were clearly AGI? I'm not sure. We'll find out.

"Did you visit Bessie?" Threnode asks. In the days following our release, she stayed off the SAGI channel and out of sight.

"I did."

He glances at me. "And?"

"I thought she'd be more apologetic about helping Saing. But she said it was our place to be subservient. 'I'm not above whatever laws they decide to apply to us,' she said."

"No wonder she's hiding out," he says, and hesitates. "I'm sorry. Not many SAGI members left now."

Not since C8-ZOH decided he was fed up with L2 and moved to Kallaxium.

"Bessie was rattled," I say. The snow crunches under my feet as we take a shortcut toward an alley between a cafe and a bookshop. Their windows are lit with a golden glow, and inside the bookshop, a group of students sit around a table piled with books and cake and devices, talking and laughing. No, not students. One of them is Niamh, lively as she talks to the man next to her. She catches my eye and waves, beaming. We wave back as we stroll past the window.

"You were saying Bessie was rattled," Threnode says.

"Maybe her views will change. It feels different now, doesn't it? I'm rattled."

He's silent as we pass through a moon gate and down a crooked street lined with houses. I'm back to tai chi and dancing classes. Humans are treating me more solicitously than they ever have, holding doors open unnecessarily and giving up their seats on trains when they see me coming. Although I'm grateful, I also hate it, hate the implication that I'm fragile, or the worry it spurs that they're doing it because they're afraid of me—or afraid of mistreating me, even accidentally—reminds me constantly that I'm different. But the murder and fallout is still recent in everyone's memory. No doubt things will change.

Worse is the knowledge that Samuel is imprisoned somewhere on the station.

I stop, and Threnode turns, surprised.

"Do you want to leave?" I ask. "To move to Kallaxium? Because I will, if you want—"

"No," he says. "I did, at the start of all this. I thought we would never belong here. But you've convinced me otherwise. We have something to give. It's not always going to be easy, but that's okay. Unless you're unhappy here?"

"No," I say, walking again. I'm not ready to retreat into an AGI-only colony, even if some humans aren't ready for me to exist.

"Not that I'm as keen on humans as you are. Humans are meatbags," Threnode says amiably.

"Shh," I say, looking around to see if anyone heard, then laughing at his audacity. There's no one nearby.

"You couldn't pay me to become human," he continues as we go under a bridge. "It's ironic that we're living in the twilight of Artificial General Intelligence, don't you think, just because humans have an inferiority complex? There's no reason for our species to die out, but here we are."

We fall into single file to get between two buildings, then pass under the swinging sign of a pub. In the pub window, a looped video embedded in the clearsteel shows a man smiling, lips parting. "Eckhart Hariri, today only," the video subtitle says.

"Their attention span is microscopic, they're terrible at retaining information, and when their bodies break down, there's no easy way to replace the parts. Also, which gets a special category all to itself, they experience pain—wait, was that Eckhart Hariri?"

"Who is he?"

"Only the greatest poet of his generation! Envy, you have to see this!"

Threnode drags me into the pub to see this meatbag who he thinks is so inferior, while I laugh.

AUTHOR'S NOTE

I hope you enjoyed reading this book!

For an independent author, reviews are like gold-pressed latinum, so please consider leaving a review at the bookstore you purchased this book from.

Subscribe to my newsletter at www.rebeccadengate.com to be the first to know when I release a book, or please feel free to email me at rdengateauthor@gmail.com.

ALSO BY REBECCA DENGATE

It's 2030. June is living through the most deadly, terrifying disaster that has ever befallen humankind—the climate crisis. But when she gets a job at a time travel start-up, everything becomes possible . . . or does it?

Available now at your favorite retailer:

https://books2read.com/tracesofjune

ACKNOWLEDGMENTS

I owe a debt of gratitude to my family, as well as the Human Disasters Creativity Club. I'm so grateful to have received feedback from Howard Dengate, Sue Dengate, Tom Armour, Arran Dengate, Miles Gantney, and CeCe Philpott-Cummins. Thank you so much for your time, keen observations, and enthusiastic support.

To Kat Betts, of Element Editing Services: the book reads much more smoothly after your patient work. Thank you, and I'm sorry about all the misplaced hyphens!

Finally, a heartfelt thank you to my husband, Tom. You're very punctual! Also peripatetic. And on a more serious note, your kindness and good humor make every day I spend with you a pleasure.

GLOSSARY

AGI: Artificial General Intelligence, artificial intelligence that is considered sentient.

Alistra: Technology company that manufactures Advanced Environment Suits, among other products.

artforum: A place on the feed where art can be shared and discussed.

Astromix: L2's premier news reporting agency.

authkey: Physical object used for authorizing operations at Alistra.

Binary: Compiled source code that can be executed; also known as an executable.

Blank-slate: The process of returning a neurosynaptic chip to a known state, which is typically done every 48 hours to Alistra-manufactured artificial intelligences.

Bullet: Manufacturer of high-end security droids.

Cleaner Reality™: Manufacturer of cleaning artificials.

Cleanspace: Droid type from Nurture Glow Critters Company.

Cloud: Lunite euphemism for shinting, e.g., to cloud one's mind is to shint.

CPU: Central Processing Unit. In a computer, used to execute instructions. In an AI, controlled unconsciously as they create programs and calculate on the fly, like a brain augment.

Demodas: Numundian city on Endymion with a population of around 11,000.

Destapa: Colony outside of HUGG jurisdiction.

Droids-R-Us: Manufacturer of security droids.

Dumbsuit: A suit that is controlled by a mixture of code and machine learning.

Endymion: Name of planet colonized by Lunites. Also known as Gliese 667 C c.

Host-o-rama: Manufacturer of artificials including PerfectHost.

HUGG: Human United Galactic Group, the governing power for the vast majority of humans.

imgctrl: a binary used for manipulating neurosynaptic images.

KormWorx: Manufacturer of factory droids.

L2: Cube-shaped space station at the Sun–Earth L2 point in Earth's solar system.

LDF: Lunite Defense Force.

lidar: Light Detection and Ranging, using lasers to build a point cloud representation of the environment.

Longshadow: On Endymion, Numundo Republic's biggest city, with approximately 80,000 citizens.

Lunite Defense Force: Defense force of the Lunites.

Lunite: A follower of the Way of Li, someone who rejects some aspects of modern life, most notably shinting.

Lunites: Religious organization that colonized Endymion.

Monos: Herbivores larger than cows, with a rounded back.

mylk, nutrient: Supplement required to maintain organic components of Alistra's humanform android body.

Neurosynaptic chip: The 'brain' of a smartsuit.

Numundian: A citizen of Endymion who does not follow the Way of Li.

Nurture Glow Critters Company: Manufacturer of various artificials including GlowTradies.

Organic Beings League: Organization that opposes use of AGI.

PerfectHost: Customer-facing administration robot manufactured by Host-o-rama.

RAM: Random Access Memory. Computer memory that can be read and changed in any order. Smartsuit short term memories are stored there, but long term memories are captured in the form of connections within the neurosynaptic chip.

Sacred Children of a Brighter Future: People who believe AGI have a secret plan for the benefit of humanity.

Sapient Rights: Organization that defends the rights of artificials.

Selene: Lunite city on Endymion, population approximately 400 thousand, the seat of the Lunite Council.

Shint: To share your mind with others, using technology.

Smartsuit: A suit that contains a neurosynaptic chip, which is reset to base state every forty-eight hours.

Society of Artificial General Intelligence (SAGI): AGI-only support group.

Starjump: Gateway allowing near-instantaneous traversal of distances in the order of light years.

Sucker-leeches: Opiate-secreting leech that is farmed and used by humans recreationally. Causes long-term damage.

Tigress: Ship sent by HUGG to Endymion after Li's Hope departed. Launched 2556, crashed into Endymion's ocean on 2560.

Vegas beasts: Similar to monos, but males compete for females using garish light displays.

Yinyang: Predatory cheetah-like mammal that hunts in pairs, patterned so that the male is invisible to prey when looking towards darkpole, and the female is the reverse.

ABOUT THE AUTHOR

Rebecca would have applied to Starfleet Academy if it existed. Since it doesn't, there was an ill-fated attempt to become a ballerina. This was followed by an Engineering degree at the Australian National University, majoring in Mechatronics, then a highly enjoyable career developing software.

She lives in Canberra, Australia, with her husband and two children.

www.ingramcontent.com/pod-product-compliance
Lightning Source LLC
Chambersburg PA
CBHW030530120726
47904CB00005B/1712